Tania Kindersl[...] the Lambourn va[...] racing. At fourteen, she grew out of horses, moved to London, discovered boys and started writing, mostly for fun, partly in the vague hope of becoming the youngest girl to write a bestseller since Daisy Ashford. She lives in London and her first novel, *Out to Lunch*, was also published by Corgi.

OUT TO LUNCH

'Just too irresistible for words'
Tatler

'Funny, cynical and full of sideswipes at the "I've got a window in my filofax" brigade'
Company

'Like champagne – frothy, fun and pure escapism'
Today

'A wickedly witty tale of love, modern manners and, not surprisingly, money'
Me

Also by Tania Kindersley
OUT TO LUNCH
and published by Corgi Books

HERE FOR
THE SEASON

Tania Kindersley

CORGI BOOKS

HERE FOR THE SEASON
A CORGI BOOK : 0 552 13709 X

Originally published in Great Britain by Bantam Press,
a division of Transworld Publishers

PRINTING HISTORY
Bantam Press edition published 1992
Corgi edition published 1994

Set in 11/12pt Linotype Sabon by
Phoenix Typesetting, Ilkley, West Yorkshire

Corgi Books are published by Transworld Publishers Ltd,
61–63 Uxbridge Road, London W5 5SA,
in Australia by Transworld Publishers (Australia) Pty Ltd,
15–23 Helles Avenue, Moorebank, NSW 2170,
and in New Zealand by Transworld Publishers (NZ) Ltd,
3 William Pickering Drive, Albany, Auckland.

Made and printed in Great Britain by
Cox & Wyman Ltd, Reading, Berks.

For Barnaby and Dinah,
with love and thanks.

1

Everyone went away, that summer. They consulted their atlases and cancelled all engagements, and one by one they packed up and went out into the world, with nothing but a change of clothes, a passport, and a defiant sense of their own adventure. It was time to fly, travel was In, everyone said so, and the more exotic the better. Equador, Bali, Nepal, Java, the Indian Ocean, the Ivory Coast, farther and farther from the beaten track. The esoteric had come into its own and the fashionable were taking up the challenge. 'Darling,' they cried happily down endless telephone lines, 'must dash, just off to Ulan Bator, you know how it is.' Someone had been reading Somerset Maugham, and the South Pacific was suddenly much in vogue (and in *Vogue*); there was great talk of atolls and archipelagos, of Vanuatu and Espiritu Santo, of Île des Pins and Kiribati and Lord Howe Island. The intrepid armed themselves with dog-eared copies of *The Moon and Sixpence*, boarded their aeroplanes, blithely waved goodbye, and said they would send a card.

Minna was left alone in Chelsea, with no particular place to go. She had never much cared for travelling, at least not the adventurous variety, all those terrifying jabs and boiling the water and cockroaches the size of gull's eggs in the bathroom, which everyone seemed to find so amusing. She continued to insist that she was an old-fashioned girl at heart. Her idea of a holiday was the Hôtel du Cap and room service round the clock and Manhattans at sundown, but everyone seemed to think all that was terribly old hat now, only indulged in by the flash money, who didn't know any better. So Minna shook her head and held her counsel and gently turned down all invitations to Christmas Island, however pressing. 'Only four towns on the whole place, you'll never believe what they are called, Poland, France, London and Banana, can you beat it? Please say you'll come.' Minna quite saw the joke, but considered it a little thin to last her all that way and said she had lost her passport, which was almost true. Besides, she was happy to stay in London, which was looking pretty in the sunshine.

The rains had come to the city, in the spring. April showers and May squalls, leaving the streets clear and clean for June to arrive, bright with promise. The traffic snarled up, jammed with pleasure-seekers out on the town with their hoods down and their music up. The urban dwellers came out on to the streets like party-goers, walking with long easy strides, freed at last from the heavy confines of their winter clothes, faces relaxing from the pinched set expression they had worn against the cold. Shopkeepers from warmer climates stood out in their doorways, basking in the heat. Girls put their hair and their hemlines up, and didn't mind so much when their legs were stared at. The restaurants and the cafés put tables out on the pavements, and the world sat and drank bitter espresso and watched the rest of the world go by. It was summer and the city was on the move.

Minna was restless. She always felt like that at this time of year. Everything happened in the summer, it always had. But now everyone had gone away and there was no-one to go and be restless with. If she had had a dog she would have walked it. If she had had a dog she could have called it after one of the Marx brothers and made jokes about it. She knew girls who had pedigree whippets called Taxi and Stop Thief, which was generally considered to be rather amusing. Minna wasn't altogether sure how amusing she thought it, but perhaps that was why she had never got a dog. So there was that possibility out of the question, and she was still restless. If she had had a car, she would have put the roof down and driven through the park and stared at boys. But she had never learned to drive.

'Oh, dear,' she said, staring earnestly at herself in the glass, 'what a useless creature I am, to be sure.'

She wandered round the house for a while, an aimless progress from one cluttered room to the next, whistling a little tune that she rather thought used to be called 'Sophisticated Boom Boom', in the Sixties. ' "Sophisticated Boom Boom",' she said. 'Really. What will they think of next?' Then she put some music on and danced a little. Someone had told her once that she had graceful arms. 'Look at the grace in my arms,' she said, executing a flawed arabesque. Then she wrote a letter to someone in Rome. Bored, she tore it up halfway through.

'Writing is just a substitute for living,' she told her reflection firmly. It smiled sadly back at her, more worldly wise than its youth pretended. 'Come along,' said Minna, firmer still. 'Let's go out and find someone to fall in love with.' So they went to Soho.

* * *

9

Minna arrived just before lunch. She put on her lipstick and over-tipped the taxi driver. 'Ah,' she said, taking in the air, 'that's better.'

Out in the sunshine, the crowds were hustling. Tourists consulted street maps with a furtive air and tried to look native. Having heard fables of the filthy English weather, they had come out equipped with mackintoshes and umbrellas, even galoshes for the more ambitious. They were not to know that their Burberries gave them away. Workmen leant on their tools, lazy in the sun, smoking hard on cigarettes they had rolled themselves, waiting for a pretty girl to pass by. Pretty girls did pass by, on their way to auditions and meetings and lunches, and didn't try too hard to rise above the whistles sent their way. Media types walked the streets with a proprietary air, on their way to each other's offices, dressed in their statutory summer uniform of jeans and white T-shirts, baseball boots optional, heavily thumbed copies of *Variety* and *Screen International* tucked under their arms. Groups of punters stood about on street corners, poised for the dive into the betting shops, papers folded back at the racing page, earnest in discussion of the prospects for the three-thirty at Newmarket. Sharp modern creations hurried past in lightweight double-breasted suits, sporting aluminium briefcases and slicked-back hair, on their way to make their million. Outside the drinking clubs, the famous and the nearly famous and the trying to be famous mingled a little ostentatiously, exchanging telephone numbers and lunch dates, still not quite sure whether filofaxes were *passé* yet. In the restaurants and bars, would-be artists waited on tables and dreamt of being discovered. Down the road, real live artists drank undisturbed in dim back rooms, just as they always had. Somewhere in the depths of the Coach and Horses, Jeffrey Bernard was unwell. Minna smiled to herself, loving it. She'd take Soho over Christmas Island any day, she didn't care what anyone said.

Eddy opened the door of his flat in jeans and a rumpled shirt that might have been silk, in the Sixties. Some things, Minna was glad to see, never changed.

'Hello,' he said, without surprise.

'Well, hello,' said Minna, putting a breathless little emphasis on the last syllable, just like all the best girls did. 'Are you busy?' She smiled up at him, as disingenuous as springtime.

'What do you take me for?' he said, throwing open the door. 'Come right along in. Bring the family.'

'Silly,' said Minna, following him up the stairs. 'I was just passing,' she added carelessly, as if it were just the merest thing, a faint whim, a twist on the wheel of coincidence. 'And there was your change of address card in my pocket and I thought, I'll just drop in and see that Eddy, he's bound to be up to no good, so you see . . .'

'I see,' said Eddy, who did. He had never sent a change of address card in his life. 'I'm up to nothing, you'll be disappointed. Just me and Jim, still together after all these years.' He indicated the record player, where the needle lisped softly to itself, stuck in the final groove.

'Ah, yes,' said Minna, remembering. 'Jim lives and all that. Don't let me interrupt you.' She looked pointedly at his record collection. 'I know you're just an old rocker at heart.'

Eddy ignored this insult. He had been ignoring Minna's insults since he could remember. In the old days he had cherished a theory that if he refused to rise she would give it up as a bad job. It didn't seem to have worked.

'So,' he said, the perfect host. 'There's beer, if you'd like.'

'Beer would be fine,' said Minna, easy as pie. 'This is nice,' she added, looking about curiously, a picture of *politesse*. The room was long and low and empty. There was an Empire bed in one corner, the sort of thing she rather thought the French might call a divan, and a saxophone in another corner, polished and shining with use, and a state-of-the-art stereo system, technology stacked up high, all matt black and graphic equalizers, and a few of those spindly gilt chairs that dowagers and wallflowers used to sit out on at dances, and a cabin trunk spilling out unironed trousers and shirts in a myriad of colours, and that was all.

'Is your furniture in storage?' asked Minna. 'Or does one just sit on the floor and lament the passing of the Sixties?'

'Minimalism,' said Eddy dismissively. 'Everyone keeps telling me it's in.' He laughed suddenly, and gestured at his room with a grand sweep of his arm. 'Don't you think I do it rather beautifully?'

'Oh, beautifully,' said Minna, faintly longing, thinking of the clutter spilling over in her house in Chelsea. But then Eddy had never believed in surrounding himself with possessions. He said they gave him an itch. As long as he had a bed to lie on and clothes to put on his back and his saxophone to play, he was happy. That was his story, and he was sticking to it. Minna, who had once thought it

12

laziness and later affectation, thought now that it was probably just him. 'Thank you so very much,' she said as he handed her a bottle of beer and led the way out on to the balcony, which was just big enough for two chairs and some cabbage roses in a pot.

Minna sat down, a little coltish still, arranging her legs anyhow around her chair, considered her beer, drank some down, and laughed quietly to herself. Eddy watched her settle in, and wondered quite what had brought her here after all this time. So like her to arrive without a word of warning, not so much as a telephone call or a by your leave, and sit on his balcony and drink his beer and laugh at him and not offer any explanation and not expect any questions. He wouldn't ask her any, not any more. He was past the age of curiosity, so he said, and anyway, he remembered about her not liking questions, and he didn't mind indulging her a little. So he smiled back at her and waited. There was no hurry.

'This is nice,' she said again, faintly inconsequential in a way she had. She looked out on to the street. 'You can watch them queueing for Ronnie Scott's, you lucky dog.'

'That's what the estate agent said. All mod cons and a room with a view.'

'What more could a boy ask for?' said Minna absently. 'And what do you do when you're not watching them queue for Ronnie Scott's? Are you still writing your songs?' She wondered what masochistic streak of Eddy's had made him decide to live above a club where he still hadn't been offered a chance to play.

'Still writing my songs,' agreed Eddy, without any great enthusiasm. Still writing the same old songs,

13

playing the same old circuit, waiting on the great break at the end of the rainbow and wishing on a star. Just like all the thousands of other hopefuls and what else was new? Sometimes he wished he could say different, but it was a little late for that now. 'Nothing much else to do.'

'Nothing much else to do,' said Minna cruelly, mimicking him. 'What a dull dog you are. You and your cabin trunk and your sax. And there I was, utterly relying on you to regale me with sensational stories of Soho life.' She rolled her r's a little, to lend herself *gravitas*.

Eddy was unmoved. 'Nothing to tell,' he said.

'What?' said Minna, arching her eyebrows into two perfect peaks of disbelief. 'No scandals? No brawling over women? No passing of counterfeit money? No hearts being broken and reputations ruined? No husbands found with other men's wives? How do you stand it?' Minna had a way of investing her version of life with a series of exclamation marks, to make it more interesting. A shameless reader of the gossip pages, she knew that every closed door hid shady dealings, nefarious practices and unspeakable acts from curious eyes. But then, Eddy only read the broadsheets and the music papers, so what would he know?

'I get by,' he said.

'Get by?' said Minna, shocked. 'What is this getting by? Getting by. I can't like the sound of it. I was utterly counting on you. It's June. Everyone's gone away.'

'Everyone?' said Eddy, verging on the quizzical.

'Everyone,' said Minna firmly. 'I did think of calling old schoolfriends,' she said, knowing this would move him. She had no old schoolfriends, after all.

'That bad?' said Eddy, more quizzical still.

'That bad,' agreed Minna mournfully. 'What's a girl to do? How do you meet people? You must know.'

'I don't,' said Eddy. 'I think I knew once, but I've forgotten. It's too long ago.'

'So long ago and far away,' said Minna. 'And you so sunk in melancholy. There's no need to get morbid, you know. It is the summer, the sun is shining.'

'Age has no respect for the season.'

'Such an OLD man,' said Minna, still laughing at him. She had always laughed at him, Eddy remembered, ever since she was twelve years old and young enough to know better. 'Should I send you a walking frame for Christmas? I expect you'll need it, with the cold weather bringing on your gout. Or is it arthritis? I forget.'

'No need to mock,' said Eddy, with dignity.

'Every need,' said Minna truthfully. 'People have been taking you far too seriously, ever since I can remember. It's that forbidding exterior, or being too tall, or something. Anyway, it's not good for a boy.'

'But I'm a very serious boy,' said Eddy, straight as a die. He had always been a very good straight man, even Minna admitted that.

'Stuff,' said Minna, with a distressing lack of elegance. 'Will you take me to dinner?' she added, changing tack without pause. 'It's my birthday.' Curiously, it was her birthday, but she had forgotten. She was still young enough to afford to forget her birthday.

'I'm too old and tired for birthdays,' said Eddy. Minna shook her head at him, not in the least

15

offended. 'There you go,' she said in reproof. 'Getting morbid again. Is it the change of life or did you just have too much spicy food for lunch?'

'It's a dirty job,' said Eddy, admitting the joke was on him, 'but someone's got to do it.'

'I'd almost forgotten about you being such a philosopher,' said Minna, laughing at him some more. He really was the most absurd creature. She put it down to too much nihilism as a child. 'Light me a cigarette, would you ever?'

Eddy looked at her in surprise. This wasn't in the script. 'What's this all of a sudden?' he said. 'The Ava Gardner season at the Electric?'

Minna was pleased that he had noticed. 'It's Sophistication with a capital S,' she said in her best pre-war drawl. 'Mark it well. It's the new me, what do you think? Note the little black dress, the definitive fashion essential, as worn by Jacqueline Onassis and Holly Golightly. Do you think it's a little too much for day?' she added, on a pensive note.

To Eddy, his eye untrained, his formative years spent reading *Melody Maker* rather than *Vogue*, it was just a black dress, and very short.

'Very fetching,' he said. 'And too old for you.'

'Precisely,' said Minna happily, contemplating her legs, which were long and pretty. Eddy saw them too, and pretended he hadn't. 'So,' she said, giving up her attempt to turn him into Cary Grant, and lighting her cigarette herself without rancour. 'Will you take me to dinner?'

Eddy had known her too long to be caught off guard.

'I never plan that far in advance,' he said blandly. 'Have another beer.'

'Make an exception in my case,' said Minna, used

16

to people who did. 'Break new ground, why don't you? It's only dinner.'

'Nothing is ever only dinner,' said Eddy. He had a feeling of foreboding about this one, he wasn't sure why. Perhaps it was all that black she was wearing, he couldn't tell. So he prevaricated, vainly, remembering her persistence.

Minna looked at him very directly. This was the new sophisticated her, putting men on the spot.

'Well?' she said, not to be deflected. Nothing was ever only dinner.

The word hung heavy in the air, not quite a question, almost a demand. Eddy pulled out a packet of the strong French cigarettes he liked, extracted one, and took his time over lighting it, taking in the smoke sharply, savouring its ugly taste, wondering quite why he was being so evasive.

'Well, what?' he said at last, frowning at her through the smoke.

'Too, too Jean-Paul Belmondo,' said Minna, narrowing her eyes in imitation. 'Shall I be Jean Seberg? Well, dinner,' she added patiently, as if translating from the Greek.

'Have another beer and stop bothering me,' said Eddy, blander than ever.

'It's all your fault anyway,' said Minna, not remotely put out. She went into the kitchen to find another Rolling Rock.

'My fault,' said Eddy in puzzlement. Now she had lost him. 'What for? What did I do?'

'All that nannying me when I was too young to know any better. Making sure I didn't stay out too late in the wrong kind of places with the wrong kind of people. And the hell you gave me when I did.' In those days, Minna, new to the art of

Always Getting Caught, seemed inevitably to bump into Eddy when he was getting up and she was going home to bed. Six, seven, eight in the morning, as she meandered happily home in last night's rags, Eddy would come walking down the same street, or emerge from a strange doorway, or jump off a bus, or draw up in a taxi with an ostentatious squeal of tyres, and he would take her by the arm and escort her the rest of the way home, and make her cups of black coffee and lecture her on the sins of staying out all night and make her feel as if she was eight years old all over again.

'You were moving with a bad crowd,' said Eddy evenly. 'Someone had to watch you.' He knew it hadn't had to be him, but he wasn't going to tell her that.

'I could look after myself,' said Minna, who quite believed that she had nine lives, like a cat. 'I was going through my wild stage, perfectly honourable and only to be expected. It was only a few late nights and some boys with long hair. I was being a Bohemian. I did do it rather well, you must admit.' She opened the fridge, intent on her hunt for beer.

'Oh, very well,' said Eddy drily. She had only been Alice in Wonderland playing at being Edie Sedgewick, but all the same, he was glad it hadn't lasted. It couldn't be good for a girl.

Minna wandered back into the room. 'Why have you got a set of manacles in the frigidaire?' she asked, all wide eyes and genteel curiosity.

'My daily woman's idea of a joke,' said Eddy. His daily woman was a peroxide blonde with endless legs.

'Do you still go to bed with her?' said Minna, handing him a beer, her voice carefully offhand,

18

as if she had just remarked on the weather and the shocking state of the government. It was no business of hers, after all.

'Is that a trick question?'

'Very funny,' said Minna, sitting down again and regarding him from under her fringe.

'That's what she said,' said Eddy, ignoring the look.

'Before she tied you up, or after?'

'During.'

'So smart, you are.'

'So they tell me,' Eddy agreed, drinking his beer.

'Dinner then,' said Minna, who thought that bondage was vastly overrated and terrible vieux jeu besides. Her mind was on more promising matters.

'Maybe. Don't bother me about it now.'

'I will though,' said Minna, who had read a copy of *Cosmopolitan* magazine once. 'It's the Eighties now, the end of the decade.'

'Not that Eighties. Some of us still have our Grateful Dead albums and wardrobes free from designer linen.'

'And some of us have no wardrobes,' said Minna, looking at the cabin trunk. 'No, no,' she said, laughing at his face. 'It's heaven, really, too, too Evelyn Waugh, I love it, you know I do. So,' she added fairly, 'now we can talk about Woodstock and the summer of love and life on Venice beach and the decline of the hippy and I don't know what, and then I'll bother you again.' She smiled radiantly, justice and verity bending down from her pedestal, allowing him a fair hearing.

'I suppose you must.'

'Of course I must,' said Minna, with all the conviction of irrefutable logic. 'A girl has to eat.'

'With me?'

'Why not with you? You brush up perfectly well and I'm not expecting the Gavroche. It really is your fault anyway, for not being away and for looking like Montgomery Clift.' Minna had what she called 'a bit of a thing' for Montgomery Clift, but that was her secret.

'And look what happened to him,' said Eddy, not to be beaten by such base flattery. Just like her to try and sneak that in, while he wasn't looking.

'That's because he didn't have me to take out to dinner,' said Minna judiciously. 'You should know when you're lucky.'

'Ah, yes. Silly of me.'

'It is rather. I wrote a story today,' said Minna, thinking perhaps she should change the subject for a while, just to let him get used to the idea of eating out.

'Did you? What about?'

'Oh, you know,' said Minna, giving an airy wave that she sometimes affected and scattering cigarette ash all over the cabbage roses, a perfect picture of insouciance, which was the idea. 'The usual sort of thing. Incest, coprophilia, sado-masochism.'

'Touching,' said Eddy, dry as you please and not to be put off his stroke. 'I didn't know that sado-masochism was still in.'

'It isn't really,' said Minna, giving up. 'I was trying to shock you.'

'You know me better than that.'

Minna looked at him over the rim of her beer bottle, all at once absurdly young in her grown-up slip of a dress. 'Do I?' she said.

Eddy didn't quite look back at her. 'Don't you?' he said.

'Oh, blast you, Eddy.' Minna ground out her cigarette and stood up abruptly. 'I'm going.'

'All right.'

'Will you buy me dinner if I go now?'

'All right.'

'Goodbye then.'

'Goodbye.'

After Minna had gone, Eddy sat some more, and drank another bottle of beer, and smoked another cigarette, since he couldn't think of much else to do. Down below him, Soho carried on being Soho, just like it always did, sleazy in the sun, but he didn't notice. It had just been another day, and he had been planning to write a song, and now he was disturbed and his inspiration, usually compliant and easy to please, had deserted him.

It really wasn't fair of her to come breezing in on the merest whim, after more than a year, all young and slim and wide-eyed. It wasn't fair that her face had grown into its promised beauty, the childish fat melting away to reveal the clear fine planes underneath. It wasn't fair that she had taken her hair out of its ponytail and let it down sleek and golden about her shoulders, or that she had taken to wearing little black dresses that faithfully followed every curve of her body. She had always been dangerous, but now she was growing fatal. She almost knew it, and perhaps she would learn, but for now she was artless in her guile, free from self-consciousness even when she thought herself at her most devious, and that made it worse.

Why had he agreed to take her out? Eddy cursed loudly, and kicked himself for being every kind of a fool. He was old enough to know better.

All he wanted was a quiet life, time to write his songs and play his saxophone and drink a little too much with the band in the pub. Minna promised anything but peace. But he was only human after all, and she wanted the company, on her birthday of all days. Any company, not especially his. Did that make it better, or worse? Eddy couldn't decide. All he knew was that he felt uncertain and unprepared and taken at a disadvantage and he didn't like it. A whiff of her scent still hung in the air, a new rich scent that made him think vaguely of Parisian restaurants and other men's mistresses, and he lit another cigarette, trying to dispel it. He was too old for this, that was all he knew, almost thirty and no illusions left.

'I'm back.' She was laughing, her face a little pink with amusement. 'You won't believe the afternoon I've had. I didn't change, do you mind? I didn't altogether think it would be formal, even if it is my birthday.'

'Come in,' said Eddy, breaking into the flow.

'Oh, you bought me champagne,' said Minna in delight, as if he had just presented her with the keys to the city.

'It's nothing,' said Eddy, muttering a little as he opened the bottle, hating to be caught out in a kindness. 'It's your birthday.'

'I shan't tell you how old I am,' said Minna, raising her glass at him, 'because then I shan't be able to lie about it when I'm older. I think all women should lie about their age, on principle, don't you?'

'Absolutely,' said Eddy staunchly. 'Let's write it into the constitution.'

'Or something,' said Minna.

She raised her glass, sparkling her eyes a little ironically at him.

'Cheers,' she said. 'Of course, it's lucky I'm here to drink this lovely champagne.'

'Of course it is,' said Eddy soothingly.

'No, no,' said Minna. 'A maniac in a Mercedes tried to run me down, just now, in the street.'

'Must have been a Mafia hit,' said Eddy.

'Not at all,' said Minna with dignity. 'The mob and I are on the best of terms at the moment, I can't tell you, it's utter love with us. It was just one of those boy racers, and then he had the cheek to say it was all my fault and started shouting at me, so I threw a bag of peaches at him, and then the police arrived and said I was causing a disturbance and moved me on.' Her eyes flashed with indignation. 'Moved me on – as if I was a prostitute or a bag lady or something. Do I look like a prostitute to you?'

'No,' said Eddy, laughing into his sleeve.

'Well, exactly,' said Minna, faintly gratified. 'That's what I told the police, but they weren't altogether charming.'

Eddy could imagine.

'I can imagine,' he said.

'Anyway,' said Minna, starting to laugh. 'It really was rather absurd. There was quite a crowd by the end, I almost took round a hat.' She laughed again. 'I kept thinking about poor Aunt Eloise. She always said I'd end up in all manner of trouble, just think what she would have thought.'

'I think a discreet veil is best drawn,' said Eddy, who had met poor Aunt Eloise, and had no doubt about what she would think.

'Well, yes,' said Minna. 'Very discreet. I said to the press, "Boys, no pictures." '

'Disappointing for your public,' said Eddy. He looked at his watch. 'So,' he said, just as if it were nothing at all, 'shall we go to dinner?'

Minna's face lit up. 'Oh, Eddy, I do love you,' she said, artless as a summer breeze.

He wished she hadn't said that.

He took her to his local pizza parlour, because pizza was what he was eating at the moment, and these were the best in London, everyone said so, and anyway, they played good jazz there.

'This is nice,' said Minna, appreciative and on her best behaviour.

'I hope you like pizza.'

'I live for pizza.'

They drank some Peroni beer, and listened to the saxophonist, who was rather good, although Minna snorted in a dismissive sort of way and said that he wasn't a patch on Eddy.

'Just another poor booby trying to be Dexter Gordon,' she said, sitting up very straight in her chair and looking boldly about her. Eddy watched in amusement as the waiter fell in love with her.

'I'm starving,' she said, callous of her new swain's finer feelings, too busy eating most of Eddy's pizza as well as her own. He remembered she had always had a huge and indiscriminate appetite.

'So,' he said, 'what are you doing now?'

'Doing?' She gave him an arch look. 'When did I ever DO anything? I am utterly good for nothing, you know that. I read books on the French Revolution, that's what I do.'

'Professionally?' Eddy always forgot about her

24

being an heiress, she was so unlike the rest of her breed. Her family had made a fortune during the Industrial Revolution, in something unlikely like copper mines or hemp looms, and had gone on to perfect the art of Marrying Well, so that the fortune, instead of diminishing with each generation, grew greater. Minna's parents, killed instantly when their car went off the road into the Bay of Naples, had died before they had a chance to spend half of it, although Minna always said that her mother gave it her best shot.

'Almost,' she said now. 'Ask me anything.'

'I don't know anything to ask,' said Eddy. 'I never much liked history.'

'History is bunk,' said Minna dreamily, picking an olive out of the ruins of her pizza and eating it. 'Who said that? Henry Ford? Do you think he was misquoted? I have a bust of Napoleon at home, the duck. Tom says he looks just like Rod Stewart, do you call that rather rude?'

'I think it's quite advanced, for Tom,' said Eddy. He had been schoolfriends with Minna's brother Tom, back in what Eddy now referred to as his wild youth, and they had got themselves into more trouble than he cared to remember. 'How is he, these days?'

'Oh, you know,' said Minna, in the special resigned voice she reserved for the foibles of her brother. 'Much the same. He's in New York, in a suite in the Carlisle, if you please. He says he's in love.'

'Oh, yes?'

'Exactly,' said Minna. 'One of those Argentinian beef heiresses, you know the ones, dressed from head to foot in Balenciaga. She's even richer than he is. They have little competitions about who can hire the longest limousine, you can imagine.'

'A match made in heaven. I can imagine,' said Eddy, who could. Ever since Tom's rather precipitate elevation to the head of the family, he had been doing his best to live up to every cliché ever coined about the young rich. Drugs, drink, fast cars, jumping out of aeroplanes, racing horses, sailing 300-foot yachts, pursuing other men's wives: he had done them all, with a rather touching devotion to his calling. As he had once said to Eddy, in a rare moment of lucidity, 'Everyone will call me a playboy whatever I do, so I might as well live up to it. Shame not to, really.'

Sent down from Oxford for driving a 1954 Bugatti into the fountain in the middle of Christ Church, which he and his cronies had considered a perfectly inspired joke, he had been on a downward spiral ever since.

Eddy still saw him once or twice a year, when Tom would descend on him, fresh from Palm Beach or St Moritz or someone's boat in the Aegean, and drag him round endless unsavoury bars, and they would drink a great deal of Armagnac and pick up girls, and each time Eddy would wake up the next day and remember why he didn't live like that any more.

'So you're left all on your own?' he said now.

'Yes,' said Minna happily. 'At last.'

The posse of maiden aunts and dyspeptic uncles who had rallied round to take Minna in after her parents died had finally given up when she ran away to London for the fourth time. There had been much muttering and shaking of heads, but little surprise. After all, everyone knew that there was bad blood on her mother's side, and they had only been waiting

26

for it to out. So Minna had lived with Tom ever since, in the great white house he had bought in Chelsea.

'And all thanks to Great Uncle James and his wild blood,' she continued. 'It's just me and the butler, but he's far too busy playing poker all night with his chums to bother with me. No, no, only joking,' she said, seeing Eddy's face. 'It's just me. Footloose and fancy free. I'm all dressed up with nowhere to go. What do you think?'

'That you'll come to a bad end,' said Eddy sternly.

Minna tried not to look pleased. 'That's just what poor Aunt Eloise used to say. Do you think I shall, really? Wouldn't it be too glamorous for anything? All the best people come to bad ends, have you noticed?' She frowned suddenly, struck by a terrible thought. 'You're not going to start nannying me again, are you?'

'No,' said Eddy, who, after all, only wanted a quiet life. 'I'm too old and tired for nannying.'

'Well, there's a blessing. I can be feckless and reckless and you won't mind a bit.'

'And what happens when you finish the Revolution?'

'I can hardly think that far ahead,' said Minna. 'I expect I could always start on the Russians. Lucky for me that so many people had revolutions, and the Bolsheviks were rather to die, wouldn't you say?'

Eddy thought that he wouldn't have put it quite that way himself, but then he didn't imagine for a moment that Minna's version of history was of the empirical school.

'So,' he said, 'I can see that you have everything quite sorted out.'

Minna ignored the edge in his voice. Some habits, she supposed, would die hard, whatever anyone said. 'I have rather,' she said. 'If only everyone wasn't away. I don't even have a dog to walk.'

2

Minna woke up to the sound of the doorbell. She looked at her watch. Ten o'clock. She didn't think she was expecting anyone, and certainly not at this hour. Even if most of her acquaintance were not in the South Seas or somewhere equally outlandish, none of them would be seen dead out of doors before eleven-thirty. She pulled on one of Tom's shirts and went downstairs.

The couple at the door were immaculate: Gucci luggage, matching suntans, very white shirt cuffs, and perfectly coiffed hair. They looked as if they had just stepped out of *Town and Country*, killing time between fundraising balls. They seemed rather taken aback by the sight of Minna, so indecorously clad and obviously not up.

'Well,' she said, not at all sure what to make of them. Whoever they were, they looked as if they had come for a long stay. 'Can I help you?'

The man cleared his throat. 'Are you the real-estate lady?' he asked, a little obliquely Minna felt, for this time of the morning.

'Not entirely,' she said, taking a beat. 'I live here.'

The couple looked perfectly baffled by this every-day statement, for all the world as if she had told them that she was a mortician of the head of the Milk Marketing Board. She put it down to the fact that they were patently American, and quite probably suffering from jet-lag.

'You see,' said the woman apologetically, 'we have just rented this house for the summer.'

'That's right,' said the man bullishly, allowing none of the genteel qualms of his wife. 'We have just rented this house for the summer,' he added in a loud clear voice, spacing his words out carefully, as if unsure whether Minna had mastered the rudiments of spoken English.

'I see,' said Minna, who didn't at all. 'Might one ask from whom?'

The man consulted a piece of paper with all the importance of a presidential aide about to read a communiqué from the White House.

'From a Mr Thomas Vane,' he said triumphantly.

'We met him in New York,' said the woman, with a reminiscent smile. 'SUCH a charming boy. It was at Effie Hampton's party, she always asks such a CLEVER mix of people, one gets so TIRED of all the same old faces, night after night, balls, openings, fundraisers, first nights, benefits for the Met . . . '

'Yes, yes,' said her husband impatiently. He obviously had weightier matters to think about. 'Thomas Vane,' he repeated, for Minna's benefit. 'A most amusing fellow, most amusing.'

Minna didn't think so. 'My brother,' she said.

'We have the contract right here,' said the man, nothing daunted. 'If you would care to look at it, you'll find it's all in order.'

'No, no, it's quite perfectly fine,' said Minna, who knew when she was beaten. 'I'm sure it's all absolutely kosher and above board and watertight. Come in, why don't you? Do you mind if I just take the time to pack a bag? There's breakfast in the fridge. Although I do think you'd be happier at the Connaught.'

'Do you want more pizza?' said Eddy, opening the door.

'How about a bed?' said Minna boldly. She held up her bag. 'I've been evicted. I really am a bag lady now.'

'Lovely for you,' said Eddy, leading the way upstairs.

'Tom rented the house without telling me, the louse. Can you believe it? Thank you,' she said, taking the beer Eddy offered her. 'Although I suppose I shouldn't be that surprised, knowing Tom. You should have *seen* the Americans who've taken it, I shouldn't think they've been west of Park Avenue in their lives. Gucci to Gucci, his and hers haircuts, and they wanted to know if I was the real-estate lady, whatever that means. Is there a false estate lady? I don't understand a word of it. Do I look like a real-estate lady to you?'

'Not in that dress,' said Eddy, laughing at her. Today it was dark orange, and even shorter than that of the day before.

'Well, quite,' said Minna indignantly. 'Some people really do have NO idea. And what am I supposed to do now? Walk the streets?'

'Do you want some breakfast with your beer?' said Eddy, concentrating on essentials. 'There's bacon.'

'Yes, please,' said Minna. 'Anyway, luckily I remembered there was you, so the day is not lost.' She gave him her best tiny-little-me-smile. She knew it never worked with him, but she always went on trying, an optimist to the last. 'Could I stay for a while? Would you mind terribly? I hardly take up any room, you wouldn't even notice I was here.'

'Of course I wouldn't,' said Eddy. 'There's nowhere for you to sleep, that's all.'

Minna fixed him with a speaking look. 'Eddy,' she said firmly. 'You are my oldest friend. Who else can I turn to? Of course,' she added, laughing guiltily, 'the fact that you are the only living person I know who isn't halfway up the Andes has absolutely nothing to do with it.'

'Nothing at all,' said Eddy, who didn't call himself a cynic for nothing. 'All right,' he said, relenting, as they had both known that he would. 'There's a futon in the cupboard. I suppose you could use that.'

'Utter heaven,' said Minna, beaming at him. 'I'm not proud. A little pallet in the corner, a crust of bread once a day, the occasional kind word, that's all I need.'

'All right already,' said Eddy. 'It's not Claridges.'

'But it's home,' said Minna. 'I know. I couldn't like it more. Have you got any marmalade?'

'With your bacon?' said Eddy.

Minna opened her eyes very wide at him. 'Isn't there toast?' she said.

Eddy sighed and put two pieces of bread under the grill. 'I don't know what the daily is going to say,' he said.

The daily had a great deal to say. She arrived at noon, after Eddy had gone out to practise with his band. She was almost six foot and as thin as a blade, with improbably blond hair, a heavy suede fringed jacket, and cowboy boots.

'Hello,' said Minna companionably. 'I'm Minna.' She held out her hand, thinking the forward approach her best bet.

'Oh?' The daily looked down at her from a great height. 'Irene. Where's Eddy?'

'Out,' said Minna, refusing to take offence. 'Practising. With the band, you know how it is. Shall I be in your way?'

'Way?' said Irene, not altogether polite. 'Are you waiting for Eddy or something? He didn't say that he was going to have visitors.'

'Oh, no,' said Minna. 'I'm not Visitors. I'm Eddy's new lodger. I live here now. Could you die?' she added hopefully.

'You live here now?' Irene started to look as if she had a bad smell under her nose.

'Well, yes,' said Minna, speaking slowly and clearly, and wondering if Irene understood any words over one syllable. 'I'm staying for a while, I'm not sure how long. I've been evicted, you see, so it was the pavement or Eddy. I know some people think it's rather romantic to sleep under the arches or Waterloo Bridge or I don't know where, but I don't think it would be quite me, do you?'

'But,' said Irene, starting to splutter. Minna had never seen anyone splutter in real life before, although she knew that people did it a great deal in popular novels. 'But you can't possibly. I mean, where are you going to sleep? There's only one bed.'

'And the futon,' said Minna helpfully.

'The futon,' said Irene in outrage. 'The futon? You can't possibly sleep on that. How am I supposed to clean round it, may I ask?'

33

'Don't fret,' said Minna soothingly. 'I can always roll it up for the day. Eddy doesn't mind, really he doesn't. He's like a brother to me.'

'He may not mind,' said Irene with a great snort, implying that she minded very much indeed. 'He may not mind, but really . . . ' She trailed off into a muttered undertone of fury.

'Have you always been a cleaner?' Minna asked, purely by way of changing the subject and making conversation, or so she told herself. She knew the importance of making small talk, whatever the occasion.

'I'm not a cleaner,' said Irene, bridling furiously and reminding Minna of nothing so much as a rather over-excited brood mare. 'I only clean Eddy's place as a favour, between jobs. I'm an actress,' she added, as if admitting that she was Meryl Streep.

'Oh, really?' said Minna, all wide-eyed interest, perfectly riveted. 'How clever of you. I don't think that I've seen you in anything.'

'I was in the last Rover advertisement,' said Irene, as if admitting that she had starred in *Annie Hall*.

'Well,' said Minna, at something of a loss. She really wasn't at all sure what the correct response to such a statement could be. She must ask Eddy when he came home.

Having exhausted her conversational powers, Irene rolled up her sleeves and got to work, giving little snorts and mutters of disapproval under her breath. Under the fringed jacket she wore a designer punk T-shirt with strategic rips in it, which she obviously considered the last word in seductive domestic wear. Minna thought it was too dated for words. She wondered what Eddy saw in this furious Amazon.

She supposed that there was, after all, no accounting for tastes. Each to each is what we teach, she thought, fair to the last.

'I expect I'll leave you to it,' she said, and went out into the Soho sunshine. The last Rover commercial indeed. It might be many things, but it was hardly Art.

Out in the street, the day was hotting up. Minna wondered quite what she should do with it. There was so much of it. What should she do with this day, and the one after that, and all the others queuing up to be had? Sometimes she wondered if she ought to get a job. After all, that was what most people did. Even Eddy had the band. But then she always came up against the thorny problem of not being good at anything except for reading about the Revolution and staying up late and eating in restaurants. She might have graceful arms but she had no qualifications.

She had been brought up with all the trappings of inherited money: nannies and governesses and ponies to ride and pretty dresses to wear and holidays on the Riviera and strangers for parents and all those other things that serve to keep the world at bay. She knew how to get out of a taxi and which way to pass the port and how to make polite dinner-party conversation. ('Rather recite the ABC, darling, than sit silent at the dining table.') She could decline Latin verbs and use the subjunctive in French and quote extensively from Byron and the Romantic poets, but none of that seemed to help when it actually came to doing anything.

She had seen people with vocations. She had

friends who were artists and writers and musicians and poets. She watched them all battling towards their respective goals, more often than not with a great deal of sound and fury, and with varying degrees of success. And she watched them go on doing it, however hopeless their ambitions seemed, and she wondered what drove them on. She supposed that they had a burning desire to make their mark on an ungrateful world. The trouble was, she had none. Sometimes she thought she might rather like a burning desire, picturing herself as a charmingly starving artist, a perfect latter-day Chatterton, perched up in a garret, living on cheap red wine and charcoal biscuits and impossible dreams.

Sometimes she thought she would rather suit a vocation, but most of the time she didn't mind so much. When push came to shove, and the swings melted into roundabouts, and life became earnest and real, and the end of the line was in sight, she had to admit that she wasn't quite sure what she would do with a vocation if she did have one. It was a serious business, no laughing matter, and Minna wasn't at all sure that she was so good at being serious.

So she floated through life, picking up people and good times as they fell about her feet and not thinking too hard about tomorrow, and for the time being that was good enough. There were limits to everything, after all, and some girls were simply not bred for impressing people with lists of achievement. Minna was a great one for knowing her limitations; in rare moments of candour she sometimes admitted that it was about all she was good at.

*　　*　　*

Looking up from her musing, she found herself outside an Italian café and went in. It was dark and cool and cramped and smelt of coffee and dim sunshine.

'Hello,' she said, smiling at the man behind the till. 'Double espresso. Please.' Eddy always told her to order two singles, that the coffee came stronger and better that way, but she liked a big cup, she couldn't help it, even if that wasn't the way they drank it in Italy.

She settled herself at a corner table, and looked about with interest. There were a few worn old men in one corner, first-generation immigrants off the boat from Palermo, playing cards with a tired intensity and watching Italian football on the television, and a group of teenage girls in another corner, arguing about boys and whether it was wise to go All the Way, or not, and two Danes eating pastries and practising their English on one another, and several advertising types in Cutler and Gross spectacles and loud ties, stopping off on their way to a meeting, busy impressing each other with sales figures and other people's salaries.

Perhaps this was where one met people. Perhaps a young Paul Newman would saunter in at any moment and take her away from all this. Minna felt that she would rather like that. Paul Newman or Henry Fonda or Cary Grant, she wasn't fussy. It only slightly irked her that all her screen idols were dead or fat or old or gone to seed. All the young actors these days were such creatures of the real world, living in odd places like Peckham and Swiss Cottage, going to bed early and never raising hell, doggedly insisting that their talent made them no different from the next man, that away from the smell of the greasepaint and the roar of the crowd they were just regular kind of folks, drinking in the pub, worrying about the mortgage, arguing with the wife. Minna was certain that this couldn't be right and yearned for the days when Humphrey Bogart and Gary Cooper and Marlon Brando were young, when film stars sailed on 100-foot yachts and drove to work in drop-head Bentleys and thought nothing of importing six tons of Alaskan snow for a Christmas party in southern California, where the oranges grew to the size of footballs and reality was damned.

The heroes Minna dreamt of were only too larger than life, giants astride a new world of their own making, inventing themselves carelessly, all raging talent and youth and glamour. Of all things, Minna admired glamour most. She felt everyone should have more of it.

'Excuse me?'

Minna looked up. A man was standing in front of her, interrupting her thoughts. Hardly even a man, more of a boy, not much older than she was. Just as she was wondering who he looked more like, Cooper mostly she thought, with perhaps just a trace of a very young Newman if one was being generous, he asked if he could sit down. Looking round, Minna noticed that the place had filled up.

'Of course,' she said, too taken with him to wonder if he was trying to pick her up. 'Just do.'

'All the other tables are full,' he observed shyly, explaining himself.

'Yes,' said Minna. 'I can see.' She smiled at him graciously, a nice indication that she had not misunderstood his intentions.

'Would you like a cigarette?' he said politely, holding out a crumpled packet, just like all those dashing GIs used to in the old war films. Minna looked at him in admiration. She wouldn't have been surprised if he had asked her to go dancing at the Four Hundred.

'Thank you,' she said, taking one and holding it up to be lit. She remembered to look at him as he lit it, through the flame, in a way that Lauren Bacall would have thoroughly approved of, had she had the good fortune to be there. Minna might not know many things, but she did know how to let a man light her cigarette. The boy blushed a little, as if not quite used to eye contact, smiled gravely at her, and then, to her utter astonishment, took a battered paperback out of his pocket and started to read. Minna bent her head to see the title. Hemingway. Well.

'I love Hemingway,' she said, which was true. How could she not when all his books were full of tortured heroism and brave young matadors and broken old colonels and hot Spanish sun?

The stranger smiled at her again, with a hint of vagueness, as if he were rather surprised to find that she wasn't Lady Brett Ashley, and returned to his book.

Minna felt decidedly put out. She wasn't sure that she was used to this kind of reaction. After all, what was the point in meeting people if they simply sat and read a book, for all the world as if they had nothing better to do? Where was the good in that?

She shifted a little in her chair, rearranging her legs to their best advantage. Minna might like to think that she had a rare lack of vanity, but like any girl she knew about men and legs. She ran a careless hand through her hair, which was long and heavy and blond enough not to need any touching up from the hairdresser, and wondered what her next move should be.

The boy was still engrossed in his book, his brow a little furrowed in concentration, quite oblivious to the rest of the world. He had light brown hair that fell over his eyes in a rather pleasing way, and a smooth untouched air to his face that said he didn't know very much about anything. Minna noticed that he had good hands, finely shaped, with long slender fingers. Perhaps he was a celebrated concert pianist, taking a break from Rachmaninov. One never knew, in this part of town. Every so often he reached out for his cup of coffee, without taking his eyes from his book. Minna wondered if he had reached the bit about the earth moving yet. She thought that it might sound a fraction forward to ask him, even for her. Only Hemingway could talk about the earth moving and get away with it. She decided to wait him out.

The clock on the wall ticked impassively through the smoke, but Minna didn't pay it any mind. She had no particular place to go. The football was still going at full tilt, punctuated by great foreign roars of joy every time a goal was scored. Minna decided she would never really understand about boys and football. It was one of life's great imponderables, like James Joyce or Rousseau's theory of the general will.

Minna ordered another cup of coffee, just for the hell of it, and lit herself another cigarette. She sat and thought about Gary Cooper kissing Ingrid Bergman in *For Whom the Bell Tolls*. She sat and thought about Humphrey Bogart kissing Ingrid Bergman in

Casablanca. She thought that some girls really did get all the luck. She wondered whether Eddy had come back from his practice to find the irate Irene spitting through her teeth, and whether they had fought or just tumbled into bed. She wondered if any cleaning had been done at all, or whether Irene had simply sat, moody in her designer rips, and telephoned to her agent. A Rover commercial. Minna, who wasn't above indulging in a little intellectual snobbery when the mood took her, snorted in derision. The boy looked up from his book in surprise.

'Sorry,' said Minna, laughing at his startled face. 'Just thinking.'

Don't mind me. I have no Hemingway to keep me company. I shall just sit here until you think you might like to talk to me. I shall just ruin my constitution by mainlining dangerous doses of caffeine, filling my lungs with the smoke of a hundred cigarettes, until you choose to relieve me. Don't mind me.

'Not very pleasant thoughts?' He was smiling at her, a little uncertainly, as if rather taken aback by his own audacity.

Minna kept her surprise to herself. 'Not very,' she agreed, thinking of Irene in her ripped T-shirt. 'Not as good as what you are reading.'

'Nothing is as good as what I am reading,' he said with finality, as if settling the point. Minna thought it probably did settle the point. She wondered what they were going to talk about next. It was all very fine, this meeting people, but what was one supposed to talk about?

'Did you get to the bit about the earth moving yet?' she said, without quite meaning to. She rather

41

thought that she had meant to say, polite and innocuous, did he come here often, but it had come out all wrong.

'Yes,' he said, looking at her in a most disconcerting way.

There was a small pause, and then they both caught each other's eye and laughed and it was all right.

'Only Hemingway,' said Minna, waving her cigarette eloquently, in that way she had.

'But of course,' he said, in that same certain way. 'Would you like another cup of coffee?'

'Your treat?' said Minna, starting to smile. 'Yes, please. Cigarette?' she added, a picture of emancipation, offering him her own packet.

'Yes, please,' he said, taking one.

Minna smiled wider than ever. She had met someone.

His name was Jay, and he had just come to London, and he wasn't very good at it yet, he said. He devised postcards, he said, which had had a sudden and mercurial success, and could now be found on every shop counter in Soho. When he wasn't writing new postcard jokes he wrote plays, he said, but those hadn't been discovered yet.

Minna thought him the most perfect new acquisition, and told him so. He smiled gravely at her and said that he was flattered. He had a shy, grave way about him that she liked. He had dark grey eyes and a slow smile and he seemed as if he didn't quite belong to this century.

'So,' he said after a while, growing a little uncomfortable with talking so much about himself, something he was not used to. 'What about you?'

'What about me?' Minna invited.

'Well.' Jay considered, not quite sure where to start. 'What do you do?'

'Oh, me,' said Minna, with a faint sigh of resignation. 'Nothing. You know.'

'Nothing?' said Jay, fascinated. 'How extraordinary.' He didn't know that there were any people left any more who did nothing, apart from those young rich one read about in the paper, always being busted for hard drugs or thrown out of university or caught speeding in other people's Ferraris, and they never seemed quite real. 'Have you done that for long?'

'Almost for ever,' said Minna, at her most worldweary. 'It's terribly old-fashioned. It's late in the Eighties now, and we are all supposed to be a fearless sisterhood of career women, dauntless in the bedroom and the boardroom.'

'So I'm told,' said Jay, who was an old-fashioned boy at heart, lucky for Minna. 'I can't ever see it myself. The point.'

'Well, neither can I,' said Minna, delighted to have discovered a kindred spirit. 'I mean, really. Pinstripe suits and power dressing and eight to eight and portable telephones and fax me yesterday and I don't know what else. It's just not sex, is it?' Minna had a curious habit of referring to everything she disapproved of as not being sex. She didn't indulge in sex that often, but it was her adjectival form of approval. Working was definitely not sex.

'No,' said Jay, in his grave way, having the grace not to take her literally. 'It certainly is not.'

Minna beamed at him. 'Well,' she said in satisfaction. 'So you do see how it is?'

Jay nodded firmly, quite seeing.

It was after four o'clock by the time Minna returned to Eddy's flat. She let herself in and danced up the stairs, hugging the thought of her new find to her. The sun was riding a little lower in the sky, but it was still doing its best, and the flat was full of it. There was no sign of Irene. Minna tried not to notice whether the sheets on Eddy's bed were rumpled or not.

'Hello,' she said, finding him on the balcony, drinking beer and listening to Mick Jagger still having his nineteenth nervous breakdown, after all these years. 'Did you have a good day at the office, dear?'

'Just dandy,' said Eddy, looking up at her.

'I brought you strawberries,' said Minna. 'From a barrow,' she added, with pride. She waved them at him. 'There, now no-one can say I'm not a good lodger.'

'As if anyone would dare.' He didn't ask her what she had been doing, out all day. Her books on the Revolution sat untouched in a corner, mute testament to her neglect.

'I met your daily woman,' said Minna carelessly, as if she didn't mean anything by it. She drew up a stool and sat down next to him, stretching out her legs for the sun to find, as if it needed any directing.

'Yes. So she said.' Eddy didn't mention exactly what Irene had said. He didn't think it politic.

'I don't think she likes me,' said Minna happily. 'She was most unforthcoming. Is she always like that, or did I just catch her on a bad day?'

'She's great once you get to know her,' said Eddy, giving nothing away.

'Really?' Minna tried to look credulous, but failed signally. Eddy gave her a sharp look. 'She tells me that she's an actress,' she said, ignoring it. 'I do think that's perfectly splendid. I must tell Richard Eyre, the next time I run into him.'

'Do shut up,' said Eddy. 'You don't really want to be a bag lady, do you?'

'Only if the bags are Vuitton,' said Minna.

3

Minna didn't quite know why she didn't tell Eddy about Jay. She had never believed in examining her motives too closely, so she told herself that the right moment had not arisen, and in the end she simply said that she was going out, and that was that. Eddy, who said he was too old for questions, didn't ask where she was going and she didn't tell him.

In the cupboard that passed for a bathroom, she put on her face with more care than usual. She hadn't told Jay how young she was, and she had a vague notion that she wanted to appear older, so she drew deep cheekbones for herself with her most sophisticated blush and put dark lines about her eyes and filled in her eyebrows and painted her lips bold scarlet, the kind of colour that would have had the maiden aunts fainting away in horror. She teased her hair into a tousled mess, then changed her mind and slicked it down with some of Eddy's hair lotion, courtesy of Mr Geo. Trumper, barber to the great and the good. Satisfied at last, she pulled on one of the dozen clinging dresses she owned and had done with it.

'Well,' she said, emerging into the light, where Eddy sat toying with his saxophone, just like all good musicians wishing on a star. 'What do you think?' She gave a little pirouette, holding out her arms for his approval.

Eddy looked her over, wishing that he didn't have to. He wished she hadn't grown out of jeans. He wished she didn't have quite such a body. He wished she didn't flaunt it in quite such a careless way, which in anyone else would have been shameless. He wondered what it was that had made her decide to stop people guessing.

'Very smart,' he said truthfully. 'And too old for you.'

'You said that before,' said Minna, pleased.

'Still true.'

'Good.' Minna came the closest she ever could to a smirk, kissed him on the ear, and left him in a rush. 'Don't wait up,' she called over her shoulder as she slammed the door on him.

Eddy was left alone in the flat, which suddenly seemed empty and silent without her. It had never seemed so empty before, it had just been his, but now it seemed dark and cold and unfriendly. Without stopping to wonder why, he left it. If he was quick, he could still catch the band at the pub.

Minna wandered down the street, darkening now, the sun spent, the deep blue dusk lighting up with street lights and restaurant signs and lurid neon promising sex sex sex and girls girls girls and sometimes the two together. The crowd, washed and primped and dressed for its evening entertainment, was on the make as ever. Hair was combed and teased and sleek with water, leather jackets were slung negligently over careless shoulders, defying the heat, and pointed boots cuffed the pavements in disdain. Taxis disgorged their occupants into the bars and clubs and theatres, and cars hooted crossly at each other, looking vainly for a place to

park. Men hung about in doorways, doing shady
deals, and the pubs and cafés were already filled to
capacity, spilling drinkers out on to the pavements,
where they preened and laughed and talked a little
too loud, for the benefit of the passers-by.

Minna was late. Jay sat at a table, reading his
book. Knowing no-one he took his book with him
everywhere, but he was happy to wait. He didn't
know very much, but he knew that girls were always
late. That was their prerogative, after all.

'I'm late,' said Minna, as if she couldn't imagine
how she managed it. 'Can you ever forgive me?' She
did it so beautifully, a vision of contrition, her smile
a little uncertain of his forgiveness, that he couldn't
mind. How could he mind when she stood in front
of him in her tiny dress, her hair slick and shining,
lighting up the night without even trying.

'It's fine,' he said, standing up for a lady, just like
Mother taught him. 'I've only just arrived.'

Minna noticed the three dead cigarettes in the
ashtray and thought that he was even more perfect
than she had at first suspected.

'Well,' she said, kissing him on both cheeks, just
as if they had been meeting for dinner for years,
'that's all right then. What are you drinking?'

'Beer,' said Jay, hoping it wasn't too infra dig. It
was impossible to know, with a girl like this.

'Beer would be lovely.' Minna smiled at him, the
most gracious of dining companions, for all the
world as if they were at the Ritz and covered in
diamonds, letting him ask the waiter for her drink,
because that was the way a real lady behaved. Real
ladies behaved that way in the old films anyway,
and that was the most reliable yardstick she had to
go by. It had never let her down yet, and so she

48

didn't stop to resent the fact that her mother had been far too busy dashing off to dances and dinners and rubbers of bridge with deposed kings to bother much with a daughter. And Jay, who wasn't used to real ladies, not like this one, felt ten foot tall as he asked for her beer, and wondered at his luck.

They ate spaghetti with clams, just like Mamma used to make, and drank rather more good Italian red than was perhaps good for them, and Minna quite forgot about being grown up and made little jokes about the other diners and waved her fork about as she talked and told him about everyone going away, and how she didn't know how to meet people.

'Just my utter luck that you picked me up this morning,' she said, batting her eyelashes at him in the most distressingly fast manner. 'Otherwise what would have become of me?'

Jay, who had never picked up a girl in his life, and wasn't at all sure how he would go about it, had drunk enough to consider this a compliment.

'I'm sure I don't know how to meet people either,' he said, thinking of the nights he sat alone in his garret, pounding away at his typewriter, struggling with what he hoped might turn out to be a masterpiece after all, and never seeing a soul. Lost in the unfamiliar maze of the city, he hardly knew where to start.

'I must have known once,' said Minna doubtfully, trying to cast her mind back. 'Shall we have some coffee? Double espresso, will you ask that nice man? Because otherwise I should never have met all those people who have gone away. But I rather think that they must have met me, not the other way round, and now look at me. Quite undone.' Minna sighed a little and looked faintly soulful. She was not above striking attitudes, when the muse took her.

'Just do,' said Jay, allowing himself to laugh at her a little. She didn't seem to mind. 'I did meet someone the other day. In a bar.'

'In a bar?' said Minna, sitting up straight in her chair, clearly impressed. A man who met people in bars, what more could a girl ask for? And there she had been, imagining he was just a sweet shy Young Artist from the provinces. It just went to show, you never could tell, not in this part of town. 'How romantic. What a dark horse you are, why didn't you tell me sooner?'

'I'm not sure that she'll remember me,' said Jay candidly. The hour had been late and the wines had been various, as the poet put it. Even struggling Young Artists have to have a night off, from time to time.

'How could she not?' said Minna staunchly. 'Do let's go and see if she's still there. I love bars.' In Minna's mind, bars were still the kind of places where Hoagy Carmichael played blues through the smoke and Lauren Bacall leant on the piano and Humphrey Bogart came in out of the rain.

'All right,' said Jay affably, thinking that he could go anywhere with this creature on his arm. 'Let's.'

The bar was crowded when they arrived. It was, Minna recognized at once, a dive. She gave a little sigh of pleasure. The lighting was as low as could be wished, and the décor was turn-of-the-century red plush meeting late-Eighties sleaze with perfect decorum. The waitresses were beautiful and willowy, rivalling Cyd Charisse in her prime.

'Aren't they pretty?' said Minna, wishing she had legs that long.

'Men,' said Jay unemotionally, an old hand already, as if it were all in a day's work.

'It's too maddening,' said Minna, not remotely put out, 'when you meet men who have better legs than you do.'

'You have perfect legs,' said Jay, expansive with all this unaccustomed late living.

Minna smiled beatifically on him. She wanted to put him in her pocket and keep him for ever.

'So,' she said. 'Where's your friend?'

'There,' said Jay, pointing diffidently, suddenly shy. 'At the bar.'

She was exactly where he had left her the last time. He wondered if she had ever moved.

'That?' said Minna, astonished into rudeness. She wasn't quite sure what she had been expecting, but it certainly wasn't this. She had vaguely thought that Jay might have found what mothers fondly call a nice girl. Pretty, a little bashful, suitably dressed, gently amusing. The creature at the bar put nice girls to shame. She was set on her bar stool as if she had been born to it, silken legs crossed, vicious black stilettos tapping the air in impatience. She was smoking a cigarette from a long ebony holder, and from time to time she paused to run a scarlet-nailed hand through her dark pink hair, just as if she was simply waiting for William Wyler to say, 'Cut'. She dripped languor.

'Yes,' said Jay, emboldened by Minna's surprise. He led her to the bar before she could protest, and touched the apparition on the shoulder. 'Lou Lou,' he said daringly. 'Do you remember me?'

The girl looked at him long and slow through

a cloud of cigarette smoke, narrowing her eyes as if to see him better, and suddenly gave a shout of disbelieving laughter.

'Well, I'll be damned,' she said, in a voice that spoke eloquently of years of dry martinis and filterless cigarettes. 'The poet, as I live and breathe. Of course I remember you, although after I was so rude to you I'm surprised you've come back for more. It was you that I was rude to, wasn't it? I thought so.' She nodded sagely and patted him on the cheek, not quite in apology. 'Buy me a drink, would you ever? The rat fink I came with has taken to the hills, damn his eyes, and I sit alone and palely loitering, which never did a girl any good, I don't care what Keats and his gang had to say about it. Augustus,' she said to the barman, who was gazing at Jay with all the rapture of the recently converted, 'earn your keep for once and get us a bottle of green chartreuse, would you ever. It's not his real name,' she added, 'but you can't get a job in this place with a name like Stan.'

'Green chartreuse?' said Jay, having difficulty catching up.

'Green chartreuse,' said Minna in admiration.

'Trust me,' said Lou Lou. 'Never trust someone who says trust me, but you can make an exception in my case, so don't fret. So, are you going to introduce me to your ladybird, or must we stare like calves all night long?'

'Minna Vane,' said Minna, holding out her hand. Jay seemed temporarily to have lost his wits. He had forgotten about Lou Lou. Their last meeting was a little hazy in his memory, but now it was coming back, sharp and clear, and he wondered how he could have forgotten. 'How do you do?'

'How do you do?' said Lou Lou, throwing back her head and letting loose a laugh that could stop traffic at sixty paces. 'How do you do? It's too much. What HAVE you been up to since I saw you last?' she said to Jay, her eyebrows rising up into two elegant peaks under her pink fringe. 'Taking my advice?'

Jay blushed and shook his head helplessly. He wondered if this had been such a good idea after all. Perhaps he should just have taken Minna home and returned to his typewriter and done some work and listened to Radio Four and gone to bed with a cup of hot milk.

'Don't look so coy,' said Lou Lou, taking her drink and draining half of it at a swallow. 'That's better,' she said, all but smacking her lips. Minna watched her in fascination. 'It's only natural, you know.'

'What advice?' said Minna.

'Sound advice. The kind of advice mothers should give their children in the cradle, before the rot sets in. I told him to go out and find himself a girl and get himself laid. No good being a poet all your life.'

Jay blushed even more and looked as if all he could think of was where to find a welcome stone that he could crawl under. He muttered something indistinct under his breath.

Minna laughed, quite dry enough behind the ears to take the rough with the diamonds.

'Well,' she said, 'he's not taking it with me, if that's what you're thinking. We've only just met.'

'That never made any difference to anybody,' said Lou Lou sternly.

'Please!' said Jay in desperation, shocked into speech at last. As Lou Lou could have told him, a girl could take the boy out of the provinces, but she couldn't take the provinces out of the boy.

Lou Lou threw up her hands, admitting defeat. 'All right already,' she said, ruffling his hair. 'Don't eat me, I beg. I have some kind of reputation to live up to. How could I know that you'd start running around with the respectable?'

'Not THAT respectable,' said Minna, who liked to think that she had something of a reputation herself.

'All things are relative,' said Lou Lou wisely, banging her glass on the bar to get the barman's attention, which was still riveted on Jay's dark head. 'And you look like a cut above the common touch to me. But then, I may be wrong.' She didn't sound as if this was ever going to be a real possibility. 'Anyway, I've been waiting for the rat fink to come out of the gents for more than half an hour, that's how much of a fool I am, and to be frank with you, I'm a little sauced, so you must forgive me.'

'Well,' said Minna, eminently reasonable and quite understanding, 'what else could you do, under the circumstances?'

Lou Lou regarded her with her worldly mascara-laden eyes, and started to smile. 'What else?' she said companionably.

'Are you really called Lou Lou?' asked Minna, curious and a little daring after her second glass. Jay was still staring at his in a vain attempt to avoid Augustus's eye.

'Not at all,' said Lou Lou. 'Is anyone really called Lou Lou anyway? I was christened Edna, if you must know.'

'Ah,' said Minna, thinking that this really was too good to be true. 'I quite see.'

'Don't you just? As I said to my sainted Mama,

no-one, but NO-ONE can expect to be romanced with a name like Edna. I hadn't heard of any Irish novelists in those days, and I don't expect it would have made much difference if I had. She couldn't take my point for any money, so I left her to it and took the first train to London and gave myself a new name and some new hair and a new pair of shoes, and here I am, which I shouldn't be except for the fink running out on me, and him promising suites in the Ritz and castles in Spain and I don't know what else. Am I making sense to you?'

'Perfect sense,' said Minna, picking up quickly on Lou Lou's strange patois, which seemed to be a curious mixture of eighteenth-century cant, modern urban slang, and B-movie cliché, all delivered with the cut-glass hauteur of a society hostess.

'Perfect sense?' said Jay, who was still writing about life in the real world. How could any of this make perfect sense? He felt rather as if he had walked into a play in the middle of the second act with no programme notes.

'Yes,' said Lou Lou. 'Perfect sense. Listen to the lady. Now do stop standing there looking like Arthur Miller and tell me about your play.'

'I'm still writing it,' said Jay unwillingly. He hated talking about his work. 'Third act, third draft.' He stared again into his glass and was surprised to find it empty.

'More?' said Augustus, who stood enslaved. No boy with eyes like that should ever have an empty glass.

'Why not?' said Minna, holding hers out to be filled.

'And some for the poet,' said Lou Lou, laughing at the barman's disconcerted face. 'He needs some inspiration, and the best inspiration I know comes straight from the bottle, no ice.'

'I had some inspiration once,' said Minna inconsequentially.

'I've got plenty,' said Jay doubtfully, remembering the days when he had been certain of it, 'But I wish I knew where it was.' He was suffering from writer's block, at least he would be if he believed in writer's block, which he didn't. He couldn't afford to start developing occupational hazards at this early stage. All he knew was that his mind was blank and recalcitrant, and it was perplexing him, and he didn't like it.

'It's all this high life,' said Lou Lou, who had known a few artists in her time and fancied that she knew about temperament. 'I dare say that I should be a poet too, if I had a nice quiet garret to live in and a Do Not Disturb sign. Don't let us tempt you out on the town every night. Before you know it you'll find yourself dissipated and thwarted and forty, and then where will you be?'

'No,' said Minna, who was too young to know any better and optimistic enough to believe she did. 'He won't be. Not Jay.'

The rat fink never did reappear, and Lou Lou said it was far too late for her to start again, so they just stayed at the bar and finished the bottle. It seemed to be the only sensible thing to do, under the circumstances.

A cabaret of heroic beauty came on and strutted their stuff, outrageous in feathers and two-inch eyelashes. Only their flat chests gave them away. Minna said she wondered what they did during the day, and Lou Lou said that she was far too young to know about things like that, and Jay said that they were probably all accountants anyway, because everyone knew about accountants. 'Straight out of Croydon,' he added obscurely. 'It's always Croydon, in the magazines.'

'Of course it is, darling,' said Lou Lou, pouring him another drink. 'There, there. Don't dwell on it.'

So they left it at that and enjoyed the show, which was reminiscent of the *Folies Bergère* and Berlin before the Wall and Marlene Dietrich at her peak, and decadent enough to please the most jaded palate.

'It's the absolute end,' said Minna, who thought it quite the most perfect thing she had ever seen. Lou Lou, who had seen it all and more before, agreed that it couldn't be all bad, and ordered another bottle, and Jay thought about his typewriter lying unused in his dark room and told himself firmly that tomorrow was another day. He didn't care to think too much how he would feel tomorrow, but then everyone knew that writers had to have at least a dash of decadence to be any good. Besides, he was enjoying himself.

The cabaret finished, and still they weren't ready to go home. Lou Lou seemed to have quite forgotten about the rat fink deserting a sinking ship, and Minna said that they couldn't possibly leave just as things were starting to get interesting. People were arriving as all the other bars closed down and they had nowhere else to go.

'Look, Jay,' said Minna patiently. 'This is all material for you. Listen and observe, isn't that the thing? How do you think Hemingway and Fitzgerald got started?'

'Not on lemonade and water biscuits anyhow,' said Lou Lou, the voice of reason. She smiled her siren smile at Jay. 'Welcome to the real world, sweet thing.'

Looking about him, Jay wouldn't quite have described his surroundings as the real world, but he recognized a worldly spirit when he saw one, and was happy to bow to a superior knowledge. The crowd which grew about him, jostling and preening and flirting, looked as if they had been born to be written into something. Men in distressed leather jackets and bare chests leant casually on the bar, butch as Sundance and twice as available, eyeing up prettier versions in subtle eye make-up and jewel-coloured shirts. A party in black tie and *diamanté* arrived on a wave of chatter and Chanel No. 5, intent on finding out how the other half lived if it killed them in the attempt.

'Too CHI-CHI,' they cried, 'Too MUCH. Too KILLING. To DIE for. Too much like HEAVEN.'

Lou Lou raised her eyes to the ceiling and blew out a particularly scathing plume of smoke.

'There goes the next cabinet,' she said with authority. 'God help us.'

'It's a dirty job,' said Minna, echoing Eddy, 'but someone's got to do it.'

'Spare me from them, that's all I ask,' said Lou Lou, stubbing out her cigarette pointedly.

Girls in microscopic skirts and six-inch-long earrings were dancing with boys in brocade coats, watched with fascination by four Japanese who had got lost on the way back from the theatre. There were cowboys and Indians and old romantics and new romantics and Georgian dandies and recycled hippies and Marilyn Monroe lookalikes, and enough beefcake to start a fast-food restaurant. There were sharp suits and *louche* suits and bunny suits and countless tiny dresses made of scraps of lace and a yard of sequins. Through it all, the waitresses shimmied in their finery, batting eyelashes and exchanging backchat, towering over the crowd and looking less like accountants than anything Minna could think of.

'Well,' she said, smiling with pleasure, 'shall we have another drink?'

'What else is left to a girl?' said Lou Lou.

The dawn was filtering through the blinds when Minna let herself into the flat, shoes in hand, and tiptoed across the room to her little pallet on the floor. Eddy stirred and muttered crossly in his sleep, but did not wake, to Minna's relief. Whatever he might say about not nannying her any more, she didn't feel up to explaining what she had been doing, out until this hour of the morning. She had a sneaking feeling that he wouldn't approve. He had an obdurate puritanical streak when it came to her, she didn't know why, and it was always one rule for her and another for everyone else. Much better that he didn't know, and then the heart wouldn't have to grieve over what the eye didn't see, and everyone would be happy.

She stared at her flushed face and smudged eyes for a moment in the glass, and decided that she didn't have the strength to do anything about either, so she slipped off her dress, letting it lie where it fell, and crawled gratefully into her bed, and went to sleep without another thought.

4

It was another sunny day. It was that kind of summer. Sunny day after sunny day, running one into another, full of promise. Minna stretched lazily, watching her bare arms rise against the brightness of the day and thinking vaguely how well turned they were. Another perfect summer's day, and what was she to do with it? She decided not to dwell on it. Something would turn up. It always did.

She got up slowly, shaking her head a little, and put on her dressing gown, an exquisite drape of wide blue and white stripes which made her think of Noël Coward and *Private Lives* and breakfast on Italian balconies.

'Good morning,' said Eddy, as she wandered into the kitchen, looking for her breakfast. She had on that vague look that told him she had been out all night again. 'Have an egg,' he added callously.

'I'm fine,' said Minna, sitting down and helping herself to the remains of yesterday's pizza. She was glad to see that Eddy was composing again. He always had pizza to go when the muse was running strong. Eddy, watching her, wondered how she could stand cold pepperoni at this hour, but he knew better than to comment on it. 'Is there coffee?' she said, smiling in what she imagined was an ingratiating manner.

'There's coffee.' Eddy got up to make her a cup, remembering to make it strong and sweet, the way she liked it. He didn't know much, but he knew how she liked her coffee, and that would do for the time being. 'So who's this boy who is keeping you out all night?' he said, before he could stop himself. It really was no business of his, after all. She was well over the age of consent, she could run around with whomsoever she wanted.

'How do you know it's a boy?' said Minna, blinking the sleep out of her eyes.

'Stands to reason,' said Eddy. He gave her her coffee, glad she wasn't taking offence. 'You always had someone whose heart you were breaking. Why should anything have changed?'

Minna smiled to herself. A heartbreaker, now there was an honourable profession.

'He's a playwright,' she said. 'I found him in a café, do you call that romantic? And I'm not breaking his heart. He lives for his art, you should know all about that. No time for girls.'

'So what's he doing, running around with you until all hours?' said Eddy.

He really did sound like one of the disapproving aunts when he took that tone, Minna thought. She would have to tell him so.

'He's got block,' she said sunnily. 'I'm helping him get over it.'

'What philanthropy,' said Eddy, trying not to sound jaundiced. 'And not even for love.'

'Don't go getting cynical on me now,' said Minna, shaking her finger at him, as if he were a wayward child. 'Love isn't everything.'

'That's not what you used to say. I never knew a girl with so many beaux.'

'Many beaux to my string,' said Minna, smiling reminiscently. There had been so many boys, in those days. That summer, hot and long and languorous, when she had first come to London, free as a bird, ready to fly. She had discovered the King's Road, and short skirts, and cigarettes, and bourbon whisky. She had learnt to stay up all night and kiss for half an hour without stopping and wind a dozen boys at a time around her little finger. Those were the days when there was a party every night, and she was always invited. And there was a different boy at every party, and she had let them all fall in love with her, let them throw their poor teenage hearts at her feet, and she had hardly bothered to stoop to pick them up.

She remembered them all, her first admirers. There was Hal, the most romantic of all, with his sleepy green eyes and his dark Byronic curls; and Johnny, who sent her armfuls of roses and bottles of scent, Opium and Fracas, far too sophisticated for her, and threatened to end it all when he found her in someone else's arms; and James, who was older and considered a bad lot and disapproved of by people's mothers; and Mark, who never went to bed and took her to all-night drinking clubs which were raided by the police; and Patrick, who was vague and hopeless and wrote poetry for her; and Davey, who watched and waited and loved her from afar, never quite daring to press his suit. And then there was Richard, after all the others, the one who took her by surprise because he didn't notice her, and suddenly the biter was bit and it was her heart that was in the dust, and the merry-go-round came to an abrupt halt, and she was left alone, hurt and baffled, and she no longer had the appetite for the chase. That was when the kissing had to stop.

Eddy had been away then, her only confidant, and she had no-one to turn to. So she took her hurt to herself, and didn't tell, and the fire in her eyes was dulled, and the parties went on without her, and she waited for a while until she felt strong enough to start again. She changed her wardrobe, bought some books on the French Revolution, and took up with another set. She carefully reinvented herself, a new shining invulnerable self. She learnt caution, learnt to avoid the knocks and blows that can bring a girl down, learnt to keep her distance, to hold a little of herself in reserve, not to give too much away. And if sometimes the strains of a half-forgotten tune reminded her of that first summer, that sweet sappy summer when she had been young and trusting and endlessly in love, if sometimes when the night was dark and still she allowed herself a secret pang of nostalgia for those lost days, no-one knew it but her. It was safer that way.

Eddy wasn't to know. He recognized the change in her, but he didn't guess at the reason, and he was too proud to ask. She would tell him when she chose, and he would listen. There was no point in reading between the lines any more. They were too old for that now, and everything was different. She would stay for a while, he supposed, and sit on his balcony in her little black dress and drink his beer and laugh at him from behind her dark glasses and keep her secrets to herself, and then she would be gone again. And he wouldn't ask any questions, because the boat didn't need any more rocking.

'Well,' said Minna now, changing the subject and pointing quizzically at his reading matter, which happened to be the *New Musical Express*. 'How fashionable you are becoming. What happened to the crossword?'

'I'm looking for a new drummer,' said Eddy evenly. He was in no mood for teasing this morning.

'I wish I was,' said Minna, laughing to herself. 'It's a pity that I can't play the drums, or I could come and audition for you. Perhaps I could take night classes, what do you think? Wouldn't a girl drummer be the absolute last word in chic?'

Eddy privately thought that it was a very good thing that she didn't play drums. That was the last thing the band needed, just when things were looking up.

'The utter end,' he said forbiddingly. 'Drink your coffee while it's hot.'

'Yes, Mummy,' said Minna, a picture of obedience. 'Must I eat up all my greens too, before I'm allowed any pudding?'

'Certainly,' said Eddy, grinning reluctantly. There was no health in her, none at all. 'So, what are you going to do today?'

'Oh,' Minna waved her hand in that careless way she had, 'I hadn't really thought. I'm rather bored with the Revolution at the moment, to tell you the truth. It's too hot for Marat. I might go shopping, I suppose. Or pay a visit to the hairdresser. Or pick up a boy and let him take me drinking in a dive somewhere. What else does a girl do on a day like this?'

'What else?' Eddy watched her eat her pizza and wondered quite how she got away with it. Her hair was muddled and old gold in the sun, and her eyes were dark with last night's mascara, and her Noël Coward dressing gown was crumpled, but she still looked as if she weren't quite real, a slight fey creature who had stepped out of another age and wasn't quite sure whether she would stay in this one. What could she do today? Anything she fancied, he supposed.

'Would you like to come to the theatre tonight?' he said, changing the subject. 'I've got tickets.'

'Yes, please,' said Minna happily. 'That would be nice. And it will give me something to do. A girl has to get ready for the theatre, it's not just a walk in the park. And of course, it will keep me off the streets,' she added, giving him the disreputable look that teased him so much.

'There is that,' said Eddy, refusing to rise. He ripped the page he needed from the NME and put it in his pocket. 'Well,' he said, 'I must dash, don't you know. I've got a drummer to audition.'

'What heaven it must be,' said Minna, laughing at him shamelessly, 'being you.'

Jay and Lou Lou were eating éclairs in a devil-may-care kind of way when Minna arrived.

'You caught us,' said Lou Lou, wiping cream off the corner of her mouth and not looking in the least bit guilty. 'Indulging. Shoot us.'

Lou Lou was blond today, Grace Kelly down to the fingertips of her pristine white gloves. Her dress was powder blue with a flared circle of skirt, and she had flung a green chiffon scarf about her head with studied carelessness, and she looked as if she were simply biding her time until Bing Crosby came along and took her for a boat ride.

'So,' said Minna, kissing them both and laughing, 'I suppose that *High Society* was showing in rep at the Ritzy last night?'

'Damn your eyes,' said Lou Lou. 'How can I be so transparent? And there I was aching to work in mysterious ways when all I end up as is plate glass. What it is to be me.'

'Mysterious to me,' said Jay truthfully. 'I think you look perfect.'

'Thank you, Shakespeare,' said Lou Lou, giving him the benefit of a flawless Rita Hayworth smile, full wattage and quite at odds with the powder blue and the white gloves. 'I can't say it isn't refreshing to meet a man who still has a little respect for the finer things in life.' She looked pointedly at Minna, who was eating the remains of Jay's éclair with a sang-froid rarely seen outside diplomatic circles, and then smiled, forgiving her, sisterhood uniting in the face of all the odds.

'I'd like a large espresso and I'd like it now,' said Minna, as if defying convention and damn the consequences. 'Would anyone like to come to the hairdresser?' she added conversationally.

'Not me,' said Jay, who went to an old-fashioned barber in the East End who was still cutting short back and sides for five bob and offering his gentlemen 'a little something for the weekend'. 'I have a play to write.'

'Oh, yes,' said Minna. 'Silly of me. Lou Lou, what about you?'

'I think it's a perfectly capital notion,' said Lou Lou. 'Just exactly what a girl needs in these dark days.'

'That's what I thought,' said Minna, pleased. She did think it rather a splendid idea, for a spur of the moment kind of thing. She didn't much care for going on her own, but with Lou Lou it would be an outing. They could gossip and read the glossy magazines and compare lipsticks, just like girls were supposed to. Minna had never been a great one for other girls, they were all too busy wondering how much of their thunder she was going to steal to be very entertaining. But Lou Lou had so much thunder herself that one could steal it in cartloads and there would still be plenty to spare.

'Well,' said Jay, beaming at them both and wiping cream from his mouth in a determined sort of way. 'That's settled. And now I must go. All play and no work and it will be the gutter for me, and no mistake.'

'That wouldn't do at all,' said Lou Lou, kissing him goodbye. 'I don't have a single thing suitable for gutter wear.'

So Jay went home to work, because he was coming up to the third act and the writing was starting to flow, and he didn't want to be out while inspiration was striking. Jay might be young yet, and he still had illusions about many things, as Lou Lou liked to remind him, but he had none about the art of writing a play. He knew only too well that 90 per cent of inspiration, the gift of the gods, that bolt of lightning, actually consisted in sitting in front of a defiantly blank piece of paper and coaxing the recalcitrant mind to think of a word, any word, over one syllable.

He had spent his first month in London in this miserable state, wondering if he wouldn't be better giving it all up and becoming an engineer, like his dad had wanted. But then he had met Minna, and the world had shifted a little on its axis, and the city had suddenly become a brighter place, and there was someone, anyone, but especially her, who called him a playwright, just as if it were a fact, just as if he had three smashes in the West End and another already sold out four months in advance, just as if he didn't spend all day tearing up useless pieces of paper that half a rainforest had probably died for, as if that made any difference. A month of misery, followed by days when the words were just leaping from his fingers, as if they could hardly wait to reach the paper, as if they had been there all the time, perfectly formed, ready to grace the page.

'That Jay,' said Minna, watching him walk away, with his head a little bowed and his hands deep in his pockets. 'He's very thoughtful lately.'

'My darling child,' said Lou Lou, summoning up her considerable worldly wisdom, 'that's what he *does*. Goes with the territory. Now, where is this famous crimper?'

'Oh,' said Minna with pleasure, 'Chelsea. That means we can take a cab.'

Minna loved cabs. She loved their diesel tick and their shiny orange for hire signs and their tip-up seats and their pull-up windows. She liked seeing them cruising empty about the streets, even when she didn't need one. Just the thought that there were taxis out there, ready to take her anywhere she should desire, made her feel that God was in His heaven, and all was right with the world. As she liked to say, she was a simple girl at heart.

'Taxi,' Lou Lou murmured endearingly, holding up one delicate hand and letting it drop with a dying fall somehow reminiscent of *Swan Lake*. 'Ballet lessons as a child,' she said, seeing Minna's admiring glance.

'Where to, Duchess?' said the driver, who knew a touch of class when he saw it.

Minna sat back in her seat with a sigh of pure happiness. This day was turning out just fine. It was the best sort of cab, one of the old kind, not tarted up with the new kind of ingratiating red and grey interior that ruined the point, but old and black and worn, with a scuffed floor that spoke of years of faithful service. This was a perfect war-horse of a cab, the kind that could have got a girl through the Blitz with no trouble.

'I love taxis,' said Minna.

'Darling,' said Lou Lou, lighting a pink Sobranie and blowing smoke out of the window, 'all girls love cabs, it's something genetic, I forget. So why the hairdresser, like a bolt from the blue?' Lou Lou had been known to like a reason for things, when the mood took her, and just now she was curious. Minna wasn't the kind of girl who spent a ritualized day having her hair set and her nails done and her pedicure touched up once a week. She would grow into that later, when she had to, but for now she had time on her side. Lou Lou strongly suspected that she was the kind of girl who cut her own fringe in the bath, sprayed it with setting lotion, and relied on panache.

'Oh,' said Minna vaguely. 'I don't know. I just felt like it. Is that so odd?'

'If you will forgive me,' said Lou Lou, 'it is rather. Horses for courses and all that, but I for one wouldn't open a book on you being one of those pampered types who employ people to pick up their handkerchieves for them.'

'Lou Lou,' said Minna, laughing. 'It's only a haircut.'

'Nothing is ever only a haircut,' said Lou Lou, with the air of one giving notes on the rudiments of existentialism. 'I know girls who go into hair shock after having their barnet seen to, and remain not at home to anyone, even their analysts, for anything up to a week afterwards. Hair can make or break a girl, and I should know.' Lou Lou patted her own lustrous locks, and gave Minna a speaking look. 'So don't give me this it's only a haircut lark, because it won't wash with me.'

Having delivered her homily on the meaning of life, as far as the salon went, Lou Lou leaned back in her seat and exhaled a telling stream of smoke from her sculpted nostrils.

'Oh, well,' said Minna, who for some obscure reason of her own didn't want to explain about deciding to give her landlord a shock. It was only some vague notion that she had cooked up that morning, tired of seeing Eddy frowning at her over his cornflakes in that avuncular manner to which he seemed to feel his age entitled him. But she was quite sure that she didn't want to go into it too deeply, and Lou Lou was bound to read too much into it, and anyway, it WAS only a haircut, she didn't care what anyone said. 'I wasn't sure what else to do today, you know how it is.'

'Dearest heart,' said Lou Lou. 'You could have gone to the National Gallery and looked at the Titians. You could have bought a new frock. You could have taken in a *film noir* or a *nouvelle vague*. You could have gone rowing on the Serpentine or taken the air in the park or visited the botanical gardens at Kew or found a nice quiet bar to drink in. All perfectly honourable pursuits for a girl over the age of consent.'

'I could have,' said Minna, who had vaguely considered some such pursuits that day and hadn't found any of them instantly appealing, not when the sun was shining and there were taxis to be ridden in.

'All right, all right,' said Lou Lou, throwing up her hands. 'I give in. All bets are off. I shan't ask another question, I swear it. Nothing beats the Dutch more than a girl who pries.'

'It's not prying,' said Minna kindly. 'You can ask me as many questions as you like, but don't expect me to have all the answers for you. I'm just an ordinary girl at heart, simple, you know. What you see is what you get.'

Lou Lou didn't believe that for a moment. She had read some Jung once, in her youth, and she knew better, but she let it ride. Everyone had their little misconceptions, and there was never any earthly point in pressing people to tell you what they didn't want to, she had learnt that lesson well enough, at least. And Minna, believing firmly in her own simplicity, wasn't telling a thing, not this morning she wasn't.

'You know,' said the cab driver conversationally, 'I had that Gerry Archer in the back of the cab once.'

'Well,' said Lou Lou, as they entered the hairdresser. She realized that she had underestimated Minna.

'You do see,' said Minna, pleased.

'Utterly,' said Lou Lou, as if she had come home.

71

The salon was the last word in baroque grandeur. Dark purple walls, dragged and distressed to a point just below pain, were hung with great gilt glasses reflecting haughtily glossy heads in various stages of coiffure. The chandelier was assuredly Venetian, the cornicing was heavy with ornate carving, and Vivaldi fluted from hidden speakers, just as if there were a full chamber orchestra secreted behind a cunningly placed screen. Across the polished parquet floor Dior pumps clipped busily, tripping from one minion to another.

The room was filled with those pampered women who devote a day each week to their hair with the kind of reverence that used to be reserved for religious practices, and their startling chatter rose confidently above the gentle hum of the driers. They sat intently in dull gold chairs, stockinged legs genteelly crossed, leafing a little too casually through *Tatler* to see who was In this month, casting furtively searching glances at themselves in the glass.

'Do you think up is really me?' they were saying. 'I mean, it IS black tie, but perhaps up is too much for dinner, these days.'

'Take it blonder,' they were saying, with the air of businessmen telling their brokers to buy copper. 'Take it shorter.' And all the time they really meant, 'Make me beautiful. Make me irresistible.'

Lou Lou and Minna allowed themselves to be draped in white linen robes and led to their seats. About them the wash of gossip ebbed and flowed as the glamorous women let drop every secret at their disposal, knowing as all girls did that they could tell anything to their hairdresser. After all, everybody knew that hairdressers heard more in a day than most psychiatrists did in a week, and took their

Hippocratic oath just as seriously as any doctor.

'She found him in the South of France, you know how one meets everyone at Eden Roc sooner or later. Rich? My dear, his idea of decorating is leafing through the Sotheby's catalogue and saying "That one". Imagine.'

'It's all very well saying he's going to send out the next three Gold Cup winners, but he still doesn't have the faintest idea of sexual etiquette. He seduces her and then Poof! Not a word. No telephone call, no flowers, no dinner invitations. Nothing. I said to her, I said, darling, please, listen to an old woman, NEVER sleep with your trainer. She's had to take her horses away, what else could she do? The embarrassment of it. I mean to say, one just KNOWS about those racing boys. They may have never read a book in their lives, but when it comes to women, they're DEVILS.'

'Four children and a perfectly respectable wife, you know the thing, she's kept her figure and had a discreet little lift, thank you very much, and there he is, running around with this leggy creature, twenty-one if she's a day, and he insists on ringing her up on his car telephone at two o'clock in the morning and talking dirty to her. And THEN he tells me he doesn't believe in the male menopause.'

'Darling heart, I can't think what came over me. It was eyes meeting across a crowded room, just like being seventeen again. He turned out to have a suite at Claridges, and the next morning he looked at me and said, "I don't think I quite caught your name." I can't THINK what I was doing. Do you think it's too terribly shaming?'

'So finally, after all these years of wondering, she took her father out to lunch and asked him, straight out, whether she was his daughter, or not. And he looked at her and ordered some more brandy and said, "Oh, darling, you know what your mother was like, I never quite dared to ask." So it could have been the milkman, or anyone, and she'll never know, unless she takes out an advertisement in *The Times* or something.'

'Well, ducky,' said the stylist, patting Minna briskly on both cheeks, by way of greeting. 'What HAVE I done to deserve this? I thought you had quite abandoned me, but ABANDONED. Or moved to Mexico or something terrifying. One never knows with you girls, nowadays. Trouble,' he added darkly, winking at Lou Lou.

'I couldn't abandon you, you know that,' said Minna soothingly. 'Lou Lou, this is Jacques, the only straight hairdresser in London.'

'Tut, tut,' said Jacques, shaking a finger at Minna. 'You shouldn't believe all you read. Very naughty. Two children,' he added to Lou Lou, 'and I've never strayed. I should be sainted, and then we could have a chignon St Jacques.'

'And we've never heard THAT joke before,' said a junior, passing by with a pile of towels.

Jacques laughed coyly, camp as a barrel full of snakes, and smoothed his carefully crumpled Armani trousers. 'That Pauly,' he said confidentially, 'he cuts hair like an angel, but my dears, he's such a BITCH. Now then, what do we feel like today?'

'Well,' said Lou Lou, patting her Grace Kelly flip. 'I think a change of image, don't you? Shall we have Jackie O or Lulu Brooks?'

'Oh,' breathed Jacques in rapture. 'Louise Brooks. The divine Lulu, your namesake, it couldn't be more perfect. The shortest sharpest bob. Shining black. Geometric. Divine. Do let me.'

'There,' said Minna triumphantly. 'I knew you'd love each other.'

When they emerged much later into the early evening sun, Minna and Lou Lou stepped out on to the street as new women. Transformed by daring flourishes of the scissors, they came out into a world which suddenly teemed with possibility. They walked out tall, silent in absorption of their newness, communing with every shop window that they passed, watching their reflections walking by, watching the men in the street watching them, wondering quite where they could have come from.

'Taxi,' said Lou Lou, breaking the silence. 'I must go home and change. It's only fitting.'

Minna quite saw that it was. She felt much the same herself.

'I'll see you tomorrow, I expect,' she said.

'I expect so, said Lou Lou, disappearing inside a cab and letting it take her quickly away. Minna watched her go, and then walked a little more, moving her head from side to side to get used to its new nakedness.

When she was ready, she hailed a cab herself, and went back to Eddy's.

5

When Minna returned to the flat, she was surprised to find it full of people. She had forgotten about the theatre.

'Oh,' she said to the crowd of strangers, not altogether polite. 'Am I very late?' She shook her head at them, not waiting to be introduced. A girl couldn't face a crowd with a haircut this new, not for any money. 'I'll just go and change,' she added, for their enlightenment.

As she fled to the bathroom, she heard a clear old-fashioned voice, the kind one can't buy any more, float after her.

'My DEAR,' it said, full of exclamation marks, 'who was that enchanting waif? Where can I find more like that?'

Waif, thought Minna, wondering if she were offended, or not. Like any heiress, she had had her moments of fancying herself as a poor little rich girl, a perfect Barbara Hutton, her life confounded by money, happiness always tantalizingly beyond her grasp, but even so. Waif. She wasn't sure she liked it.

She faced herself manfully in the glass, ready for the moment of truth, staring hard at her new hair, so close now to her head. She ran her fingers tentatively through the silver slick, feeling the back where it was shaved close, pulling it this way and that, enjoying the cowlick that fell teasingly over one eye. She examined the fine planes of her skull, now revealed, turning her head back and forth, and then she counted to ten. It was the last word, she decided, smiling rapturously at her reflection. It was daring and brave, a faultless gladiator of a cut. It was the most modern thing she had seen on a head, and it was all hers. She pouted at herself lasciviously, batting her eyelashes, just checking that it wasn't too butch. She felt rather like that girl of Hemingway's in *The Garden of Eden* who has her hair cut and cut until she goes mad.

Waif, she thought, snarling benignly at the glass. She would give them waif. Tonight she would be sophistication: she could be Audrey Hepburn and Ava Gardner and Gloria Swanson and then some, and perhaps Eddy would stop treating her as if she were five years old and caught stealing blackberries.

'*I've been to a marvellous party*,' she sang vaguely to herself, just like Noël Coward used to, '*With Nounou and Nada and Nell.*'

She stepped into her little black dress, that other essential to urban living besides dark glasses. A little black dress could take a girl anywhere, from dinner at the Ritz to breakfast at Smithfield and back again. This one was a prince of the genre, lovingly cut, the kind every girl should have in her wardrobe.

'*It was in the fresh air, and we went as we were*,' sang Minna, pausing to admire it, giving it the moment's respect that such a miracle of engineering deserved. '*And we stayed as we were, which was Hell.*'

She put on her eyes and brushed her cheekbones with rouge and painted her lips scarlet, and thought how fast all the uncles and aunts would think all this powder and paint.

'*Poor Grace started singing at midnight, and didn't stop singing till four.*'

She stepped back to admire herself, a consummate urban girl, ready for anything. Something was missing. She pulled thoughtfully at her cowlick, wondering what it could be.

'*We knew the excitement was bound to begin, when Laura got blind on Dubonnet and gin.*' Pearls, that was it, she thought, catching inspiration as it struck. A dress like this simply cried out for pearls. '*And scratched her veneer with a Cartier pin, I couldn't have liked it more.*'

Wondering how she could have been so remiss, Minna slung three ropes of pearls round her neck, fingering them devoutly, as a Catholic might count her rosary. Minna had a deep love for her pearls, legacy of a long-dead grandmother. She often slept in them, knowing how they declined and lost their lustre if deprived for too long of contact with human skin. These were no ordinary jewels, no amusing pieces of paste, countless oysters had died for these, and Minna treated them with the respect they deserved.

She gave herself a final supplicating look in the glass, and stepped out to meet the crowd. She walked out into the room, her head shining silver and gold into the evening sun, her mouth curved into a half smile that gave nothing away, and that same old-fashioned voice greeted her arrival with a heartfelt 'WELL' of utter approval, and Eddy, surprise writ absurdly on his normally deadpan face, stepped forward and said rather weakly, 'Minna, this is Oliver Skye.'

The voice resolved itself into a slight and immaculate creature who took her hands in his and looked her up and down with miss-nothing eyes and smiled with pleasure and said laughingly, 'My dear, but Eddy didn't warn us that his house-guest is quite so bewitching. How like him. Who is it that does your hair, do tell. I can spot Leonard, or even Hugh for that matter, at twenty paces, but I have to confess that you have me baffled, unless it's that ducky barber in the Old Kent Road. It isn't, is it? No? But then, I can't really picture you in Kray territory, even for that amount of perfection.'

'It's just a man in Chelsea,' said Minna, for all the world as if hairdressing was something she hardly had time to think about, as if this miraculous cut had been dealt her quite by chance, just as if she had been passing and gone in on the merest whim, sat down carelessly, her mind on something else, and said in an abstracted voice, 'Darling, deal with it.'

Oliver smiled wider than ever (he had enviable and extremely expensive teeth which he took lovingly to a certain Manhattan dentist who specialized in stars of stage and screen), recognizing a well-kept secret when he saw one.

'Well, my dear,' he said sincerely, 'I congratulate you. I do.'

Eddy, having recovered himself, thought that Minna had had quite enough extravagant praise for one evening, and introduced her to the rest of his guests.

There was Alabama Skye, not looking at all like an award-winning playwright with her faded jeans and wayward blond hair, but then, Minna wondered, quite what does an award-winning playwright look like? Also her sister, Venice, another matter entirely in a king's ransom of scarlet chiffon and a sunbeam curtain of hair that fell down her back. She was, Minna knew, something of a legend in certain circles, a consummate good-time girl, a girl who had been pictured on the arms of more playboys, princes and potentates than were dreamt of in most people's philosophy. She might have been invented for the gossip columns, and she posed happily for them as they charted her progress from Rome to the Riviera, from Portofino to Positano, from Chantilly to Klosters.

It was Venice who had provided the only high spot of the year before, a year woefully short of scandal. It was a year when no heiresses had run off with confidence artists, when the crop of débutantes had dutifully come out and flirted becomingly with stockbrokers and guards officers, when the flotsam of international white trash, who could usually be relied on to kick up some kind of fuss, had instead discovered the newly fashionable health spa at Biarritz, and spent all their time taking interminable rest cures. It was a year when, worst of all, England's foremost aristocratic rogue, the one whom all mothers warned their daughters of, the one whose love for fast cars and faster women kept the columnists in clover, the one whose penchant for drugging and drinking had sent enchanted ripples of shock round every dinner table worth its salt, had suddenly declared himself cured of his various habits and married a painfully respectable girl from the Home Counties, whom he had met while buying a lampshade for his mother in Nina Campbell.

Society, reeling from the blow, had bowed its head and attended the wedding in deepest black, confounding all the fashion writers who had spent the last two months extolling the joys of colour and most particularly New Age White. Telephone lines burned up all over London as harassed style gurus filed desperate last-minute copy. 'Black is back,' they cried *in extremis*. 'What the chic woman is wearing. Funereal, unrelieved black. Black on Black.' Chanel sold out of its definitive black suit and had to wire to Paris for another shipment. Grandmothers who never received anything but duty visits at Christmas and illegible postcards from distant beaches found themselves besieged by chattering relatives who just happened to be passing ('Berwick on Tweed is just on the way to EVERYWHERE, Granny, so we thought it too silly not to drop in'), and stayed only long enough to ransack attics and trunks, their magpie eyes alighting unerringly on the Fortuny model that had been worn to the Four Hundred and the Café de Paris and the Milroy. This was the dress worn by the girl who had danced with the boy who had danced with the girl who had danced with the Prince of Wales, and now its day had come again.

While the noble scion and his interior design-ing bride settled down to nuptial bliss, bovinely contented in gumboots and thornproof tweeds, raven-clad hostesses were left disconsolate, deprived of the joyful expectation they had felt when opening the morning paper. Where were they to turn now for stories of seduced seventeen year olds and written-off Ferraris and clandestinely snorted cocaine?

It was at this moment, when things seemed quite at rock bottom, impossible to get any worse, that Venice stepped in to save the day, creating such a delicious scandal that no-one could bring themselves to talk about anything else for weeks afterwards. Always visible, this season Venice was doubly so, having felt no need to go into mourning over the reform of a rake. She had been one of the seduced herself, in her salad days, and she knew that his reputation as a Lothario was built on shifting sands. (Although whenever the forbidden rumour went round that, 'My dear, could you die, but I have it that he's not altogether . . . ' Venice refused to comment. She might kiss, but she wasn't given to telling, a startling inconsistency in a girl otherwise so endearingly indiscreet.)

The talk started when Venice, so conveniently easy to spot in the blaze of colour that stood out against the inky uniform of her peers, calmly hooked a fish not only big, but previously considered quite Out Of Bounds. Tempting but unobtainable, everyone had always said about the incorruptible David Maxwell, so serious, so straight and so rich, with his multi-national conglomerate and his jet and his bridge-playing wife. He was a collector's item – this tycoon with no known vices except for his predilection for Victorian water-colours. Could this be the man who set Venice up in her own apartment and paid her court with such flagrance? It was hardly to be believed. Telephone lines that had lain dormant for days sprang to life as the news was passed generously from mouth to mouth. The tree-lined avenues of the chattering classes echoed with the sound of Tiffany earrings falling on to glass as the eager wearers shed them so as to press the receiver closer to their ears.

'My DEAR,' they cried in ecstasy, 'have you HEARD, let me tell you, Belgravia that's all, and a Monet over the chimneypiece, and an account at Cartier, and fittings at St Laurent, and out every night, what CAN he tell that dreary wife, working late in the office, dear, it's too much, and don't tell a soul, but they say that he . . . well . . . I can hardly bring myself . . . TIES her up . . . you know, remember Archie, hanging them from the chandeliers . . . can you IMAGINE?'

Venice, her number of invitations doubled at a stroke, was seen everywhere, and if people wondered why she had taken to affecting quite such large ruby cuffs on her wrists, they didn't quite like to ask.

Just as the tirelessly wagging tongues started to slow, having discussed every aspect of the liaison, Venice pulled her ace out of the bag. As if the cachet of landing such a prize had started to pall (the word sugar-daddy was never mentioned by the gossips: it was an expression so outmoded as to be vulgar, and vulgarity was something they spent most of their waking lives avoiding), she left him, casting his worldly goods aside as if such baubles meant nothing to her. The leaving itself would have been enough to send society into a perfect fever, but Venice also contrived to serve them with the ultimate twist of irony besides, the most deliciously convoluted exclamation mark at the end of the affair. Not only did she leave him, not only did she forsake all the jewels and the pictures and the clothes, but the man she left All This for, hardly even a man, was David Maxwell's own son, newly sent down from Oxford, and due to a strategic net of trust funds, almost as rich as his father.

Undreamt of delight rippled round the salons. The columnists abandoned their tables in the fashionable watering holes where they had gathered, disconsolately waiting for something to happen, and returned to their typewriters, silly season blues quite forgotten. Rumour abounded. There was hushed talk of unseemly brawls, policemen paid off, threats parried.

Venice sailed through it all unruffled, dressed in a new and curiously understated style that every woman in London studiously tried to imitate, dining out every night with her new escort, so young, so golden, so much prettier than his father. And just when, wondered the babblers, would Sebastian Maxwell take his new inamorata home to meet Mummy?

As she shook hands with him, Minna didn't wonder that Venice had made such a controversial decision. Sebastian went a long way to being any girl's dream. Tall and *louche* in an eccentric suit made of red baize and cut two sizes too big, he had a vaguely distracted air, as if life were just a little too much for him. In an age when undergraduates preferred bitter beer and parkas to plover's eggs and white tie, Sebastian was a throw-back to another era. He was Percy Shelley and Sebastian Flyte and every man who had ever fallen in love with Zuleika Dobson. And sent down too, Minna thought in admiration. She had done her best to be expelled from three schools, and failed miserably. It was not a subject she liked to dwell on. She was not used to failure.

'And this,' said Eddy, 'is Milo Oranmore.'

Milo Oranmore, thought Minna, shaking his hand and smiling with a shy charm she had picked up somewhere along her travels, the man whom everyone said Alabama Skye would marry. She had read his books, and seen the profiles that the Sunday papers so loved to run on him, and she knew him for the Young Literary Sensation that he assuredly was. He had rather fetching eyes. It was, Minna thought to herself, just like Antonia Fraser and Harold Pinter all over again, except prettier. Oh, the literary mafia, see how they run.

'So what are we going to see?' she asked politely, knowing the importance of making conversation. She hadn't thought to ask, but to Minna theatre was theatre, and she liked to see the bad as well as the good, so that when people talked about how embarrassingly dire the new show at the Aldwych was she was in an informed position. Besides, she trusted Eddy's taste. It wouldn't be Andrew Lloyd Webber, at any rate.

'What are we going to see?' said Oliver in amazement. 'My dear child, what a question. There's only one play that anyone could be going to tonight.'

'It's the first night of Alabama's new play,' said Eddy, laughing a little.

'Oh, dear,' said Minna. 'I am past a joke. Please forgive me.'

And of course everyone did, because it was impossible not to, and anyway, it was time to go.

The press almost missed them when they arrived, busy looking hopefully into every stretch limo that pulled up. How typical, everybody said later, of Alabama Skye to walk to her own first night. How like her to arrive in jeans and accompanied by a bunch of unknowns. Avid readers of the gossip columns recognized Venice of course, and she was kind enough to stop and pose happily for the photographers, most of whom were her utter slaves anyway, and Oliver was a familiar face from the glossy magazines where he appeared frequently, pictured at every new collection and opening and ball, but who, people wondered, was the blonde beauty with the shorn hair, and who was the dark young man on her arm, so carelessly dressed? Should one know who they were? Should one have them for dinner? Should they be taken up at once and asked everywhere? It was a terrible dilemma.

Once Alabama was spotted, the usual barrage of household names and so-called personalities who always turned out to such events were unceremoniously elbowed aside as the cameramen pounced on her. Shots of Alabama in public were rare as hen's teeth, and they were far too old hands to miss such an opportunity. You could get Joan Collins or Jane Seymour any day of the week, hardly trying, but Alabama Skye, now there was a prize.

'Alabama,' they cried, pleading. 'Over here, give us a smile, just here, Alabama, hold it there, lovely, just one more . . .'

Alabama, who didn't much like the press and made no secret of the fact, kept on walking.

'Come on, Milo,' she said, 'we're holding up the queue.'

'What it is,' said Milo, to no-one in particular, 'being Mr Alabama Skye. Perhaps I should go on *Wogan* after all.'

'Please, Alabama,' cried the photographers with one plaintive voice, 'just one more.'

'What do you think?' said Milo.

'Screw 'em,' said Alabama sweetly.

'Don't worry, boys,' said Venice, who didn't mind holding up the queue at all, and proceeded to do so for another five minutes. 'Get my good side, there's a duck. She's probably got the change of life or something. You never know with these Artists,' she added darkly, pouting at the man from the *Daily Mail*, who was a particular favourite with her. 'Temperament.'

'Love you, Venice,' crooned the pressmen. 'Fabulous, darling, who's your boyfriend?'

'Old hat, boys,' said Venice lovingly. 'Ask your editors. Last week's news.'

'What it is,' said Sebastian, to no-one in particular, 'being Mr Venice Skye.'

'Well,' said Venice reasonably, 'you're not as pretty as I am.'

'Oh, do come along,' said Oliver impatiently. 'One for the gossips, darlings,' he said to the photographers, presenting them with his perfect profile. 'And now I want a drink.'

Minna wondered at their polish as she let Eddy take her arm and guide her into the theatre, hardly noticing the danger she was in from flying photographers, who had spotted Bill Wyman arriving just behind her. She supposed it took years of practice to be quite so carelessly *au fait* with the press.

'Just think,' she said, turning to Eddy, 'when you're a famous musician, you'll have to fight them off as well.'

Eddy grinned his twisted grin. Just now, he thought that he had about a snowball's chance in hell of making it, what with the drummer running off with the bass guitarist to an ashram in the West Country, and the keyboard player threatening to have his second nervous breakdown, and inspiration decidedly thin on the ground, and him almost thirty and getting too old for this particular game. A small but devoted following round the jazz clubs had been heady when he was twenty-two, but now it wasn't enough. If he could have thought of anything else to do, he would have packed it in by now, but he couldn't, so he went on hoping, but sometimes he felt that his hope was running dangerously thin, and even bourbon didn't help as much as it used to. But he couldn't tell Minna that, she was too young to be told that playing a saxophone unrecognized wasn't as romantic as she thought it, so he just smiled and said that he supposed he would, and they went inside to face the crowd.

And what a crowd, thought Minna, looking about with interest. Screen stars smiled rather stretched smiles at each other, eyes wandering restlessly across the lobby in search of more photographers, and discussed each other's salaries.

'A million a picture now he's got that Oscar. Only six months ago he was lucky if he got fifty grand . . . '

'My dear, they wanted Redford, but he was in Utah, then they tried Costner, but he was already committed, Julian Sands couldn't do it, Dan Day-Lewis couldn't do it, so finally, they send it to him. I mean to say, I know it pays the mortgage, but it's hardly complimentary, is it?'

'Suddenly he doesn't want to do it, but he's under contract, of course the only answer is to get fired. So he goes to the producer, and says he wants his make-up artist, his hairdresser, his analyst and his dog flown out from New York to be with him, all with their own trailers on the set. Then he says he thinks they need a co-producer and his brother Mike is free right now, why don't they put him on the payroll. Then he says that he needs tickets to go to Paris every two weeks, first class from LA if you please, to visit his sick mother-in-law. So he sits back and waits for the call to tell him that they've got Charles Dance instead, and the next Sunday the producer rings up and says, "Darling baby doll thing, love you senseless, you can have everything you want, and we start shooting on Friday."'

The serious English theatrical contingent, intense in stubble and slightly crumpled suits, stood a little apart, safe in their superiority at not having sold out to Hollywood and never having allowed *Hello* magazine into their houses for an exclusive interview.

'Bloody press everywhere,' they said. 'I wouldn't do this for anyone but Alabama . . . She wrote me such a dream of a part in her last play, I felt I should come . . . Isn't that Ken over there, must just have a word . . . Hello, Alabama love, can't wait to see the show . . . '

In between the stars of stage and screen, the usual contingent of glamorous women who could be relied on to be seen in all the right places, glittered and shimmered through the crowd, intensely chic in their tiny little Ozbek confections, alighting now and then with small cries of delight on the hard-faced men in suits who were the power behind the throne, the money men, the oil that kept the wheels of the entertainment industry running smooth.

'Darlings,' cried the glamorous women. 'It's been such ages, a hundred years since we've seen you. We must have lunch, so busy with Goodwood coming up . . . We're giving a little dinner next week, terribly quiet, just us and the Attenboroughs . . . '

The money men puffed lugubriously on their cigars and said that they would love to, but that they would have to look in their books.

'Call my secretary,' they said, hidebound by a lifelong habit of never committing themselves. 'We'll be in touch. Give my love to Dickie.'

Theatre critics, eyes alight with expectation, discussed Alabama's last play, trying to decide which was her best work, wondering which direction she would take this time. Young bucks from the *Evening Standard* Diary wandered through the crowd, looking for clues. There was an undercurrent of excitement tense in the air, cutting through the chat. After all, a new play from Alabama Skye had become an Event, and nobody wanted to miss out.

Finally, it was time to go in, and the glitterati and the literati and other assorted luminaries took their seats, and the talk was suddenly hushed as the curtain went up.

And everyone concentrated on the play, and took champagne in the interval and discussed technicalities in loud voices, and went back to watch the second half with no idea what to expect, which was what Alabama liked to do to an audience.

And when it was over and the curtain fell, there was an infinitesimal pause, and then the applause broke out, ringing as sure and triumphant as a marriage bell, registering a hit. Alabama stirred impatiently in her seat, uncomfortable with such lavish praise. It was just a job, after all.

'Come on,' she said, 'let's get out.'

They slipped out of the side door, escaping the crowd, scorning those waiting for taxis.

'We can walk,' said Alabama, who always did, striding out through the late-night streets in her pointed boots, needing the respite to accustom herself to another success.

Minna following obediently behind, wondered what it must be like, writing to such applause. She wondered if Jay's play would have such success, whether he would arrive at his first night to find London at his feet, if he would take them by their carefully tended throats in the same way, and hold them there until he had had enough. She wondered if he would become fêted and exclaimed over in the same way, if his star would rise quite so inexorably. She hoped so. He would make such a perfect celebrity, studiously not allowing fame to go to his head. She must introduce him to Alabama, and they could talk plays and strings could be pulled. Minna was a great believer in strings. She often wondered how anything got done without them.

Eddy, watching her face as she pondered these things, remembered her habit of arranging things in her mind until she had them in some kind of manageable cosmic order, and knew better than to interrupt her. Unlike some girls he knew, she didn't make demands for baubles and fast cars and champagne and foie gras, she didn't expect to be wined and dined and paid extravagant compliments, but she did demand a freedom from questions, from unsolicited intrusions. People who had overstepped the mark had found themselves quite ruthlessly cut, before they knew quite what was happening. Until this summer, Eddy would have liked to think that such a Siberian fate would never befall him, that he could overstep the mark and survive, but now he was not so sure.

It was bad enough her turning up out of the blue like this, fey and feckless in her tiny dresses, skating carelessly round him, staying out all night with nameless escorts, refusing to answer any of his unspoken questions, but now there was this new hair. Eddy was of Lou Lou's mind when it came to the salon: just as it was never just dinner, it was never just a haircut. And this one was a gesture of defiance, a sartorial exclamation mark, revealing her finally as a beauty, as a grown-up, as a woman, and however hard he tried, there was no possible way that he could pretend she was fifteen and someone's little sister any more. Eddy frowned to himself, not wanting to wonder quite why he found it so disturbing, and Minna looked up at him and saw the frown and thought that Jacques had done his work to perfection and laughed happily to herself.

'What's that look?' she said boldly. 'Think what would happen if the wind changed.'

Eddy looked noncommittal and didn't answer, asking her instead if she had liked the play. There, on safer ground again. He breathed a small sigh of relief.

'Oh, yes,' said Minna seriously. 'I loved it. It was very strong.' Strength was important to Minna, who liked life cut clear. 'Clever,' she added sagely, as if settling a hotly contested debate. 'Imagine.'

Eddy did imagine, although he tried not to. Dreaming never got a boy anywhere these days, everyone knew that.

'Don't worry,' said Minna, who had no such qualms and could afford to laugh at him. 'Soon it will be your first night and you can pick up the laurel wreaths as if they mean nothing to you.'

'Don't you start,' said Eddy, giving her his most forbidding glance, which slid off her as easily as water off glass. He had forgotten about these little flashes of accuracy that she would just pull out of the bag whenever one was in danger of writing her off as another blonde. Not dumb, but very blonde, and everyone knew what that meant, at the end of the day. 'I may be engaging in the honourable artistic struggle, but I'm still your landlord, so watch it.'

'Have a care,' said Minna, ignoring him and laughing more than ever. 'The upward path is easy, but there's no turning back.'

'It's a dirty job,' said Eddy blandly, giving up.

'But someone's got to do it.'

'Please, children,' said Oliver in a special chivvying voice that he had copied from his grandmother on his mother's side, to some effect, 'I shan't tell you how enchanting you look from this angle, or you might start getting ideas, but if you don't stop coffee-housing and start hurrying along, we're going to miss the grand entrance, and I for one am not going to miss out on a free ride on Alabama's coat tails.'

'It's these heels,' Minna grumbled.

She would far rather have made the grand entrance out of a cab, one silken leg appearing slowly before the other, tantalizing all the gawpers for a teasing moment, until the whole creation emerged to smile for the cameras. Minna often thought that she would have been rather good as one of those Hollywood starlets in the Thirties, endlessly crossing and recrossing the Atlantic, their lives one long ocean voyage, and all so that they could sit on their eight pieces of matching luggage at either end and strike careless poses for the barrage of photographers who followed their every move.

'A girl was never meant to walk in heels like this,' she added, to clinch her point.

'Heels indeed,' said Oliver, sounding just like his nanny used to when she was told that there was crème caramel for pudding ('Cream caramel indeed! We'll have a nice plain rice pudding and some jam, IF you don't mind'). 'It was heels and heels alone that made King Edward lose his throne. Now come along, do.'

6

The first-night party was being held in one of those post-theatre restaurants that the thespian world had made so much its own that it had become more of an actors' club than anything else. At the eight-thirty sitting, anonymous suited couples could enjoy what they happily termed Authentic Italian Food ('So rare to find proper polenta outside Tuscany'), but they were only tolerated on the strict understanding that they would give up their tables on the stroke of eleven o'clock. It was at this witching hour, when normal diners disappeared home to their beds and their gardening books and the highlights of the day's golf, that the real clientele arrived, borne in on a wave of thick theatrical gossip, to be greeted by a kiss from the siren on the door and envious looks from the waiters, who were all actors themselves, filling in between commercials.

As Milo opened the door, the roar of the crowd came rushing up to greet them.

'Actors,' said Oliver darkly. 'These theatrical parties are all the same. Everyone's so busy PRO-JECTING. I ask you.'

Alabama started to look faintly green. 'Couldn't we just get a take-away and go home?' she said.

'Come along,' said Milo steadily, taking her arm. 'Just remember that you're taller than Derek Jacobi, marginally less bearded than Anthony Sher, prettier than Ian McKellen, and younger than Peter O'Toole. Apart from that, you don't have anything on these people.'

'Oh, Milo,' said Alabama gratefully. 'You're such a bitch.'

'I taught him everything he knows,' said Oliver.

The stairs curved down into the restaurant, and Alabama paused for a moment at the top, contemplating the grand entrance that she so wanted to avoid but which Oliver and Venice, crowding in behind her, felt that they had been invented for.

'Is my mascara straight?' said Oliver anxiously, getting out his compact.

'Heaven,' said Venice sincerely. 'And such a pretty shade of blue, you are clever. Cousin and sister of award-winning playwright, and don't we just LOOK the part? Could anyone ask for more? Do you think Alabama should be frantically proud of us? Oh, bugger,' she added, looking round. 'I've lost Sebastian again.'

Sebastian was still outside, studying the menu, quite unaware of how perilously close he had come to missing his moment in the limelight.

'Do you think they use buffalo mozzarella, or the other kind?' he enquired, as Venice retrieved him.

'Idiot,' she said lovingly, readjusting his collar, which was standing up on one side.

It was time to go.

'Just pretend that I'm famous and you're with me,' said Minna to Eddy, charitable to the end. 'I shan't tell anyone different. At least not unless they pull my fingernails out or pay me or anything.'

'All right,' said Alabama, squaring her shoulders gamely like a good brave playwright, and putting on a once-more-into-the-breach kind of face, like the one that had so nearly won Kenneth Branagh his Oscar. 'Let's do it.'

'Let's fall in love,' said Oliver as they went downstairs.

The restaurant was already filled to capacity, all the famous faces milling about in a carefully aimless way, kissing each other breathlessly and asking each other with delirious interest how they were, REALLY, for all the world as if they had just survived a hazardous Amazonian canoeing expedition when everyone knew they'd only come from Notting Hill Gate.

As soon as Alabama was sighted, pandemonium broke out. Everybody stood up and started clapping and exclaiming a little louder than the next person, so as to be noticed. The three most upmarket of the photographers, who had managed to get in ('Only the ones we can utterly trust, darling, and they're such old chums I couldn't say no,' said Alabama's producer), started contorting themselves into faintly sado-erotic positions to get a good shot and letting their flashbulbs off in everybody's eyes. The waiters, who had been watching for their cue with the patience of all good rep actors, began opening magnums of champagne with a great deal of ostentatious cork-popping. ('Just like Alain Prost after winning a big race,' said Oliver, licking his lips.) The crowd surged forward, desperate to be the first to kiss Alabama in congratulation.

'My public,' said Oliver, quite forgetting about racing drivers in his despair. 'They didn't even notice the mascara, and it took me weeks to find this colour.'

'Really,' said Venice in derision. 'What do they know?'

'Come on,' said Eddy, steering Minna through the crush. 'Free hooch.'

'I hope,' said Minna severely, 'that when you become famous you will give up saying such vulgar things in front of a lady.'

The crowd around Alabama was growing thicker.

'Darling!' they cried, trying to look intellectual and ecstatic at the same time. 'Too much like heaven. Rabelaisian. Chekhovian. Ibsenite. How the last act caught one unawares.'

Milo, well-trained in such occasions, and comfortable in the knowledge that he had a book launch next week when it would be his turn centre stage, wandered off in search of a drink. Alabama was doing perfectly well without him. At the bar, he was pounced upon by those ubiquitous society girls whose sole purpose in life was to attend three parties a night. As Oliver naughtily insisted, they would go to a philatelists' convention in Weston-super-Mare if they thought Imran Khan was going to be there. All long blond hair and long blond faces and most of the lights on but never quite anyone at home, they wore the space-to-let signs on their foreheads with all the pride of a Ph.D. in Pure Mathematics. They called everyone darling with a touching spirit of egalitarianism, not so much out of any affectation, but because they could never quite remember the names of all the people they met. They liked Milo because his large estate in Ireland, respectably decrepit and feudally tenanted, proclaimed him as one of them, and his literary success was putting him a cut above, into the 'someone everyone should know' bracket.

'Darling,' they cried, bearing down on him with

all the devotion of birds of prey. 'What a perfectly ducky play. Why don't you ever bring Alabama to St Moritz, Ernst Poellenberg's party, my dear, you would have died, Bobo came disguised as his own mistress, two marriages broke up, and Cecil arrived with a Sudanese pianist called Edgar, can you beat it? You should have come to Sienna, we've just this minute got back, Ferdie's facelift is SUCH a success, everyone was asking where you were.' (These were the kind of girls who were exceptionally good at issuing invitations to other people's houses.)

'Really,' said Oliver, who was mingling with a divine intensity seldom seen outside SW1, 'how Chiantishire goes to people's heads.'

Eddy and Minna stood a little apart, surveying the mêlée with unconscious disdain. Minna, although bred to the high life, had never embraced it, judging from a young age that it required too many changes of clothes. Eddy had been part of it, in his youth, when boys graduated without a thought from the great public schools to the great country houses, when everybody knew everybody else as a matter of course, when parties were given every night and people were hardly asked but found their way instinctively to wherever the fun was, gathering in garlanded marquees and aubusson-carpeted drawing rooms and Mayfair nightclubs to discuss each other and have their picture taken for the *Tatler*.

It was a triumph of decadence over snobbism, meritocracy and aristocracy jostling for gossip and champagne and a tip for the three-thirty at Ascot. Rock stars mingled with marquesses, gun runners joked with pederasts, starlets chattered with débutantes. Nancy Mitford's caveat on the dangers of slipping from correct U-speak was rendered obsolete as Old Etonians affected the diction of barrow boys and vice versa. Young blades destined for honourable careers at the bar and in the Foreign Office roared around Belgravia in mobster pin-stripes, greeting each other in their idea of East End patois. 'Wotcher, Grandad,' they told their bewildered papas, dropping t's and h's like autumn leaves, secure in the knowledge that the Sixties were only just over and class barriers were now as old hat as the Bastille, the barriers of privilege stormed, and the Rolling Stones invited to all the best houses.

Eddy had taken his place on the invitation list as if by right, partly because it was expected of him, partly because he couldn't think of anything better to do. University had thrown up no lures to him, and of the splinter group who did go up, most could be found in London four nights a week anyhow, decked out in their Bullingdon tails and complaining how provincial the proctors were. ('My dear, too like prep school. I tried to explain that we were only climbing the wall for a bet, but he wasn't having any of it. "It's off to the Dean with you," he said, so off I go the next morning with the mother and father of a hangover, AND bloody Archie's pinched the last of my Fernet Branca. Lucky for me the Dean's such a poppet, he gave me rich tea biscuits and a £200 fine, which I suppose someone will have to pay, I told him to put it on battels and not worry about a thing . . . ')

So Eddy had followed the crowd where it led, drinking until dawn and sleeping until lunchtime, seducing the right girls and making the right jokes and taking the right drugs, until he woke up one afternoon with a lurking malaise that was not merely due to the questionable quality of the brandy from the night before. When he realized it was boredom, he packed his bags and left the Mayfair squat that he shared with a Lithuanian showgirl and a Scottish earl. Without a backward glance, he left the Meissen vases filled with Trinidadian grass, the Venetian-looking glasses used for cutting lines of cocaine, the crystal glasses in which the dregs of last night's claret still lingered. He left behind the parties and the rags and the one-night stands, the glitter and the roar and the sound of breaking glass, the girl who was torturing him with faithlessness and rendering his nights sleepless.

No-one came after him as he disappeared into an unfashionable Chelsea backwater, no knocks fell on his door as he sat at his window watching the cherry trees blossom and drinking cheap red wine and playing his saxophone. He was only one in such a crowd, and the merry-go-round would carry on spinning without him. Like a divorce where both parties are too eager to be free for bitterness, Eddy and society parted, neither looking back in anger or regret. If he did think on it at all, if he saw a familiar face in the street or passed a door which had once held such promise, he thought that he was well out of it. How could he not be, when the sweet-smelling jasmine flowered so pretty on his balcony and he had songs to write and Minna came to tea and teased him about his art and her virginity. That was when she first came to London, just out of school and full of the freedom of the city. She would walk past his window most days, one way or another, and sometimes she would wave and pass by, and sometimes she would come up, and they would sit on the balcony and drink beer and smell the jasmine and Eddy would ask if she were still a virgin and she would say yes, unless she wanted to annoy him and claim herself the victim of some nameless seducer.

'Who is he?' Eddy would demand furiously, always taken in, infuriated by the idea of some jaded rake taking her carelessly after too much brandy.

'No one, no one,' she always said, laughing mercilessly at him. 'I'm quite touched by your concern, but I'm still intact. I promise you'll be the first to know. Anyway, I'm saving it for my marriage bed.'

And then she would assume the beatific smile of the utterly innocent, as if lustful thoughts never crossed her pristine mind, and tell him about the three boys she had kissed the night before. He would look at her sternly and tell her not to trample so carelessly on all the poor hearts thrown at her feet, and she would laugh some more and blow smoke rings at him and tell him not to be such an old woman. It was that kind of summer.

Standing on the edge of the party now, seeing some of the old faces, Eddy found them merging into one another in his memory, confused in a profusion of late nights and various vintages. Was it the blonde talking to Milo whom he had lived with for two illicit weeks while her fiancé was playing polo in Argentina? Or was it the other one, almost identical, who had been married three times since, and was now stepping out with a Texan oil baron. It seemed so long ago now, and all he could remember clearly was the crusading sense of liberty he had felt in that first summer on his own, and how fresh-minted Minna had seemed after those glossily jaded temptresses. He remembered the lightness of her step as she climbed his stairs, her delight in drinking beer at tea-time, her sinful pride in the number of her gentlemen admirers.

'Oh, my gentlemen admirers,' she would sigh, in a vain essay to appear weary of the world and all its diversions. 'What CAN a girl do?' And then she would sparkle her eyes at him from under her fringe and steal one of his cigarettes and tell him he was the only man for her.

'My only love,' she would say, not meaning it. 'What would I do without you?'

When this flirtatious mood took her, Eddy let himself join in, making her promise to save herself for him.

'Don't throw yourself away on one of those callow boys,' he said. 'Wait for me.'

'And you such a man,' Minna would laugh, feeling his biceps, which were as nothing compared to those of her schoolboy admirers, used to rowing and cricketing and playing fly half. 'How could I resist?'

But she had resisted, moved on, as careless of him as she was of all the others. When he saw her again, she was changed, she had found an affair, shot herself of her innocence.

'So what happened to you?' she said, when challenged. 'I waited so long I was growing old gracefully. I had to ask someone else to teach me.'

Eddy, who had enjoyed the joke as much as she had, suddenly found it grown stale, and was shocked by his urgent desire that it had been him. She didn't tell him who it was and he didn't ask, their old mood of confidences somehow over, and the subject was closed. She had slipped away again, to wherever it was that she went, tripping heedlessly away from him, taking her secret with her. And Eddy had moved to Soho, and formed his band, and played his jazz in those smoky basements where the cognoscenti gather in search of echoes of Charlie Parker, and told himself to think no more about it.

'Do you know ANY of these people?' Minna asked, breaking into his musing. He might have grown into one of these strong silent types, but a girl could only take so much strong silence, and she wanted to be entertained. 'Because I don't.'

'I knew some of them once,' said Eddy.

'Hark at you, Methusaleh,' hooted Minna. 'Was it all a terribly long time ago, in your salad days, and you green in judgement? Were you young and foolish? Tell me everything, I long to know.'

'Have another drink and don't bother me,' said Eddy, hailing a passing waiter.

'More champagne for the lady,' said Minna inconsequentially. 'How I love it when you put me in my place. Shall I be sent to bed with no supper?'

Oliver came waltzing over, having worked the room to his satisfaction and found himself back where he started. He held out his glass for more wine, batting his blue eyelashes at the waiter, who stood unmoved, like the rock of ages, having seen it all before.

'They stood among them, but not of them,' said Oliver in reproof. 'Just look at you two, giving everyone marks out of ten. Lucky for me I'm a confirmed eleven, or I might worry. No need to look so disapproving, ducky,' he said to Eddy, lighting one of the small Turkish cigarettes that he affected. No matter that they tasted of carbolic soap, they came in the smartest packets imaginable, with a gold crown stamped on the front, and one could only buy them from a tiny tobacconist at the right end of Burlington Arcade, and that was enough for Oliver. 'I remember days when you could be seen at four parties a night, twice as decadent as this, so don't give me that born-again look, because I know better.'

Oliver was the only relic of Eddy's old life to have followed him into the new. But then Oliver was beyond categorization, everyone knew that. Although he rejoiced in society, graciously accepting his acknowledged position as arbiter of taste from Belgrade to Belgravia, attending every soirée, every dinner, every first night, with careless devotion, he could hardly be written off as just another socialite. As he tripped about Europe for the season, he revelled in keeping everyone confused. When in Paris, he was seen at the Ritz bar, the Comédie Française and the front row of all the couture shows, which was only to be expected. What was not expected was his presence in the fringe theatres, the obscure galleries where struggling artists paid to have their work shown, the tiny smoke-filled cafés in the wrong *arrondissements* where he could be found discussing Cocteau in effortlessly colloquial French with perfect old nuts of men in worn tweed coats who lectured at the Sorbonne. The same double life took him through all the great cities of the continent, and back to London. 'I don't know much,' he had once said, in a fleeting moment of self-deprecation, 'but I know what I like.'

So he moved, clever as a chameleon and twice as canny, from salon to bar, assuming the argot of each with the skill of a born linguist, switching from the staccato tattle of the society hostess to the hurried intolerance of the intellectual, from the muted enthusiasm of the jazz buff to the measured consideration of the art critic, with the most careless of ease. 'I simply don't know how Oliver does it,' people said, and he never told.

So when Eddy had disappeared, Oliver alone noticed, and late one night Eddy had been surprised to see that unmistakable figure, resplendent in a perfect rose-bed of a shirt, sitting quietly upright at a corner table.

'My dear,' said Oliver, when Eddy joined him. 'No-one told me that you play like an angel. Whom does one ask for brandy round here? I've been making eyes at that waiter for quite half an hour. Do you think he's playing hard to get, or is it just me?'

Still in his early days, starting his apprenticeship, Eddy was playing in one of the more seedy of the late night dives, high up in the north of London, where the music mattered more than the décor. It was not what he imagined Oliver was used to.

'Slumming, darling,' said Oliver, when pressed. 'Allow me my little foibles. And since I've come all this way, and WHAT a way, you might let me take you for dinner next week.'

So, in between slices of high life, Oliver carefully fitted Eddy into his regimen, drinking with him in the crowded aromatic pubs of Soho, eating with him in restaurants that had never heard of balsamic vinegar, carousing until late in the kind of bars where they didn't watch the clock and membership wasn't required. Oliver, as he liked to claim when the egalitarian mood took him, was not a snob. He didn't give a hoot for strawberry leaves or coats of arms or paragraphs in *Debrett* (although of course, he always knew who had them). His snobbism was purely aesthetic, born of an adoration of talent in all its guises. He liked people to be beautiful or witty or brilliant, that was all. He had spotted Eddy early on, marked him down on his private dance card as one to follow, and so he kept alive a friendship that might have died with the season, worked at it as a gardener might tend his roses, watched it with satisfaction. Apart from anything else, he liked Eddy. He might not say much, but he was Worth It. Something was always Worth It, with Oliver.

It had been Oliver who had decided to bring his cousins to Soho that night. Alabama knew Eddy from a long time back, never intimately, but well enough to recognize a fellow traveller, and that, with Alabama, was always enough. Oliver had called his talented cousin, as he liked to do most days, if only to check that she was still writing award-winning material, and suggested they meet at Eddy's. Alabama, too nervous to argue, had agreed to everything.

'*Edouard, mon brave*,' Oliver had said, brooking no opposition. 'We're coming to you for drinks. Alabama needs a few allies on her big night. And you can tell that lodger of yours to put on her party frock and have a civilized night out for once.' Eddy didn't even begin to wonder how Oliver knew about Minna. Oliver always knew everything, that was part of his charm. 'Oliver will know,' was a kind of incantation heard on painted lips all over London.

For his part, he had been eaten with curiosity ever since he first heard about the mysterious lodger. Someone who knew someone had told tales of Tom Vane's sister, out on the town in Soho, drinking all night in transvestite bars, moved in with Eddy. Genes will out, this someone passed on sagely; after all, didn't everyone remember Tom in his wild youth, and not so young either, out all night, breakfasting at the Savoy still decked out in his evening rig, black tie askew, unflagging, demanding champagne wherever he went, a different girl on his arm each night?

Oliver had been intrigued, knowing Eddy for the misanthropist he had styled himself. Eddy was not the kind to pick up strays, however deserving, and particularly not Tom Vane's sister, not if she were anything like Tom.

And now, in the middle of this glittering celebration of a party, while the famous dazzled and shone about them, Oliver decided it was time to come to terms with this lodger, to take her up and discover her.

'So,' he said, facing her squarely, eyes alight with interest, 'imagine you being Tom Vane's sister.'

Minna, finding herself confronted, bit back the smart retort that rose to her lips, remembered about grace under pressure, refused to let herself become rattled in this alien environment, counted to ten, lifted her chin a little, batted her eyelashes twice, took a long drag on her cigarette, and said on a perfectly composed note, 'Well?'

Later, when Oliver knew and loved her, he often looked back and wished that he could recall the exact flight of her voice when she said that first quizzical 'Well?' Try as he might, he could never quite recapture it in all its frigidly intimate suggestion. Touch, but touch me not, where had she learnt to do that? He had to count to ten himself, to give himself time to readjust. Perhaps youth had changed since his day, or perhaps it was just this youth, but he recognized at once something to be reckoned with, and he silently took his hat off to Tom Vane's sister, who had obviously learnt, somewhere between the nursery and the street, that being someone's sister was not enough.

It was at this moment, in that pregnantly telling pause, that one of the society blondes, oblivious to atmosphere, peeled herself off someone's arm and came in their direction. She had spotted Eddy from afar, and now, with a delicate lack of timing, decided to make her move.

'Darling,' she cried, draping herself over him. 'What utter heaven. And after so long.' Was there a note of reproach in her voice? Eddy, who still couldn't remember if she were the one he had slept with for those short illicit weeks, was taken at a disadvantage.

'Hello,' he said helplessly.

'Come and talk to me,' she said, taking this for a yes. She bore him away, with the air of an archaeologist who has just unearthed a rare artefact from the second century BC. Minna and Oliver looked at each other, hardly bothering to restrain laughter, all at once conspirators, gathered together on the same side of the fence, and neither with any doubt that it was the right one.

It was Oliver's turn to say, 'Well?' with all the wealth of meaning that only he could put into one syllable, and Minna, seeing that Eddy had retreated to a safe distance, gave way to her laughter, which escaped in absurd gusts, enchanting Oliver more than he could have thought possible.

'It's his past,' said Minna, wiping her eyes. She had never seen Eddy at quite such a loss before, 'catching up with him.'

'And WHAT a past,' said Oliver in admiration. 'I could tell you stories about her that would make your toes curl, but CURL.'

'Oh, please do,' said Minna. She hadn't known that the girl was part of Eddy's past, just guessing, taking clues from the proprietorial way her arms had folded about his neck, as if reclaiming some long-lost prize.

It was at times like these that Minna realized how little she really did know about Eddy. The English devotedly preserved the convention of time telling, the years making all the difference. 'I've known him from way back,' people always said, with a proud sort of finality. 'We were at prep school together,' they said with triumph, securing their claim. Those years had fooled Minna for a while. 'I've known Eddy FOR EVER,' she said, when asked. It was only later, when confronted with a piece of his past that didn't fit into her particular jigsaw, that she began to realize that knowing someone first doesn't mean knowing them best, that she couldn't really claim the knowledge of years, just a short time of intimacy a long time ago. And that summer, that halcyon summer, had been so sweet and short-lived, cloaked in all the unreality of a shimmering heat haze. After all, what had they really talked about, all those afternoons on the balcony with the jasmine flowering about them? Kissing and late nights and short skirts and the best way to break hearts. And Minna, who thought at the time that they were baring their souls, who felt superior in having an older man with whom she discussed Life, looked back, her perspective levelled, and wondered. All that summer she had play-acted, a perfect Sarah Bernhardt of invention, making up roles as the mood took her, veering from sophisticate to *ingénue*, temptress to blue-stocking, every feminine cliché from Lolita to Cleopatra, trying them out as a dedicated shopper might try on one Chanel suit after another, wondering which suited her best, faking it with heedless candour, keeping everyone guessing.

And on the strength of that fleeting summer, she slept on his floor, because she had nowhere else to go, and this man standing in front of her, this immaculate aesthete with his knowing eyes, was her only clue. So when she said 'Please,' she meant it, for all the careless levity in her voice. Oliver, who had seen more than he cared to remember in his peripatetic life, heard the plea behind the smile, and thought to himself that there was more to this lodging arrangement than met even his observant eyes, and grew interested.

'My dear,' he said, gathering up a bottle of champagne and guiding her to a corner table, laid for two and strategically placed with a view of the room, a table that might have been designed with Oliver in mind. 'Come with me and I shall tell you everything. But first, you must promise to leave me your pearls, should anything unfortunate happen to you.'

The party rolled on into the night. Alabama stood tall in the middle of the room, drinking the sour mash bourbon she preferred, while the beau monde paid court to her with a shamelessness hardly ever seen since the heyday of Versailles. Venice, perfectly filling her role as the decorative and delectable sister, and Girl About Town in her own right, tripped from arm to arm, each more famous than the next. She treated them all with a touching disdain. 'Darling,' she said to a man who could command £10,000

110

to open a supermarket, 'this suit! Did you have it made with a knife and fork?'

Sebastian, whose vagueness verged on the eccentric, and whose appetite was legendary, had settled himself at a centre table, and was busy eating a large dinner with utter concentration, oblivious of the curious looks sent his way. He paused from time to time to question the waiter on the ingredients of a certain dish, or to smile amiably at one or other of the glamorous women who chose to light on him, picking faddishly at his plate and telling him what a complete disgrace he was. His interest was only really riveted when the chef, scenting a disciple at sixty paces, emerged, voluble and Italian from the kitchen, and sat down over a bottle of Barolo to discuss sauces.

'Sweet Sebastian,' said Venice, rather to the dismay of London's youngest and most sought-after director, who was trying to tell her about Chekhov. 'He's another Escoffier. He really only likes food and me, so we thought he had better open a restaurant. Of course,' she added loyally, 'he's terribly brilliant, but you can't make a living out of THAT, can you?' Despite the obvious and enduring brilliance of her sister, Venice still equated academic excellence with antiquated dons in ill-fitting tweeds, and held little brief for it.

Milo, who was much of Alabama's mind when it came to parties, and avoided them as a general rule, had closeted himself in a corner with a bottle of Armagnac, a Russian prince and the most scathing of the theatre critics, and was busying himself tearing the latest theatrical offerings to shreds, with a blatant disregard to the fact that half the assembled company was in them.

'Don't worry, ducky,' he said consolingly, when bearded by reproachful looks and obviously hurt thespian feelings. 'It's not you we object to, it's the damned play.'

'That Milo,' said the ruffled artistic spirits. 'Not very sporting of him, when he should be celebrating Alabama's success.'

'That Milo,' said the glamorous women, jealously eyeing the prince he had cornered. 'Talking to Sergei about Wittgenstein again, I shouldn't wonder. It's unfair of him.'

Over on the other side of the room, Eddy was being tossed from blonde to blonde with all the bemusement of an infant thrown into the deep end for the first time without armbands.

'Darling,' said the blondes in their well-bred voices, 'such bliss such heaven such a long time.'

They lit cigarette from cigarette, blowing smoke carelessly in his eyes, holding their glasses out automatically for more champagne, bending their heads for more compliments, stretching their necks for more admiration. It was a life's work for them, simply being themselves, and no small matter. Eddy watched them, all at once out of his depth where once he had been master of the situation, answering in monosyllables as they asked him with breathless disinterest about his ducky sax and his dinky jazz clubs and how it was that he found time to go out when he was working so terrifically hard at being an artiste. Eddy didn't think it worth the time, explaining it, since the sum total of their musical knowledge was garnered from going backstage to see the band at the last Rolling Stones concert.

And all the time, Oliver sat with Minna, enjoying the way her eyes shone a little brighter with each glass of wine, utterly approving of her minimal hair and maximum jewels, gleefully pouring Eddy's history into her ear, undiscriminating, hardly pausing to edit, telling her of the parties and the good times and the wine and the women, allowing her to fit into place all the missing pieces of the jigsaw, to piece together this man she thought she knew.

Just as he was finishing, running down a little, an apparition separated itself from the crowd and bore down on them.

'Well,' it said, throaty as Mae West and twice as promising. 'And little Bo Peep insisting that all her worldly goods were in Christmas Island or I don't know where. Coming it too rich, Cinderella.'

'Lou Lou,' cried Minna in delight. 'How quite perfect that it's you. Sit down at once. This is Oliver Skye. Have some champagne, we've got a bottle.'

'More than my date ever did for me,' said Lou Lou, larding more intimations of sex into a sniff than Tallulah Bankhead ever had. She held out a hand heavy with *faux* diamonds for Oliver to kiss, which he did with a kind of reverence, his keen sense of the original scenting a one-off. 'And I was such a nice girl once,' she continued. 'How a party can pall in the wrong company. Do you think it's just me, or is the male sex composed entirely of rat finks? What's a girl to do?' She took out a gold Sobranie and fitted it carefully into a foot-long cigarette holder. 'So,' she said, letting Oliver light it with a pretty condescension, 'what's the news? How's Shakespeare? Where's Shakespeare? Surely he should be here, learning the ropes.'

'In his garret,' said Minna, with regret. 'But it must be his turn next, don't you think?'

'So cries the optimist,' said Lou Lou, graciously allowing Oliver to fill her glass. Tonight, transformed by Jacques at his clever best, she was Louise Brooks, shining jet into the night, a sonnet in drop-waisted chiffon, sparkling reminder of the heady days of the Twenties when Scott and Zelda sported gaily in fountains and Dorothy Parker threw cultured pearls before swine and Isadora Duncan drove in fast cars.

'Well,' she said, turning to Oliver, who sat, breath bated, wondering if she might not turn into a pumpkin on the stroke of midnight. 'Where did Minna find you? Or did you paddle all the way back from the Andes just for the party?'

'Friend-of-Eddy,' said Minna, a little unwilling, suddenly aware of a line being crossed, that her oil and water worlds were about to mingle, not sure if she were pleased or not.

'Ah. The elusive Eddy,' said Lou Lou, waving her cigarette holder with a grandiose air that was the first indication of how much champagne she had drunk. 'And which one is he, pray?'

'One-over-there,' said Minna, pointing diffidently, her last defences dropping away. Lou Lou's magpie eyes followed, across the room, to the tall blonde-hemmed figure.

'But *ma foi*,' she said, resorting to French. 'And only your LANDLORD?'

The wealth of meaning Lou Lou managed to put into the word made Minna uncomfortable. It was all very well telling about Eddy, but revealing him in the flesh, having to see him through someone's else's eyes, was quite a different matter. And especially Lou Lou's eyes, which observed everything through a positively indecent haze of sex.

Minna stood up abruptly.

'I'll leave you with Lou Lou,' she said to Oliver, taking on that faintly dizzy manner that always served as her best defence. 'She's the last of the great courtesans.'

'Well,' said Oliver, watching Minna disappear into the crowd. 'There's no telling with that one. What do you really do?' There were no flies on Oliver, he had brushed them off a long time ago.

'I'm an actress,' said Lou Lou, calm as you please. 'More off stage than on at the moment. *Plus ça change*,' she added, with an expressively deprecating shrug of her alluring shoulders.

'A command performance, if I might say so,' said Oliver easily. He was used to receiving confidences. His unshockable air of having seen it all before drew out secrets as surely as the sun brought out blossom in springtime. 'But wasted all the same. Let me see who I can introduce you to.'

Eddy was asleep when Minna finally came home, or that was what he told himself. He had left the party soon after two o'clock, just when someone had arrived with the first editions of the morning papers.

'Reviews,' they had cried, and everybody had crowded round to look, half-afraid of failure, half-assured of triumph. The critics had been generous with their praise, lauding the company, the set, the lighting, but most of all the play. And Alabama's star had risen a little higher, confirmed in its brilliance by the approval of her peers, and Eddy, having nothing left to do, paused only to kiss her in congratulation before leaving.

He thought of taking Minna with him, but there

115

seemed little point. She had planted herself in the middle of a crowd of men and was watching herself grow, so he left her. Eddy had never believed in competing too hard, whatever the prize. It was no business of his, after all, if she wanted to stay up all night with a gaggle of strange hangers-on.

And she had stayed up all night, letting her new band of admirers take her from nightclub to bar without ever discovering their names. What were names anyway, at this time of night. Oliver and Lou Lou had come some of the way with them, and an older man called Robert or Richard or Roger, who engaged Lou Lou in deep conversation all night.

The dawn was filtering through the Soho streets when the hardiest and most devoted of her new swains dropped Minna off. The pavements were slick and wet where they had been hosed down, and the crates of empty bottles and discarded vegetables stood sentinel outside the shuttered restaurants, and the tramps and the strays slept quietly in doorways, clutching empty bottles of meths. It was the last hour of slumber for the city, the quiet hour of rest between the night dweller's return and the rising of the early shift. A solitary taxi rumbled through the pause, and somewhere a bird sang hopefully, waiting for his fellows to join him.

'Goodnight,' said Minna politely to her escort. 'Don't do that,' she added kindly as he attempted to kiss her. She turned her cheek away from his unsteady embrace and let herself into the flat, pausing to watch him amble off into the growing morning, unoffended. There would be plenty of girls for him to kiss the next night, and the one after that. He usually tried, liking to do what was expected of him, nothing daunted if his compliment was returned to sender.

Minna laughed a little to herself, and climbed the stairs.

'Sweet buffoon,' she murmured, wondering what his name could have been, her vanity lively enough to be pleased at his attempt at seduction.

And Eddy, pretending sleep, had heard the voices and her quiet laughter, and drew the inevitable conclusions, and thought angrily to himself that she hadn't changed at all.

7

'Oh, good,' said Minna. 'I hoped I'd find you. I seem to be rather late this morning, what with one thing and another.' She laughed a little guiltily to herself, remembering the strange man she had allowed to bring her home. She hadn't done that for a long time, considering herself past the age of teasing. She wasn't altogether sure what it was, but there was something about this particular summer that was sending her sliding back into all her old bad habits. She had seen Eddy's disapproving look over the crossword at breakfast and ducked out of the flat before she could be called on to explain herself. She really did think that the new hair might have persuaded him that she didn't need nannying any more, but old dogs and new tricks didn't seem to go together any better now than they ever had.

'Oh, stop it,' she said, seeing Jay's face break into a great goofy smile of amazement. 'It's just a haircut. The new me, what do you think? You don't have to tell me if you hate it, it'll grow.'

'It's perfect,' said Jay truthfully. How could he hate anything on such a vision? She looked like something out of *La Dolce Vita* in her green dress and her hair glinting silver in the sun and her sunglasses blackest Italian and her arms laden with heavy silver, and she put Anita Eckberg to shame without even trying. 'I love it.'

'The sweetness of you,' said Minna carelessly, trying to pretend she wasn't pleased. She looked a little furtively round the café, wondering if anyone had noticed the change, but no-one seemed to be very interested. It was the same as it always was. The same old men, gnarled and argumentative, watched the same game of football on the same television. The same clock ticked impassively on the wall, and the same small groups of girls discussed boys and lipstick and whether the Wag was all it was cracked up to be. Media flotsam and young lady novelists drank small cups of espresso and smoked untipped French cigarettes, and in one corner two Parisian boys sat thick in discussion of the mysteries of *le Style anglais*. After all, everyone, but everyone in Paris this year was wearing tweed coats and Prince of Wales check and those particular yellow corduroy trousers and Gucci loafers and even cravats, for the more daring. But since they had been in England, they hadn't seen a single person in such a uniform, and they were starting to wonder if they had been misled. Could *Vogue* be wrong? It was too perplexing for words and not at all what they were used to.

'Poor ducks,' said Minna, listening with obvious enjoyment to their Gallic postulations. 'Do you think we should tell them?'

'Not at all,' said Jay laughing. 'And have their world come tumbling down about their ears?' Having no sartorial pretensions himself, he wore a perfectly serviceable writer's uniform of nondescript black trousers and a white shirt, rather darned in the sleeves. His one extravagance was a pair of Chelsea boots, the kind Mick Jagger used to wear in the Sixties, which had to be custom-made in the backstreets of Limehouse, and which he wore with half-concealed pride.

'I did know a man who wore yellow corduroys once,' said Minna absently. 'I rather think he was a friend of my parents. But he was half Australian or something terrifying, and had to work terribly hard to be received in the best houses.'

'Careful,' said Jay, who had never met anyone who wore corduroy trousers, much less yellow ones. 'Your background is showing.'

'What background?' said Minna, trying to bluff him out.

'Nanny and mater and pater and tea on the lawn and even croquet, I shouldn't be surprised,' said Jay airily, allowing himself to tease her a little, wondering at his own bravery. There was something about Minna that brought out the daring in him.

'Oh, that,' said Minna dismissively. She was a great believer in forgetting one's past, whatever anyone said about it catching up with one. 'Don't start getting on your high horse and going all snobbish on me, I couldn't bear it. I promise to try harder.'

'Harder at what?' asked Jay, a little bemused at her train of thought, which he already knew to be erratic at the best of times.

'Harder at having the air of mystery which is so essential to all us artists. You know,' she said patiently, seeing that Jay was still having difficulty keeping up. 'So people can't tell if our parents were lords or lorry drivers, or counts or coal miners.'

'Or dukes or dustmen?' Jay supplied, glad to be of use.

'Precisely. You can't win either way, why do you think I had my hair cut? The only answer is to be utterly mysterious, unless of course you come from Serbo-Croatia or somewhere, in which case it goes with the territory.'

'Serbo-Croatia or Christmas Island, I suppose?' said Jay, vastly enjoying the lesson for today. It was better than *Listen with Mother*, he didn't care what anyone said.

'That sort of thing,' said Minna approvingly. 'My friend from Bikini Atoll, you do see.'

Jay didn't quite see, but then these flights of fancy were still one step ahead of him, and who was he to reason why. He would do and die for this vision, that was all he knew, and nothing less than she deserved.

'When I say us artists,' Minna continued, 'gracious of you not to take me up on that, I mean you really, I only included myself to make it less confusing. Anyway, I feel sure I must have been a poet or something in my former life, because otherwise I should be working in a merchant bank or married by now, or something equally dread, wouldn't you say?'

'Of course,' said Jay weakly, wondering if his arithmetic was up to it. 'I absolutely would say. You're totally and deliciously right.'

'Now, Jay,' said Minna, who was less of a fool than she let herself believe. 'Don't let's get facetious.' She fixed him with what she fondly believed to be a gimlet eye, although she never quite knew what a gimlet eye was, and stubbed her cigarette out rather pointedly in the tin ashtray.

'No, no, not at all,' said Jay ingenuously, taking a diverting bite out of his Danish and smiling innocently through the crumbs. 'Don't let's. I mean, I won't. How could I?'

'Pah,' said Minna eloquently. 'There's a great deal more to that boyish artistic soul of yours than meets the eye, so don't think none of us have noticed or anything short-sighted like that. We can't fool all of the people all of the time.' Minna sometimes thought that one could fool most of the people most of the time, but only in her more optimistic moments.

Looking at her then, Jay thought that quite probably he would lay down his life for her if she asked him, and he thanked the fates, or whoever it was that decided such things, that it wasn't the Middle Ages and he was no Roland. He had always rather fancied himself as another Roland, but that was before he had met Eleanor of Aquitaine.

'Well,' said Minna, glad to have got things straight. 'I am glad to see that you're feeling as ill as I am.' Jay, still so new to the metropolis, had not yet got himself kitted out in all the vital accessories to urban living. Unlike Minna, who considered herself born to walk the streets, whatever Eddy said, and who proved it by having sixteen pairs of sunglasses in different tints, Jay had none. Banning the rays, so essential to anyone who ever presumed to call himself streetwise, had not filtered down to him just yet. So his eyes were open for all to see, a delicate shade of pink, slightly swollen, sure betrayal of excess. He blinked them now, under Minna's exacting scrutiny, and started to wonder about the desirability of shading them from the glare.

'Working late last night,' he said, mumbling a little into his coffee and going rather pink about the ears. How could he tell Minna that he had met a girl in his local late-night corner shop and found himself buying a bottle of brandy and asking her home to drink it with him? How could he possibly tell Minna that after the brandy was finished his new lady friend, quite uninvited but with a great deal of enthusiasm, had performed several unmentionable and unimaginably exotic acts upon him, leaving him only when dawn started to break, with a companionable peck on the cheek and no questions asked. It was all very well Lou Lou thinking it a huge joke, telling him to go off and find himself a girl, but now in the cold hard light of the morning after, he was feeling rather confused, faintly guilty and not a little pleased with himself. But he certainly wasn't going to tell Minna that.

'You couldn't feel ill,' he said defensively. 'Not looking like that.'

'You should have seen me first thing this morning,' said Minna innocently. For all her sixteen pairs of sunglasses, there were still some things she hadn't learnt. Jay swallowed manfully and tried not to imagine.

'Shall we have another cup of coffee?' he suggested, changing the subject.

'Why not?' said Minna blithely, smiling on the sinful. 'Just let's.'

Across London, Oliver was sitting up in his bed having breakfast (Colombian coffee, two croissants, and Frank Cooper's Oxford), and making his usual morning round of telephone calls. He had already called Alabama to congratulate her on being so clever, and Venice to congratulate her on being so beautiful, and now he felt it was high time he rang Eddy, just to tease him a little, because really, how could a boy resist.

'My dear,' Oliver said clearly, as Eddy picked up the telephone. 'My felicitations. You must be proud.'

'Proud?' said Eddy unhelpfully. He was feeling crusty and quite his age this morning, and not like a bright young musician at all. He blamed it on too much champagne, which he wasn't used to, not these days. 'Proud of what?'

'That ravishing new lodger of yours, of course,' said Oliver, too much of an old hand to be daunted. Besides he had more than an inkling of the way this particular wind was blowing, and he didn't want to miss a single gust of it. 'What a boy you are for hiding lights under bushels. How is it that you have never introduced me before? I'm quite beside myself with enchantment.'

'She's a law unto herself,' said Eddy unwillingly. 'Besides, she doesn't like society.'

'Unlike her dear brother,' said Oliver, with a hint of indulgence. Everyone knew Tom Vane was beyond the pale, he was famous for it, but one had to admit that there was something vaguely cheering about such unabashed excess in these dark days of recession and the tottering economy.

'Fortunately,' said Eddy, who didn't have to admit any such thing, and who had no desire to dwell on the Vane family, not this morning.

'Yes, well,' said Oliver, in the conciliatory voice he kept for difficult cases, 'really, I couldn't agree more, one in that family is more than enough. Anyway, darling, I shan't keep you. I know time is money for you Artists.' He could tell Eddy was in no mood for light conversation. He sometimes thought that he had a seventh sense about such things. 'I only called to ask you to a little supper party I'm giving on Friday, just the tiniest thing, but who knows, it might be diverting. Do say you're free.'

'I'm free,' said Eddy, camp as a rattlesnake.

'Don't mock,' said Oliver sternly. 'A simple yes please will do. Really, I sometimes wonder how you get asked anywhere.'

'I don't,' said Eddy. 'Far too anti-social now I've discovered my Art, don't you know.'

'Yes, well,' said Oliver with feeling. 'One can forgive people for making the mistake. Anyway, you can put on your best frock and bring that delicious lodger with you, and she can have a nice time, even if you don't.'

'I'll ask her,' said Eddy, not altogether helpful. 'But I can't be answerable if her calendar is impossibly full.' He thought of Minna's erratic hours and painful neglect of the Revolution, just when it was crying out for her, and wondered who would be keeping her up until dawn tonight.

'Tut, tut,' said Oliver in reproof. 'Of course she'll come. Now I should just get back into that Empire bed of yours and try getting out of it the right side. I mean to say, darling, I can take it, everyone has their dark side, no-one knows that better than I, but think of the poor lodger, how utterly terrifying it must be for her, having such a landlord. Take your happy pill and think of England and I'll see you on Friday.' And Oliver, his work quite done, put down the receiver and turned back to his address book, which happened to be a very fetching shade of green calfskin, with his initials discreetly engraved on one corner. He did so long to have a coronet above the initials, but the only excuse for that would be to marry a duke, and Oliver didn't think that terribly likely, with the law being what it was.

When Minna came back that afternoon, she found Eddy drinking beer on his balcony, watching the world wag.

'Hello,' she said brightly, in very good spirits after half a bottle of Pouilly Fussé and a tiny Armagnac snuck in when Jay wasn't looking.

'Hello,' said Eddy. He held up his bottle. 'Do you want to join me?'

'Yes, please.' Minna headed for the fridge, where two six-packs huddled reassuringly, like quarter backs warming up for a big game.

'How's your hangover?' said Eddy, as she joined him.

'What hangover?' said Minna, who had quite forgotten the morning. It seemed such a long time ago, a lifetime, before lunch. She seemed to remember that she hadn't been at her best.

'The one you woke up with,' said Eddy, trying not to laugh. She was a disgrace, there was no other word for it. He wondered who she had been drinking with all this time. And where. Somewhere up-market that was for certain. She gave off that rich smell of scent and liqueurs and other people's cigar smoke, and she had a bright look in her eyes which told him that she hadn't been sipping Perrier. No new woman this; no aerobics and callanetics and designer water and abstinence. She was an old-fashioned girl down to her fingertips. She was feckless and reckless and quite without regrets, born into the wrong age. He supposed they didn't make girls like this any more, and a good thing too. She reminded him of the girls they used to make in the Twenties, the kind who drove men to drink and destruction. She was Gloria Gilbert and Daisy

Buchanan and every girl who was ever driven in a Stutz Bearcat, and there was no excuse for her at all.

'Oh, that one,' said Minna, laughing herself. It seemed so ridiculous now, that she should have had such trouble getting out of bed. But then, with a bed so near the floor, what could a girl do? She longed for one of those Empire beds, like Eddy's but grander, the ones that rise three feet off the floor, the kind that Josephine had lingered on, waiting for Napoleon to come home, sweaty and triumphant, from the Italian campaign.

She waved her hand dismissively at Eddy, indicating that she was not the kind of girl who suffered from hangover, that the dry tongue and bleary eye of the morning-after were strictly the province of ordinary mortals, that her stumbling entrance into the kitchen this morning had been the merest tease, a perfect joke, a momentary pretence that she was human after all.

'That one,' she repeated dreamily. 'I'd quite forgotten it.'

'Dark glasses at breakfast,' said Eddy conversationally, 'are considered something of a giveaway. Just so you know for next time.'

'Rat,' said Minna. 'You don't let me get away with a thing.'

'It's good for you. You know what people do with enough rope.'

'Oh,' said Minna in exasperation. 'Cut me some slack, skipper, why don't you? Drink your beer, it's getting warm.'

'Warm beer and cold rain,' said Eddy, looking at the impeccable blue of the sky, and trying to remember what rain looked like. 'The curse of the English.'

'What about *le vice anglais*?' said Minna, just to show him that she knew the facts of life.

Eddy looked at her sternly. 'What does a nice girl like you know about things like that?'

'I gave up being a nice girl for Lent,' said Minna carelessly.

'Pity.'

'What do you know about nice girls anyway?' she asked, curious. 'Not at all your bag.'

'Don't overestimate me. There's plenty about me you don't know.'

'The man of mystery. Strong and silent. An enigma of our times. Get you.' Minna laughed at him shamelessly and went into the kitchen for another beer. Eddy watched her go and wondered why she didn't get fat.

'So,' he said, as she came back and settled herself on her stool. 'Oliver wants us for dinner on Friday.'

'Us?' said Minna. 'How positively domestic you sound. Here, I forgot, I brought you a doughnut. Shall we sit down and have tea and imagine we're just an old married couple at heart?'

'I've got some beer,' said Eddy, who considered that some remarks went far too near the bone.

'So you have,' said Minna, who prided herself on her powers of observation. 'Let's just pretend we're Scott Fitzgerald and drink ourselves to death while the town burns. I'll be Scott and you can be Zelda,' she added, charitable to a fault.

'Thank you so very much,' said Eddy. 'I suppose that means that I have to dance in fountains and turn cartwheels outside the Plaza and take ballet lessons and have affairs with dashing French airmen?'

'And go mad,' said Minna fairly. 'You don't get all the good bits. Although they do say that those sanitoriums in Switzerland are as grand as the Ritz, these days, so it shouldn't be too drack for you.'

'I'm enchanted by the prospect,' said Eddy, dry as a bone. 'I expect you'll just go ahead and write *The Great Gatsby* and make me frantically jealous?'

'Frantically,' said Minna happily. She had, after all, always rather fancied the idea of herself as a great artist. 'I shall wear duck-white shoes and drive the high corniche, and slick my hair down, and write the Great American Novel, which I very much fear will push you over the edge altogether.' She looked immensely taken by the thought.

'I'm touched,' said Eddy.

'So when do we go to Oliver's?' said Minna, moving swiftly on. 'I love Oliver, I never met a man who knows so much dirt about people.'

'A walking distillation of fifteen years of gossip columns,' agreed Eddy, who wasn't above appreciating a little tattle when the mood took him, even if he didn't know all the names any more. 'Friday. He begged me to tell him that you were free, but I said that I couldn't possibly commit you, your social schedule being what it is.'

Minna, whose sense of hearing was as sharp as any girl's, caught the edge in his voice, and decided to ignore it. She really didn't feel strong enough to explain away her choice of dancing partner, not on a day like today, with the sun shining so bright and beer to be drunk and the evening stretching ahead, full of uncertain promise. 'Friday,' she said, carefully ignoring the pitfalls that lay beneath her perfect feet, 'would be fine.'

The week rolled on. Oliver busied himself with his dinner party, staying in constant telephonic contact with his caterer, his florist, his hairdresser and his medium. 'I sometimes wonder when I get five minutes to myself,' he said. Eddy wrote a song and practised with the band and had beer at tea-time with Minna and allowed her to tease him and told himself that he wouldn't let anyone else get away with such liberties. Jay started on the fourth draft and walked about in a state of constant agitation, and Lou Lou just did whatever it was that Lou Lou did, and let everyone draw their own conclusions. Minna merely carried on being herself. She had an irresponsible feeling of being on holiday, and quite often woke up surprised that she wasn't in St Tropez. Most days she had breakfast with Jay, and let him tell her about what she referred to as his creative angst, and sometimes Lou Lou would join them and it would be a party. In the evenings, they took to the town because, as Lou Lou said so sagely, someone had to teach Jay about life. Jay, bemused but happy, was only too willing to be taught. So they went to see stand-up comics on Brixton Hill, and cabaret in downtown Balham, and undiscovered rock bands in Harlesden. They danced to reggae in Ladbroke Grove, and rap off the Charing Cross Road, and soul in Covent Garden.

They drank in late bars down in the wrong end of Chelsea, run by Greeks and Cubans and Italians, where they locked the doors after one o'clock and let you drink until five, and Lou Lou always looked knowledgeable and secretive and muttered about Mafia connections and protection money and people having the police in their pockets. Some nights they went to fringe theatre in cramped upstairs rooms, and some nights they ate *dim sum* in steamy little restaurants in Chinatown and caught a late-night film at the Empire, and some nights they just stayed in Soho and drank in the bars and wandered into Ronnie Scott's to hear the jazz. And if sometimes Jay looked a little jaded at breakfast and had an extra cup of coffee and an Alka-Seltzer and complained of his head, Lou Lou always said that it was the price of an education.

And then, of course, there was lunch. Lunch, needless to say, had been another of Lou Lou's ideas. Jay and Minna had been comparing hangovers over a Danish and trying to remember whether they had actually danced on tables the night before or whether they were hallucinating, when Lou Lou swept in in a tortoiseshell wig, a shocking red dress reminiscent of Ava Gardner at her most daring, six-inch stilettos, and vermilion winged sunglasses, the kind you can't get any more, and suggested lunch.

Minna had been enchanted. Lunch, she decided, was just what every girl needed. Lunch was the last word. It was all very well having nothing to do but the Revolution, but there was the rest of the day to fill, and it was no small matter. If, of course, one was a *demi-mondaine*, or *petite cocotte*, or whatever it was (the French had a word for it, just as they have a word for everything the English don't, but Minna couldn't quite think what it was), but if one was one of those things the French have a word for, then there was no problem. Then the day was hardly long enough to fit in all the manicures and pedicures and coiffures, all the shopping, the visits to the couture houses and the florists and the lingères, to the hatters and the shoe-makers and the palmists.

If one wasn't, then there were great stretches of the day to use. If one had eight dresses and was done with it, and one looked hell in hats and did one's own nails and didn't travel everywhere with great bunches of flowers hanging from one arm, then one had to think again. Lunch, Minna considered, was the perfect answer. She wondered that she hadn't thought of it before. But then, she supposed she had thought of it, even suggested it, but those people she knew, the ones who were off in Nepal and Bali and the South Seas, didn't really do lunch. They could sometimes do things like snatch a bite, or grab a sandwich, or meet for a quick drink, but it wasn't the same as lunch. They were always far too busy composing their next symphony or rushing to rehearsals or writing to a deadline or dashing to see their agents. They seemed to spend large chunks of their lives talking about or talking to or going to see their agents. Minna wasn't remotely surprised that none of them were married. How could they be? No time to fit in a wife and an agent?

She supposed it served her right for not having normal nine-to-five friends who did something respectable with unit trusts, but they were said to be even worse. People in offices had Meetings, even Minna knew that. She could never quite imagine whom they Met all the time, or why, but she didn't like to dwell on it. All she knew for sure was that lunch would be no good at all for that sort, and she rather thought that she was well out of it. She had been taken out by a City boy once, when she was too young to know any better, palmed off on him by her brother, but none the less willing. Her willingness had turned to resignation when he started talking about the balance of payments and the Exchange Rate Mechanism and the trade deficit and take-overs and insider trading with all the zeal of missionaries in early nineteenth-century Africa. (He himself had seemed rather taken aback to find her staring at him with the same kind of bemusement that natives in early nineteenth-century Africa must have shown when the same missionaries tried to explain to them the rudiments of rugby football.) She had gone home feeling shamefully ignorant and good for nothing, and hadn't even asked him in, which she would normally have done, although not for the purposes he imagined. Ever since, she had made a small pact with herself never to feel like that again. It didn't do a girl any good, whatever the pundits said about adversity being character forming. So she hung about with the kind of people she could understand, and due to her catholic tastes in literature and her deep respect for the theatre and the concert hall, they turned out to be the kind of people who didn't know any more than she did what a unit trust was. Which was all very fine and dandy, except when it came to lunch and they were all too busy with their agents.

So Lou Lou's brainwave came as an utter godsend to Minna, and now, whenever Jay could be tempted away from his typewriter, there was lunch to look forward to.

8

'Darlings,' said Oliver, rapturous in Scott Crolla and bottle-green mascara, 'don't you look an utter picture? How clever you are. Come in and scintillate my guests.'

'The kindness of you,' said Minna, kissing him on both cheeks. She had her little black dress on this evening, the one that Eddy so disapproved of, and she wore her king's ransom of pearls as if they were nothing at all. Eddy, who had never believed in dressing for the occasion, stood tall in black Levis and a white shirt.

'Afraid my black tie is still at the cleaners,' he said, shaking Oliver's hand with grave formality.

'Don't be silly,' said Oliver, patting him affectionately on the cheek. 'You look like a dream. The understated look can never go out, in my opinion. Now, who do you know?'

In Oliver's wide drawing room, butterflies of all descriptions flitted between great urns of roses and orchids, talking in high fluting voices and peering over each other's shoulders to see who had just arrived. Eddy was amused to see that Oliver's idea of a little dinner was at least forty people, most of whom were instantly familiar from the gossip columns.

'I suppose you asked me for the token low-life element?' Eddy said.

Oliver giggled, a little coyly. 'Darling heart,' he said. 'I always think it's so important for people to see how the other half live. Have some champagne and don't be such a snob. Alabama,' he added, catching his cousin on the wing, 'come and cheer Eddy up. Alabama,' he whispered conspiratorially, 'affects to hate the high life as well. You can keep each other company.'

'I'm such a slut,' said Alabama, kissing Eddy. 'I sell all my principles down the river for a glass of free champagne.'

'It's terribly shaming,' agreed Eddy, letting an extremely pretty waiter make eyes at him while his glass was being filled. 'I'm certain that David Hart never goes to parties like this.'

'No need to rub it in,' said Alabama in reproof. 'A girl has to hang up her typewriter some nights.'

Eddy looked at her with affection. 'Shall we get terribly drunk and justify ourselves till dawn?' he said.

'Really,' said Oliver, leading Minna away from the ungrateful. 'I wonder why I bother with those two, really I do. You, on the other hand, are quite another matter.' He smiled at Minna's face, shining with anticipation. 'I can see I'm going to have half London in love with you before the night is through.'

Minna found herself thrust into a group of darkly beautiful men who were discussing a party they had been to in St Tropez the week before.

'My dear,' they said in horror, 'people throwing custard pies, can you believe it? Effie Hampton's Valentino was ruined beyond repair, crowned heads walking out, Ernst Poellenberg slipped on the mess and broke his ankle, I hear he's threatening to sue, could you imagine.'

'Absolutely perfectly frightful,' said Minna staunchly. 'People these days.'

'Darling,' said the beautiful men, their eyes lighting up. 'Heavenly dress, where did you get those pearls, I haven't seen pearls like that since I was in Paris for the collections, do you know Ferdie Waterloo, he used to wear pearls like that, before the accident.'

'I always heard they were cultured,' said Minna, lying disdainfully.

'Don't tell us,' said the beautiful men, besides themselves. 'It can't be true, Teddy angel, come here, you'll never guess, remember old Ferdie and his pearls, not real, darling, too shaming, how could he hold his head up in public, I always said he was rather bogus, didn't I always tell you how bogus that family was, you never could quite find them in the *Almanach de Gotha*, however hard you tried.'

Minna left them to spread the news, and wandered away across the party.

'Come and talk to us,' said Milo, who was drinking Armagnac in a corner with Sebastian. 'Let us explain to you about the high life.'

'I don't understand a word of it,' said Minna gratefully. 'Who is Ferdie Waterloo, and why does he wear five strings of pearls?'

Milo laughed and poured some brandy into her glass. 'Don't ask,' he said. 'Poor old Ferdie. Not really my neck of the woods.'

'Poor old Milo,' said Sebastian. 'He's just a young literary turk, he knows nothing. You'll have to forgive him.'

'It's so demoralizing,' said Milo, 'being me.' He looked vastly pleased at the thought.

'Utter hell,' said Sebastian vaguely. 'Do you think

it's too vulgar to fall on the food? I'm dying of curiosity.'

'New caterers,' said Milo, for Minna's enlightenment. 'Oliver had a set-to with the last ones because they used *faux* caviar instead of the real thing. There was talk of him having to skip the country altogether, to get over the shame.'

'Luckily for him, everyone thought he was setting a new trend,' said Sebastian. 'So now all the grandest hostesses are simply throwing Danish lumpfish roe at each other, and telling everyone how common Sevruga is. Oh, dear,' he added, his eyes wandering across the room. 'Venice is breaking hearts again. She WILL do it, however hard I tell her not to.'

In the midst of a gaggle of men, Venice was sparkling bright as the evening star, and twice as dangerous.

'Now now, boys,' she was saying as her admirers fought to light her cigarette and fill her glass and get her telephone number. 'One at a time. It's no earthly good looking so soulful, you know I'm quite the most taken girl here.'

The crowd swayed and weaved and re-formed into little groups intent on influencing friends and making people. A momentary gap appeared, revealing Eddy and Alabama, leaning against a wall and making faces at people's backs.

'Why,' said Milo conversationally, 'is the beat of my heart making up to your landlord in that shameless manner?'

Minna, who was wondering much the same thing herself, shook her head. 'I shouldn't begin to know,' she said, 'being a well-brought-up girl myself.'

'A well-brought-up girl?' said Lou Lou, appearing out of the crowd in nostalgic sequins and swinging geometrical hair. 'My dear, a positive collectors' item.'

'Lou Lou,' said Minna, pleased. 'What a surprise.'

'Oliver's taken me up,' said Lou Lou, knowing better than to take offence. 'Furthering my career in that madly philanthropic way of his.'

Minna said nothing, rather thinking that a discreet veil might best be drawn, what with one thing and another. Besides, she didn't want to betray her ignorance of sexual jargon.

'Where's that lovely landlord of yours?' said Lou Lou, her eyes roaming restlessly across the room.

'Oh,' said Minna, waving her hand carelessly, 'he's off somewhere flirting with award-winning playwrights. You know what boys are these days.'

'I do indeed,' said Lou Lou, interest kindling in her old-fashioned eyes. 'Lucky there's a positive hundredweight of the eligible and irresistible floating about, quite spare. To take your mind off it, you understand.'

'Pity they only want to talk about parties in St Moritz,' said Minna, getting her saints mixed. 'Still, they are rather pretty. Do you think I should try again? For the aesthetic value?'

'Indubitably,' said Lou Lou, who didn't like to see edible flesh going to waste. 'Dash back into the breach, why don't you? I would join you but I have bigger fish to fry, you know how it is. No rest for the wicked, do you call it unfair that the pure at heart get all the luck? But then, I don't expect I should go the distance with the simple life. Sin is rather more satisfying, somehow.'

'All I can say,' said Minna, laughing, 'is that it's a very good thing that Jay isn't here, to hear you talking like that.'

'Oh,' said Lou Lou, getting out her cigarette holder and unfolding it like a telescope to its full twelve inches. 'He'll grow to love it. Look at all those biologists who go and live up trees and end up just like parrots, it's all adaptability. After all, someone has to teach him about life. We can't be rolled in cotton wool all our lives, it's the law.'

The party unfolded into the night. People started to eat, discussing the new caterers in discreet under-tones. Milo and Sebastian filled their plates and sat on one side of the room bitching genially about half the assembled company, while Eddy and Alabama dined off a bottle of bourbon they had found in the kitchen, and bitched rather less genially about the other half. Venice, too hemmed in to get to the food, allowed her admirers to bring her choice morsels to tempt her tiny appetite. 'I eat like a bird,' she said apologetically. 'It's too dull of me, so EARLY Eighties. What can you do?' Lou Lou was kept too busy to eat by Oliver, who kept taking her off into corners and introducing her to middle-aged men. Minna really did think it a tad blatant, in polite company. 'Darling,' said Oliver, passing by on the wing, 'no need to look so disapproving, it's only networking. So lucky you introduced me to Lou Lou, the contacts I can help her to make, her career is going to take off, you are clever.'

'Quite,' said Minna, who liked to think of herself as progressive and open-minded. 'Absolutely.'

Having had quite enough of the beautiful men, she lit on a hard gambling core who were discussing the prospects for Saratoga in one corner, and spent the rest of the evening playing craps with them for high stakes. Oliver's glamorous female guests were perfectly horrified by the sight of their escorts, sleeves rolled up and hair askew, crouching on the floor and throwing dice, occasionally letting out a vulgar shout of triumph, but Oliver was enchanted. 'Too, too *Guys and Dolls*,' he said happily. 'How I died for that Sky Masterton.' Minna personally felt she was doing more than her duty in keeping the party lively, what with Eddy being so blatantly anti-social. After all, Alabama Skye wasn't the only girl in the room. She would have to have a word with him about it at breakfast. But just now, breakfast was a long way off, and she was winning.

As it was, Eddy was out when Minna rose the next day, so she put on her lipstick and went to meet Jay and Lou Lou for lunch.

They went to one of their favourite haunts, long and low and green, with the kind of clientele who looked as if they had been hand-picked from all aspects of the media, and the kind of waiters who looked as if they were only waiting on tables until they could break in to all aspects of the media. It had, Minna thought, a pleasing kind of symmetry to it. The *maître d'hôtel*, or whatever one called the man who greeted one (the French of course had a word for it), fell on Lou Lou's neck like a long-lost brother and led them with great portent to the very best table he had. 'Here with a view of the room, I keep it for my most special guests,' he said unctuously. In return for such treatment, Lou Lou gracefully removed her sunglasses, somehow managing to invest this simple gesture with all the loaded meaning of a woman disrobing, and gave him a bat of her eyelashes which sent him reeling back across the room into a junior waiter carrying a trayful of soup. By some divine dexterity, the junior waiter saved the day and his job by executing a graceful pirouette in the right direction and carrying on as if nothing untoward had happened.

'Well,' said Lou Lou, 'that one's destined for the Royal Ballet and no mistake.'

'I should give him a raise,' said Minna to the greeter, who had taken appreciably longer to recover his composure and was covering up the fact by making a great fuss of spreading out their napkins for them and clicking his fingers at minions to bring them menus, bread and iced water.

'I don't think I'll have anything to eat,' said Jay plaintively, pushing his menu away. He had been up all night battling with the third act and was feeling all his artistic temperament. 'Not hungry really.'

'Don't take any notice of this one,' said Lou Lou conspiratorially to the waiter, the greeter having retired from the fray to powder his nose and take another valium. 'He's suffering from one of those strange artistic maladies. Writer's block or hangover, or some such. Bring him the head of Alfred Garcia, medium rare, and a nice bottle of Chablis.'

The waiter, who was inordinately well read but only infinitesimally talented, laughed appreciatively, and wondered if his latest manuscript had got lost in the post. He was sure that publishers didn't take six months to read a slim novel. Novella really, if he was being brutally honest, but it was so perfectly turned that he had been certain that no-one would notice the lack of plot. Besides, people didn't really mind about plots any more, did they? After all, it was the Eighties, and everyone, but everyone was talking about style over content.

'Now then,' said Lou Lou, turning to Jay, 'that's

quite enough of that. Us girls have come here for stimulating conversation and erudite discussion and we utterly rely on you to provide it, so if it makes you happier, you can start singing for your supper and stop looking as if you had passed your sell-by date, that's all.'

'What Lou Lou means,' said Minna, 'is that some people are good for one thing and some are good for another and each for each. So since we're no good at writing, we can be good at paying, and you're broke again, and so it's our treat, and let's not be bourgeois about it.'

'Oh, all right,' said Jay, bowled over by Minna's logic. 'I accept. I bow to your largess. I suppose I can always repay you by dedicating my first play to you both.'

'Yes, please,' said Minna. 'Does that mean we can come to all your launches and literary parties and meet Stephen Berkoff?'

'Certainly,' said Jay staunchly. 'First nights and interviews on *Wogan* and press conferences too, I shouldn't wonder.'

'Oh,' said Minna in rapture. She dreamt of holding a press conference, with all those lean young men intent on a story holding out microphones towards her and hanging indecently on her every word. She sometimes felt that she had been born to give press conferences.

'Isn't that Harold Pinter over there?' said Lou Lou, stretching her neck aristocratically and taking in the room without seeming to look.

'Where?' said Jay, turning around and staring. He hadn't yet learnt the urban art of staring obliquely. The other lunchers were so well versed in this practice that they all seemed to be devoting their utter attention to their own tables, when all the time they were frantically busy taking in who was with whom, and who wasn't. There would be questions to answer after this lunch, as always. Why were the girls from Bloomsbury looking so friendly with that strange young man, for example? And what could the most prominent of the literary agents be doing with the equally prominent theatrical agent? Could Kenneth Branagh be writing another autobiography already? And quite what was Harold Pinter doing with the fat American film director with the ulcer? Was he writing another film? And if so, was it cast yet? And who would be first past the post in the race for the distribution rights? It was never too early to start thinking about these things, everyone knew that, which was why they spent so much of their working week at lunch. Otherwise how would they ever find out what was going on?

'Jay,' said Lou Lou firmly, looking mournfully at Jay's fascinated face, 'drink up and stop staring in that calf-like manner. It doesn't do a man any good at all, being seen staring. Pretend Minna and I are the last of the Bluebell girls and that everyone else does something clever in investment banking. That should do the trick.'

'What trick?' said Jay, turning back to Lou Lou obediently, waiting for the meaning of life.

'The trick of seeming not to care,' said Lou Lou, taking a good slug at her Chablis and fixing him with a gaze that had been described as hypnotic by the kind of people who should know. 'It's like riding a bicycle. Once the stabilizers come off, you never forget how.'

'Oh, Lou Lou,' said Jay, blinking at her gravely. He was feeling the provincial in him strongly today, and

143

whatever Minna said about the provinces making a comeback ('Look at Dennis Potter, he lives somewhere extraordinary like the West Country') he didn't like it. 'I don't expect I'd be a very quick study.'

'Practice,' said Lou Lou, sagely, wagging a finger at him. 'That's all anything takes, these days. Eat your steak.'

'Perhaps I am hungry after all,' said Jay. He wondered if nannies were like this.

'I don't know about anyone else,' said Minna, looking at her snails with love. 'But I'm starving.'

'The greed of the innocent,' said Lou Lou approvingly. 'So rare, in this neck of the woods.'

'The bust is making a comeback,' said Minna happily. 'Everyone says so.'

'When did it ever go away?' said Lou Lou, looking down at her own cleavage, which was the sort bad girls were given at birth, just to make sure they got into enough trouble.

'When indeed?' said Jay, laughing into his plate. He felt sure they didn't make girls like them any more. Girls like this were strictly limited editions, only available to the favoured few, and hard to find. Harder to keep he imagined, wondering what kind of men did keep this kind of girl. He knew so little. The more he saw the less he knew. He supposed life was like that.

'So,' said Lou Lou, 'you should have seen Tinkerbell here last night, running a crap game with the ten most eligible men in London. Which one of them did you allow to take you home?'

'I think he was called Xan,' said Minna, insouciance herself. 'But I didn't really bother to find out.'

144

'I can imagine not,' said Lou Lou, with one of those utterly suggestive looks that she had made so much her own.

'Lou Lou,' said Minna, in reproof. 'I sent him home at the door. We can't think of sex all the time.'

'I can,' said Lou Lou simply. 'Anyway, I hope that landlord of yours noticed.'

'He was far too busy closeted with Alabama Skye, disapproving of people, mostly me,' said Minna crossly.

'Alabama who?' said Jay, choking into his drink.

'Quick,' said Lou Lou, slapping him on the back. 'The poet is having a seizure. Did you bring your smelling salts? Really, Shakespeare, someone is going to have to take you in hand.'

'Well,' said Jay, smiling sheepishly at them and wiping his streaming eyes with a napkin. 'It's a good thing I've got you two, isn't it?'

'Very good,' said Minna.

By three o'clock, people were starting to leave, strolling back to their offices to pick up their scripts and their galley proofs and their messages before going home to get ready for the dinners they all had to go to, so the circus could start spinning all over again.

'That was nice,' said Minna, finishing her brandy with a fine bravado flourish and smiling genially on her companions.

'I must go and do some work,' said Jay, trying to sound businesslike. He knew it was only once a week, but he still couldn't quite get over his lingering puritanical guilt about drinking at lunchtime. For him, still so new to the city, it was a revelation, the last word in decadence.

'You must,' said Lou Lou, who had no such qualms. 'All work and no play makes Jay a clever boy. And don't forget the dedication.'

'I have to write something first,' said Jay ruefully, 'before I can dedicate it to anyone.'

'So get out your typewriter, Shakespeare, and don't get led astray by girls like us.'

Minna smiled. She liked being girls like us.

'Lord love a duck,' said Lou Lou, grabbing a waiter's arm and looking at his watch. 'And there's me with an appointment, late. I must fly.'

And that was the last Jay and Minna were to see of her for quite two weeks.

'Don't ask,' said Minna, seeing Jay's face. 'Just don't.'

9

Minna woke with the sun on her face and a vague but insistent feeling that, wherever she was, she had felt better. A pain in her head fought grimly with a rumbling discomfort in her stomach, the whole overlaid with a Gothic disorientation that was no help to either. Closing her eyes, she tried to start the day again. She presumed it was the day, for otherwise how could it be so heartlessly sunny?

Raising herself slowly on to one elbow, she gazed vaguely at the wall opposite, getting her bearings. There was a cabin trunk she was perfectly sure she recognized, and a trail across the polished floor that was testament to her going to bed the night before. Shoes first, at a crazy angle, obviously tipped off; one stocking, a snake of limpid discarded black, followed closely by the other, half unrolled; and finally a dress, a dark slip of crumpled material, hardly recognizable, dropped as it fell. There the trail stopped, and Minna's eyes came to rest, contemplating one tiny foot, protruding obscurely from a pile of rumpled bedclothes.

'There,' she said to herself, 'is my foot.' She shook it tentatively, watching the perfect toes move on her whim. 'Ergo the rest of me must follow.'

Having found herself, she felt comforted and more at home. Movement was next, and she rose carefully from the bed, dropping sheets behind her, arms spread for balance. It was a true test of stamina, but she gritted her teeth and passed with colours, if not flying, at least intact.

'There,' she said again, with a hint of firmness, 'I'm up.'

Up was a great improvement. She put on her dressing gown, remembered she was at Eddy's, and found her way to the bathroom. Pieces of last night started to filter back to her. She had gone out on the town with Jay, that was it. She vaguely remembered a very dark bar, and a group of rather disreputable but very charming men, and then someone's flat, and doing the foxtrot, and rather a lot of rough Spanish brandy, which was all anyone seemed to have to drink. Oh, dear.

'I've been to a marvellous party,' she sang tonelessly. *'Elise made an entrance with May.'*

Her reflection stared balefully at her, not looking in the least like any recognizable character from *Private Lives*. The Master was absolutely right about people's behaviour away from Belgravia. It was quite shocking.

'You'd never have guessed from her fisherman's vest, that her bust had been whittled away.'

She would clean her teeth first, that's what she would do. And then she would remove the worst of the eye black.

'Poor Lulu got fried on Chianti and talked about esprit de corps.'

And then she would take several Alka-Seltzers which everyone swore worked like a charm if one couldn't stand the taste of Fernet Branca. And then she would take a deep breath and wash her face.

'Dear Baba arrived with a turtle.' And then she would put on some lipstick, which was always good

148

for a girl's self-esteem. '*Which shattered us all to the core.*'

And then she would be ready to face the day, such as it was. Whichever day it was.

'*I couldn't have liked it more.*'

Eddy was in the kitchen, eating eggs and doing the crossword.

'Good morning,' said Minna firmly, hoping it was the morning. 'Isn't it the most perfect day? I never saw such a day, did you?' She felt rather like Grace Kelly after the party in *High Society*, except that Eddy didn't even look a little like Bing Crosby, and there were no healing waters on hand to help her in her predicament.

'Perfect,' said Eddy, looking up from his eggs. He took in the black sunglasses, and the Coward-esque dressing gown drooping hopelessly from one shoulder, and didn't ask her how she was feeling, which he felt was more than she deserved. He had seen the trail of discarded clothing strewn across the floor, and had drawn what conclusions any man would, or at least any man knowing Minna as he did. Besides, he wasn't feeling altogether like a breath of springtime himself this morning, what with one thing and another. He had gone out with the band, and they had picked up some girls who sang backing vocals and found themselves drinking shots of tequila until late in a bar someone knew where they did that sort of thing. Lick the salt, drink the shot, suck the lime. In unison, the way they did it in Mexico, not that any of them had ever been. But then everyone knew that, since tequila had become so fashionable. All Eddy knew was that it made him morose, and that was why he had put off going home for so long. That was the most sense he could make of it, and he didn't care to make any more, not this morning with the sun shining far too bright into his half-open eyes.

Pleased that she had got it right, and it was morning after all, Minna sat down and started to eat some cold Chinese takeaway straight from the carton.

'Coffee?' said Eddy, watching her curiously. He never would get used to her eating habits.

'Yes, please,' said Minna, smiling her most winning smile.

'It's only instant today,' said Eddy, busy with the kettle. 'Do you mind?'

'Not at all,' said Minna. 'I'm such a heathen I rather prefer it. Grounds, you know. Like fish bones, not really worth the bother.'

'Here,' said Eddy, adding before he quite meant to, 'so, did you have a nice time last night?'

'Very nice, thank you, Nanny. And I got home way past my bedtime, and there is no hope for me, none at all.' Minna beamed at him without a trace of contrition. 'Did you?'

'Fine,' said Eddy, grinning reluctantly. 'The band, you know.'

'I know.' Minna didn't know at all. She had never met the band, and she certainly didn't know any girls who sang backing vocals and drank tequila down in one. But she smiled wisely at him, and nodded sagely, and imagined them all in some smoky bar, composing through the chatter, rather like the Jockey must have been in Paris before the war. She didn't imagine dank pubs and beer slops, or stale carpets littered with cigarette butts, or thick foul-tasting tequila with the worm lurking in the bottom.

'So,' she said absently, intent on her chow mein. 'What might you do today?'

'I thought I might write a song.' He had been going to do that yesterday, but somehow he had never got round to it. Such was the way the muse went. That was how he explained it to himself, anyway.

'How wonderful.' Minna looked up in admiration, opening her eyes as wide as they would go behind her dark glasses. 'How lucky you are to be you.'

'That's what the man says.'

'Don't go getting so cynical so early in the morning. And on such a morning. I wish I could write a song.'

'You're better off with the Revolution.'

'History can pall in the heat,' said Minna, at her most insouciant. 'I love the Revolution, you know I do, but a song might be nice all the same.'

'Might be.' Eddy nearly asked her if she had any plans for today apart from the Revolution, but he stopped himself. He had to keep reminding himself that she wasn't fifteen any more, as if he could forget with the new hair and the new dresses and the five strings of pearls. She was well over the age of consent and none of his business any more. It wasn't for him to remark that it seemed rather odd that she was out every night when she insisted that every living soul she knew had gone to Easter Island or Christmas Island, or whatever the place was called. Eddy had travelled some in his youth, but never in the South Seas, and he didn't know Bikini Atoll from a hole in the ground.

He wondered what they might talk about next. There he was with all those unspoken questions

151

on his lips, and there was she with all the un-spoken answers on hers, and it wasn't getting them anywhere, and Irene would be arriving any moment, and then what? It was really too early for all this. Not quite eleven, and the sun still nowhere near the yard-arm, and far too bright for both of them.

'So,' they both said in unison, and looked at each other, and laughed, and suddenly it didn't seem to matter any more.

'I'm sorry,' said Minna. 'Is it a bore me being here? I never really asked, did I? And what with Irene and all the songs you have to write, and all . . . '

'It's not a bore,' said Eddy. It wasn't. Anything but a bore. 'It's nice to have you. We couldn't have you walking the streets.'

'Except I look so pretty, walking the streets,' said Minna, who sometimes rather fancied herself as a lady of pleasure. She laughed at him unrepentently and lit a cigarette.

'Pretty, but quite unsuitable.'

'In one so young?'

'In one so young. What would people think?'

'Well,' said Minna judiciously. 'It's a dirty job.'

'I know, I know,' said Eddy in resignation. 'But someone's got to do it.'

'Do what?' said Irene, barging into the kitchen in a flak jacket and studded boots. Minna wondered quite where she had stumbled on her fashion sense. 'This flat is a pigsty. I'm not clearing up after two, you know.'

Minna took one look at her furious face and heartlessly fled, muttering vaguely about luncheon appointments, leaving Eddy to deal with the fall out. Some things were just too much for a girl at this time of the morning.

It was too late for Jay at the café, and Lou Lou seemed to have assumed a life of her own lately, and was strangely unavailable, so Minna took a single cup of espresso and pretended to read the paper until it was time for lunch. Deciding that she felt like oysters, she headed off towards St James's, winding her way out of Soho, down Bond Street where the shop windows glittered with tempting prizes of jewels, water-colours, silver and cabin trunks. The pavements were filled with smart women in their summer linen, heading for Gucci and Chanel and Hermès and Tiffany's, mingling with the art dealers coming out of their galleries in curiously old-fashioned pin-stripe suits and fob watches, off to meet each other for lunch and discuss the precarious state of the market.

Outside the discreetly grand portals of Sotheby's, Minna stopped at the news-stand to buy nice thick copies of *Vogue* in English, French and Italian. She crossed Piccadilly, jammed with lunchtime traffic, limousines bumper to bumper and tour buses disgorging loads of tourists intent on culture into the Royal Academy, and headed off down Duke Street, where she bumped into two of the beautiful men from Oliver's party.

'Darling,' they said, kissing her gracefully. 'What heaven to see you.'

'Italian *Vogue*,' they said, their eyes alighting on her reading material. 'The cleverness of you. The new collections are to die for, Armani has surpassed himself this time, we had such fun with him in Venice in the spring, Harry's every night, angel, one's HEAD. Purgatory, that's all, do you wonder why we do it to ourselves? Anyway, we must dash, lunch with Granny at Claridges, could you die? We simply had to go to Floris first, if we forget to take her a gallon of rose geranium she's bound to die and leave all her money to our terrible cousin Geordie, not at all the thing, he lives north of the Park, can you beat it? Let's have lunch, we'll make a tiny *coup de téléphone*, must fly, utter heaven to see you . . .'

Minna waved them prettily goodbye, wondering vaguely what it was about the beau monde that always seemed to leave her slightly breathless, and went into Green's, where she settled herself at the bar, made her best eyes at the barman, and ordered a dozen oysters and a glass of champagne, just for the hell of it. Minna sometimes liked acting as the rich are supposed to, so as not to disappoint her public.

Across the room, a screen idol who lived nearby, ageing gracefully in W1, took an equally solitary lunch, and in a discreet corner a young marchioness ate fishcakes with her lover, who was rumoured to run guns to the Middle East. Minna didn't pay them much attention, rather more interested in St Laurent's latest confections for the evening. She might not care for wearing couture, but she loved looking at it, and it did make a nice change from the Revolution in this heat.

After lunch, she wandered out into the sunshine, dreaming her way through the shoppers and the tourists and the businessmen on their way back from expansive expense account lunches with their mistresses, insensible to the admiring glances cast her way. Outside the Ritz, she took a bus, perching on the top deck, watching the London roofs slide by in the sunshine, riding high above the park, glossy green below her, until she reached the Portobello Road, where she caught a double bill at the Electric, happy to sit in the cool darkness with her popcorn and her feet up on the seat in front, watching Gérard Depardieu being blond and French. She wondered what he would be like to kiss. She wondered what it was about the French. (She had always had a bit of a thing about the French, ever since Napoleon, whom she worshipped, despite the piles.)

As the film ended, she suffered a sudden pang of homesickness, deciding that she had been away from Soho for too long. Passing the six o'clock shift of actors waiting for their bus to take them up to the West End, she hailed a cab back to her local bar, where she settled herself at a corner table with her three copies of *Vogue* and ordered herself a glass of champagne, which seemed to be what she was drinking today, and pondered her night-time plans, which so far were uncertain. She thought of those people who planned their lives, who bought themselves Filofaxes bound in crocodile and wrote down their social obligations for months ahead in crowded black script, not leaving a moment's space for doubt. Minna had never had a diary, and was not sure what she would do with one. Her life had an unfashionable air of immediacy about it which she liked, every day a surprise.

The place was filling up, the tide of players washing in, ready to be seen, painted and primped and full of promise. Every seat was full, lounged and slung and posed upon, the crowd spilling over the edges, lurking round the bar, looking over each other's shoulders, gossiping and pouting and smoking and discussing where they would make fashionable that night. Minna found herself surrounded, with a stranger at her table. Her interest quickened, as it always did when confronted by something new, her gold-digger's instinct for the strike aroused, but not by a flicker of her eyes did she betray it. She summoned the waiter, no mean feat at this time of the evening, with every hipster in Soho vying for his attention, and ordered her wine with a bland lack of curiosity for the man sitting opposite her. He was a man too, not a boy like Jay, and he had no copy of Hemingway, just an untouched edition of the evening paper and a martini, and he was staring at her in lazy examination, quite without shame.

Minna looked carefully into the middle distance, wondering if she should be offended by such scrutiny, considering whether she might grow haughty, put up her chin and send him about his business. The canons of proper behaviour, which well-brought-up girls received from their model mamas, were all a mystery to Minna, whose education in etiquette had lasted only until she left the nursery. Thanks to her nanny, she knew how to eat soup without making unseemly noises, that Don't Care was made to care, that toast crusts would make her hair curl, and that she would have to eat up all her greens before she got any pudding. After that, with her mother off in a whirl of lunches and teas and balls crammed with crowned heads, she had had to make it up as she went along. People who should know, the despairing aunts and uncles, shook their heads over her, saying that she would end up in all manner of trouble, and tutted indignantly over stories of her walking stockingless through public thoroughfares and dancing barefoot till dawn. Girls like that came to bad ends, married bad lots, and ended up as recluses in nameless hill countries, everyone knew that. Minna sometimes thought that she wouldn't mind a bad lot.

So it was after a brief internal debate that she decided to play this stranger at his own game, sitting up quite straight and staring impertinently back. She didn't stop to wonder if her decision had anything to do with his adventurer's face, full of uneven planes and startling shadows. He was the kind of man that eighteenth-century mothers would have regarded as a thorough-going rogue, the kind of man who would have inevitably been packed off to India after disgracing the family name. He had disarmingly light green eyes and black hair that fell over his forehead and a crumpled suit made of some dark stuff and long fingers that tapped with light impatience on the table top. Minna studiously avoided asking herself whether any of this influenced her bold behaviour. After all, she liked to fancy herself working in mysterious ways, not believing in questioning anyone's motives, least of all her own. She liked to fancy herself in pursuit of the unexpected in those days, heedless of the consequences, for tomorrow was another day when we might grow old, or die, or lose faith, settle for second best, too tired to look for any more. So she stared back at this man, liking the way his eyebrows grew so thick and straight, wondering where he came by the scar that lent an old-fashioned raffishness to his left cheekbone. He didn't seem remotely disconcerted by her returning his gaze, but continued to look, letting his Martini grow warm beside him.

Finally, as the noise about them from the swelling number of evening drinkers grew to a pitch that made their own silence ostentatious, Minna drew out a cigarette. The old black and white films that served as her almanac of Fitting Female Behaviour had taught her that cigarettes were always produced at moments of tension, dramatic punctuation marks for the main action. Just now, the convention worked as well as it had when Bette Davis was a girl. The stranger produced a heavily worn gold lighter and lit her cigarette, and she in turn offered him her packet, and he took a cigarette for himself, and lit it, settled back in his chair and let out the smoke with a sort of satisfied sigh, and said in a low voice, 'Thank you. I'd run out.'

It was a start at least, and Minna was not quite so young as to blunder into the breach. She blew out a little smoke of her own, and watched it in an interested sort of way, waiting for him to continue, as she knew he would.

'Do you always drink alone?' he said, some hidden note of amusement in his voice saving the question from offensiveness, as if he were implying that he would like to be much more personal, but would observe the proprieties and play the game for a while longer.

'Do YOU?' said Minna boldly, letting him see that he wasn't going to have it all his way, not yet anyway.

He didn't take his cue to get on the defensive, smiling at her instead, a crooked smile full of the kind of dangerous promise that nice girls were warned about from the cradle. Minna, starting to enjoy herself, thought that it was her luck that she wasn't a nice girl. Absence of parental advice had left her still guessing quite what kind of girl she was, although her father, in an uncharacteristic rush of paternal intimacy, had once advised her never to marry an Irishman.

'Sometimes. Tonight anyway,' he said, raising his Martini at her and cutting to the chase. He was still smiling that reckless smile. 'Why don't you have dinner with me?'

Minna bridled instinctively, eyes flashing with a touch-me-not menace quite at odds with her tiny pink dress.

'Do I,' she said, haughty as a duchess dismissing a servant caught at the gin, 'look like the kind of girl who allows herself to be taken to dinner by men without even knowing their names?'

'Yes,' he said disarmingly. 'I'll tell you my name if it makes you feel better. It's Casey. There now.'

'Casey WHAT?' said Minna, as unbending as a society hostess faced with a gatecrasher.

'Seamus Brendan Parnell Casey,' the man said, giving an ironic grandeur to the fullness of his name. 'But people call me Casey.'

'So you're Irish?' said Minna.

'A little lapsed, but yes.'

'Oh, well then,' said Minna, as if that made all the difference. 'In that case I'd love to have dinner. Shall we go?' Which just goes to show the effect a little well-timed parental wisdom can have.

'Now?' Casey looked momentarily taken aback. 'Don't you want to change, or anything?'

'Should I?' Minna looked down at her dress, at the pretty pink suede stilettos that went with it, at the single strand of pearls she had slung on that morning, just for the hell of it, suffering a tiny unfamiliar pang of doubt. She had never had to consider her sartorial decisions before, not having anything to dress up for, happy in her slips of dresses

159

that always seemed quite able to take her anywhere she wanted to go. Perhaps she didn't look quite suitable. But suitable for what? Perhaps he was the kind of man who only dined at the Ritz. He didn't look to be the type, but a girl could never tell, these days. Perhaps he only knew the kind of girls who changed three times a day and spent their lives in Versace, the kind of girls who wore Chanel at breakfast.

She looked up at him, questioning.

'Don't I look suitable?'

'You look perfect,' he said quickly, seeing that he had blundered. Casey had roamed all over the world, from Rome to Paris to New York and finally back to London, and he had been kept waiting by more women than he cared to remember, impatiently pacing about hotel rooms while a constant flow of chatter from the bathroom issued promises that the lady in question was 'so nearly ready darling, just one more tiny minute'. And the tiny minute stretched inevitably into a tiny half hour as lipstick was changed and hair was teased, stockings straightened, shoes chosen, cast aside and then restored to favour. This decisiveness, this instant 'Shall we go?' was quite new to him, and had surprised him into rudeness, he who had been described as the most charming man in Europe by the kind of women who should know.

Minna, who didn't know, and wouldn't have been much impressed if she had, smiled again, reassured. She took out a tiny compact and reapplied her lipstick, dabbed some scent behind her ears, pouted at herself in the quarter inch of glass, and was ready.

'Let's not go far,' she said, having a yen for dirty old Soho that night, with all its intimations of sleaze and drunks and dubious sexual practices. Besides, this man, this rogue Irish, looked right here and that was the kind of thing that gave Minna satisfaction.

'Let's just not,' he agreed, feeling much the same. He had been in the country that day, and all the rolling fields and grazing cows and waving sheaves of corn had made him uncomfortable. Too much pastoral serenity can rot a boy's soul, turn him soft and indulgent, and he was happy to be back in the squalor of the city, in the bosom of the shameless old whore of a quarter that Soho was. And picking up girls too, at his age. He felt footloose and fancy free and quite irresponsible. He felt like behaving badly and staying out all night and drinking more than was good for him and not giving a damn.

'What?' said Minna, watching him laugh to himself.

'Nothing,' he said, shaking his head at his own folly.

'Well, that's all right then,' said Minna, with an air of finality. She didn't want him getting ideas, not yet anyway, not before the first course at least. She had some idea of what was proper, or that was what she told herself.

They went to a small French restaurant, dark and plush and curiously old-fashioned, teetering on a fine line that managed to be sexy and shabby-genteel at the same time.

'Well,' said Minna. 'All dark corners and *flambé*, what a turn-up for the books. I hadn't taken you for that kind of boy.'

'My heart beats where the steak is Diane,' said Casey, lighting her cigarette without ostentation.

Minna liked that. These days, most men lit a girl's cigarette as if they were Sir Walter Raleigh, throwing his cloak over the puddle all over again.

'And no prices on the menu,' she said, blowing smoke in his eyes, just to confuse him. 'Don't they think that I'm a fearless career woman with her own American Express card?'

'Do you want to look at this one?' said Casey, laughing a little, calling her bluff.

'But not at all,' said Minna in reproach. 'I never argue with managerial policy. Besides, it does a girl good to be kept guessing from time to time. Why don't we go all the way and let you choose for me?'

'Daring,' said Casey appreciatively. So far, she wasn't missing a loop. 'I hope you like suet pudding.'

'Clever of you to guess,' said Minna. 'What else makes life worth living?'

And so they ate, and exchanged the sort of banter that seemed to be passing for conversation that evening, and Minna found herself impressed at the way he ordered a wine with an obscure name and didn't make a great fuss about tasting it, but simply said, 'I think you might like this.' Minna, who didn't know a great deal about wine but knew what she liked, thought it delicious, but didn't say so, because she felt that if he was so utterly *au fait* with such matters he wouldn't need telling, or he might think she wasn't used to such behaviour. He had plenty of polish, she thought to herself, wondering where he had learnt it. She knew, had known at once, that she was dealing with quite a different quantity from Jay, that this man had been round the block more than once, that this was not just meeting people, but a player to be reckoned with. So she watched herself, not wanting to give too much away, not realizing that she had given herself away the moment she had said, 'Shall we go?'

Looking slyly at his raffish face through her eyelashes, she wondered at her daring. She might like to fancy herself with a reputation to protect, but she thought she might have overstepped the mark this time. It was all very well being the kind of girl who cared nothing for convention, who did nothing in a work-a-day world, who was only one step away from a bag lady, who allowed young playwrights to buy her coffee in strange cafés, but it was quite another matter to let herself be invited to dinner at a moment's acquaintance by a man who was quite probably a practised seducer. He had that kind of indented mouth and roving eye that suggested he had known many women, that kind of air that was only a thin line away from being utterly suggestive. He had a lazy way of giving his absolute attention as she talked, never overdoing it, nor pushing or intimidating, just listening, letting his eyes trawl carelessly over her in appreciation, intimating in some way that she was the only person in the world he cared to talk to. Men didn't learn that overnight, even Minna knew that, and they certainly didn't learn it so that they could go home alone.

And as they parried platitudes, as if to say, 'this is not all we are capable of, but we shall observe the proprieties for form's sake, and so as not to upset the waiters,' she thought that perhaps she had not been so wise after all, and rather wished she had Eddy with her, to send her home in disgrace.

It was at this point that she threw caution to the winds, and decided to come clean. If he didn't like it, he could always leave. Emboldened by the sheer controversy of her decision, Minna waved away the pudding menu the waiter was trying to sell her, asked firmly for a large brandy, stretched her neck a little, as if to remind herself how long and slender it really was, faced him full on, and said, 'So, I expect you must think that I'm shamingly easy? Well,' she added, without letting him have time to speak, 'I have to tell you that I have been known to be quite alarmingly difficult, so you can leave now if you want to.'

Casey, who hadn't thought any such thing, tried to think of a suitable rejoinder to this unprecedented remark, failed to discover one in his extensive repertoire, mouthed a little, and started to laugh. He would not begin to describe Minna as easy, and he had known, and had, a few easy women in his life, so he should know. He tended to avoid them, these days, having learnt that those women who are easiest to have are hardest to get rid of. One moment they insist that they don't believe in steady relationships, and the next they are discussing china patterns.

'What?' said Minna, watching him laugh at her. She wondered if she could have inadvertently made a joke. 'Really,' she added, in tones of admonition. This was not what she had expected at all.

'Not easy,' said Casey, still slightly at a loss. 'Really, not at all.' He smiled engagingly at her, to prove his point.

'Oh, well,' said Minna, who had begun to be rather taken with the vision of herself as a woman of loose virtue and slack morals. 'I suppose I shall have to try harder. How did you guess? Was it the pearls? Not slutty enough? Or the way I took my fish off the bone?'

'You're confusing me,' said Casey, falling back on an old Fred Astaire film he had seen once. 'And I resent that in any woman.'

'That's my line,' said Minna, thinking that she probably had confused him. She had certainly confused herself, but perhaps that was just the brandy. 'What a perfect cad you are.'

'That's what my mother told me.'

'Don't be silly. Boys like you don't have mothers.' There she was, calling him a boy, just as if she were reassuring herself that he would be incapable of impropriety. She had a sneaking feeling that he was the kind of man who kept a suite somewhere, on the off chance. But this was irrational. No-one kept suites any more, not even the peerage.

'Have some pudding,' said Casey, hoping to change the subject. He wondered quite why he had mentioned his mother. He never did that. It was bad for his image.

'Too late,' said Minna, as her second brandy arrived. The first seemed to have gone so quickly, but she supposed that was life. Here today and gone tomorrow. 'So,' she went on, thinking perhaps that he was right, and a change of subject was called for, now that she had established herself, 'aren't you going to ask me anything? I never met a man who was so uncurious.'

'It's a policy objective,' said Casey, nodding at the waiter to bring the bottle. He could do with some brandy himself. 'Never ask questions.'

'Never complain, never explain,' said Minna absently. 'Was it Margot Asquith, or Emerald

165

Cunard? Don't you wish you were called Emerald?'

'Reverently.'

'Naughty,' said Minna, shaking her finger at him. 'When I was being general, and you go all literal on me. Unfair.'

'You're blinding me with science,' said Casey, pouring himself some brandy and drinking it with the kind of concentration usually found in golfers at the nineteenth tee.

'Take me out, coach,' said Minna, laughing at him. 'And you running rings around me, all charm and practice and so many conquests behind you. It's just not sex.'

So there they were, back to sex again, as if it had ever gone away, and Casey shook his head in bewilderment, and watched Minna laugh at him, and then the door of the restaurant opened and a crowd arrived and Minna looked up and said, 'Oliver!' and suddenly she was surrounded, being kissed and exclaimed over, and Oliver turned to see who she was with and said, 'Minna, what a dark horse you are,' in heartfelt admiration, and the waiters gathered around and produced more chairs and menus and bottles of champagne and all the paraphernalia of a late supper, and the crowd resolved itself into Lou Lou and Jay and an older man Minna felt sure she recognized, and Oliver, resplendent as master of ceremonies, his eyelashes newly dyed for the occasion, and it was a party.

'Really,' said Oliver with half-hearted resentment. 'I hear of this lodger but two weeks ago, and before I can do a thing to find out who she is, I discover she knows everyone in London. It's too naughty of you to have neglected me,' he told Minna in his stern voice, taking it for granted that she had known Casey for ever. 'What with Casey being the wickedest man in London, and me a saint, but a perfect saint, and you don't have dinner with me, however many Ave Marias I say before brunch. It's too unkind.'

Having said his piece, Oliver subsided into geniality and introduced everybody. The older man turned out to be called Roger Middlemarch, and was something of a big shot as producers went, which was a long way.

'Don't take the blindest bit of notice of Roger,' said Oliver sincerely. 'He will slum with us, however hard I tell him not to. He's all the rage at Cannes, but does it mean anything to him? I ask you.'

'Where have you been?' said Minna to Lou Lou. 'It's been an age since we've seen you. Jay thought you had been abducted by white slavers and shipped to Morocco in a laundry basket.'

'Oh,' said Lou Lou, looking vague. 'Nothing so exciting. How I long for a white slaver to come and brighten up my life.'

'Me too,' said Oliver.

'The woman of mystery,' said Jay in admiration. 'We miss you terribly.'

'Isn't he heaven?' said Oliver, looking at Jay. He was at something of a loose end at the moment, his last love, a South American bongo player, having run off with a Polish violinist, to live in sin in Gdansk.

'Now, now,' said Lou Lou, allowing Roger to light her purple Sobranie, 'don't go getting ideas about Shakespeare here. He lives for Art.'

'Who's Art?' said Oliver, with interest.

'So, Oliver,' said Casey in his lazy way, not seeming remotely put out that his intimate dinner had been so rudely interrupted, 'what's been happening? You know how I rely on you to keep me up to date.'

'Oh,' said Oliver, clasping his bosom in ecstasy. 'And there I was quite forgetting how long you'd been away. Charming of you to call Minna the moment you return and not even a tiny bell for *moi*, but I shan't hold it against you. Where to begin?' But here Oliver was being rhetorical, because he always knew where to begin. True to form he plunged into a positive orgy of make-ups, break-ups and general misdemeanours. 'Maria Vittadini's purple party, my dear, Effie Hampton dyed her Great Dane mauve for the occasion and now she can't remember what colour it was before, to have it dyed back . . . She's divorcing him on grounds of mental cruelty, she says that he won't let her fly first class any more, I can hardly blame him, I'd send her cargo or not at all . . . So he went crawling back, on his knees, ready to beg forgiveness, and he found her having a "massage" from three very large negro gentlemen, I could think of other words for it . . . '

Minna quietly drank her brandy through the barrage, listening with half an ear to the comprehensive social history of the last few weeks while she doodled on her napkin and slyly watched Casey through her cowlick.

'So,' said Oliver breathlessly, when he had finished. 'There you are. Could you DIE? Where shall we go now? These waiters live for me, but LIVE for me, can you blame them, but even they get a little sniffy if one stays too late.'

The waiters were clearing up about them with a resigned sort of ostentation, putting chairs on tables

168

with a desultory heavy-handedness in a vain hope that people might take the hint.

'Don't worry, darlings,' said Oliver, favouring them with a bracing smile. 'Just take away this man's credit card and we'll be laughing all the way to the bank.'

Casey handed over his card.

'Well, thank you, darling,' said Oliver, as if quite surprised. 'I won't say no. Now come along everybody and let these poor boys go to bed.'

10

Afterwards, Minna decided that it was entirely Oliver's fault. After all, if he hadn't arrived in such a rush of people, it wouldn't have thrown her and Casey into the false intimacy that had proved fatal. It was us and them all of a sudden, children caught sneaking off school by an indulgent grown-up.

'You two,' Oliver would keep saying, quite unnecessarily, Minna felt. 'Oh, you two.'

And did he have to assume quite such an expression of complicity, that discreetly vulgar prima donna smirk? It really wasn't the kind of thing a girl needed when she was trying to have a perfectly respectable dinner with a man she had never met before. And Lou Lou didn't help either, sitting there with that kind of look that simply oozed sex, the kind of look that Elizabeth Taylor would have hocked her diamonds to achieve. That this was merely Lou Lou's usual expression didn't excuse her at all. There was a time and a place for everything, after all.

And had Oliver really had to insist that they went drinking to a certain late-night bar he knew where the lighting was low and the pianist sang gravel-voiced songs about lost love, those old songs that slink through the smoke and lead the mind astray.

'Come along, you two,' he said. (AGAIN? thought

170

Minna. Had they mysteriously become fused at the hip?) 'I know you don't have homes to go to.' And just what was that supposed to mean?

It was a banquette kind of bar, with booths, and Oliver elected to sit on the outside, so that Casey had to move up next to Minna, his leg against hers in a most unsuitable manner, his arm brushing against hers every time he reached for his drink, his roving profile too close to hers, shadowed in the gloom. Lou Lou sat opposite them, watching the room with those suggestive eyes and laughing quietly to herself from time to time at some private joke which could have had something to do with the follies of the world in general and the decline of the yen in particular, but then again, might not.

If things had been different, Minna told herself firmly, she would just have thanked him for dinner and smiled a suitably distant smile and gone home to Eddy's and slept on her pallet and no-one would have known any better. But somehow the bar became her undoing, and when the others left – 'Us poor mortals, wending our weary way. What it is to be young,' had been Oliver's parting remark, and quite uncalled for – Casey had turned his knowing smile on Minna and said, 'I'm going to have another brandy, will you have one?' she had given up and let the evening take her.

'Of course,' she said, waving her hand in that airy way she sometimes affected. 'I might as well be hung for a sheep as a wolf.'

'So I'm a wolf now, am I?' Casey seemed rather taken by the idea.

'Or a sheep,' said Minna cleverly, sneaking it in

under the wire. 'Funny of you not to take that option.'

'I have some kind of reputation to protect.'

'Bet you say that to all the girls,' said Minna, growing lippy with the lateness of the hour and the shameless intimations of sex that hung heavy in the air. 'Reputation, what does that mean anyway? Oliver says that you are the wickedest man in London.'

'Oliver is given to overstatement,' said Casey, calm as you please.

'No shit, Sherlock.'

Minna drank her brandy, wondering at herself. This wasn't like her at all. She was behaving like some broad in a 1940s B-movie. Any moment she would lean forward and pout over the rim of her glass and ask him if it were true what they said about Irish boys. What did they say about Irish boys? She must look it up when she got home.

Casey was laughing at her now, and the pianist was playing that ridiculous song about then I go and spoil it all by saying something stupid like I love you, which Minna considered should at least carry a government health warning after ten o'clock, and the night wasn't so young any more and everything was getting quite out of control.

'Don't laugh at me, you brute,' said Minna, flipping her cowlick at him in a last ditch attempt to save the day and her virtue. 'I didn't ask to be picked up and taken to a dive like this. I didn't ask to be fed brandy until all hours. Nobody warned me.'

'I blame myself utterly,' said Casey, who somehow seemed to be holding her hand across the table. 'I do.'

'You should,' said Minna affably, pleased that he

172

agreed with her. Perhaps there was some hope for him after all. 'You really should. Leading girls astray at your age.'

'And you way past your bedtime,' said Casey, more serious still.

'Way, way past,' agreed Minna happily.

'So had I better take you home?' asked Casey, solemn as a priest reading the banns.

'Yes, please,' said Minna.

Casey lived in a little artist's cottage down in the tree-lined whiteness of Chelsea, a forgotten reminder of the days when it had been a bohemian quarter populated by painters and poets and wild-eyed girls who spent their days lying naked on overstuffed sofas for anyone who would pay them.

Inside, a tiny hallway cluttered with architectural prints led up to a great studio room crowded with plinths and columns and busts, the kind of thing that might have been rescued from the folly of a bankrupt noble. Minna picked her way past a headless nude and an orange tree and went over to examine the bookshelves which ran along one wall. Bookshelves, she always felt, were even more revealing than address books and a nice point to start conversation besides. She felt light-headed and rather irresponsible, and curious as to quite what she was doing here.

'What would you like?' said Casey, taking his jacket off and draping it irreverently over a bust of Voltaire. 'Brandy, champagne?'

Minna longed for champagne, but she felt on consideration that it would be altogether too much of a cliché in such a set up. Champagne, after all, had oiled the wheels of seduction since boy met girl and suggested dinner, and Minna wasn't so sure that she wanted to be seduced yet.

'Have you any green chartreuse?' she asked, conversationally.

'Of course,' said Casey. He liked a girl who knew what she liked.

'So,' said Minna, as he gave her her drink. She shook the glass a little, reassured by the clink of the ice. 'Are you a closet intellectual?' She walked along the bookshelves, reciting as she went. 'Trollope, Macaulay, Pepys, Rousseau, Tolstoy, Eliot, Faulkner, Fitzgerald. Fitzgerald? That's a little too much like light relief. What do you do – read him on Sunday afternoons when you're feeling like a rest?'

'Have to have something to impress the ladies,' said Casey, sketching an attempt at a southern drawl. He had never quite recovered from his Oxford education. He had been brought up in a house that contained one book, and that was *Ruff's Guide to the Turf*, and he had been collecting knowledge ever since, like some kind of insurance against his heredity. A long line of gamblers and drunks stretched behind him, back into the murky reaches of a family tree littered with duelling fatalities and bankrupt suicides, but he wasn't telling Minna that. It was the kind of thing she would have found quite ravishingly romantic, if only he had known. So instead he shook his head and tried to look bland.

'So you are a wolf after all,' said Minna. A wolf who read Voltaire. How confusing this boy was. 'And does it work?'

'Sure,' said Casey, admitting the joke was on him. 'Byron by candlelight. How can a girl resist?'

Ray Charles suddenly seemed to be singing all about Georgia being on his mind, and the night was dark blue through the high arch of window, and the room was getting smaller all the time, defying physics. How could a girl resist, Minna wondered.

She wasn't at all sure that she would be able to, but she wasn't going to rush into any decisions just yet. She wasn't the kind of girl who believed that letting a man take her home made anything inevitable. She might just decide to leave, after all. She might take a bath, or read some Macaulay, or recite an ode. The night teemed with possibilities.

For the moment, she felt like a walk. She took one around the room, while Casey sat on the sofa and watched her with those lazy eyes that she wouldn't quite look into, not yet. She was looking for clues, adjusting herself to the alien environment, making the room her ally. After all, everyone who ever watched a B-movie knew that there was no earthly way to kiss a girl unless she offered herself up to be kissed. It was all a question of geography. So for the moment she was on tour, summing up the evidence. For such a modern boy he certainly liked his things old. No chrome and glass for him. Just an old-fashioned boy with an old-fashioned room. She gave him an old-fashioned look, just to make sure.

He laughed, startled.

'What was that for?' he asked.

'Just checking,' said Minna obliquely. She stood on one foot, just to show that she could, and watched him watching her. He knew how to look, she would give him that. What was she doing here? She wished he would ask her to stay so that she could say no, make a grand outraged exit at such impertinence. 'What shall we do now?' she added, thinking perhaps that she might say yes and throw caution to the winds. 'The crossword?'

He laughed again.

'I never was any good at crosswords.'

Minna raised one eyebrow at him.

'And you with your classical education?'

'And what would you know about my classical education?'

'Oh,' Minna said carelessly. 'I can spot a Christ Church boy at sixty paces. All that arrogance and charm. They don't teach you that in the redbricks, not the last time I looked.' Surrounded from a young age by Tom and his ebullient Oxford friends, there were some things Minna could spot in a man.

'Magdalen, actually,' said Casey, dignified as you please.

'Beg yo' pardon,' said Minna without a hint of contrition. 'And a scholarship boy, I presume? Hand to mouth on a grant and STILL managing to get credit at all the best tailors? The romance of you.'

Casey, who had been told that he had a way with women by the sort of people who should know, wasn't used to them laughing at him. Not the sort of women he knew, anyway.

'How did you know?' he said, lighting himself a cigarette and trying to look ironical.

Minna crowed with delight. She had been shooting in the dark, trying to catch him off balance. Luck be a lady tonight.

'Some things a girl just knows,' she said, looking sage. She folded herself on to the sofa beside him, having asserted herself. It was one thing being Easy, but there were limits. Pushover was so dated. She waved her arm vaguely at the room. 'All This,' she said judiciously, 'very well chosen, very tasteful, very good cover. And all to impress the ladies.'

'And are you impressed?'

'Wildly. An adventurer with a bust of Voltaire. They don't make them like you any more.'

Casey very much wanted to kiss her. Instead, he got up and poured her another drink. He had never met a girl who could take so much chartreuse without any discernible effect. The books hadn't worked, nor the Ray Charles, nor the drink. And his charm, which people said was raffish and sure fire, was sliding off her, and she was laughing at him. When women sat on his sofa in the usual run of things, it was in a languorously inviting kind of way, asking to be seduced. But this girl, this absurd strip of a thing in her pink dress, was quite upright, cross-legged, looking about her for more ammunition to throw at him.

'You're laughing at me,' he said, sitting down again, facing her squarely, as if that helped with three unbridgeable feet of sofa between them.

'But of course,' she said, as if asked whether she spoke French and was proficient at the piano-forte. 'What did you expect? I didn't read enough Margaret Mitchell in my youth to go a-swooning. Crinolines and fainting fits went out with yankee doodle dandy, or didn't you notice?'

'Perhaps I should have tried the Byron after all,' said Casey in resignation.

'Too late,' said Minna happily. 'All your props are gone, what to do?'

'Crawl back into my hole to lick my wounds,' said Casey, trying to look soulful. He would never understand women, not if he lived to be a hundred and got a telegram from the Queen. Just when you think you've got it taped, they send up a maverick like this to test you.

'And you a broken man,' said Minna callously. 'No-one said it was going to be easy.'

She set down her glass. Afterwards, she could never quite decide what it was that made up her mind. Perhaps it was just that time of night, that still empty time when it seems the whole world is asleep. Perhaps it was just that she didn't feel like any more chartreuse, couldn't be bothered to brave the streets looking for a cab, didn't have the energy to move any more. Or perhaps it was something to do with the curve of his mouth or the way his eyes watched her or how he let her laugh at him without minding so much.

Whatever it was, she was at once sure and clear and wanting to be kissed. So she set down her drink and leant towards him and took the half-smoked cigarette from between his fingers and put it out and smiled at him, still half-mocking, and he smiled back, wondering what he had done to change her mind. But Ray Charles had gone through his repertoire and gotten back to Georgia, still on his mind, and it was, after all, that time of night.

Eddy was battling with the crossword when Minna returned the next morning. A plate of half-finished eggs and a pot of cold coffee sat balefully in front of him, and he had on the kind of face that parents assume after waiting up all night for a child to return from its first grown-up dance.

'Well,' said Minna, who was still feeling curiously irresponsible and not quite herself at all. 'Aren't you going to ask me what sort of time I call this?'

'Not at all,' said Eddy, obdurate and stuck on twenty-two down.

'How disappointing.' Minna went to look in the fridge, noting with interest that the handcuffs seemed to have disappeared. She felt it was rather too Freudian for this time of the morning. 'And there you are, looking Victorian and all.'

Eddy muttered incoherently into his copy of the newspaper, something about fifteen letters down ending in Q. Minna took no notice, found some salami and a half-finished pot of olives in the fridge, and settled down to eat them.

'Breakfast,' she said logically.

Eddy averted his eyes and muttered some more. How anyone could eat olives stuffed with anchovies for breakfast was quite beyond him.

'I'm not looking Victorian,' he said suddenly, struck. 'And what does that mean anyway? Victorian?'

'Oh, you know,' said Minna vaguely, finishing off the olives and lighting a cigarette. 'Horse-whipping and pistols at dawn and no daughter of mine shall commit such an unnatural act and continue to darken my threshold.'

'Wrong century,' said Eddy, bitchily for him. Minna noticed and pretended not to. She was rather too busy wondering why her perfect pink dress, so suitable the night before, seemed so naked now. Live fast, die young, the pundits said, and everyone knew that staying out all night was an essential set piece in any girl's repertoire, so there was no earthly reason that Eddy had to look quite so cranky, for all the world as if he had just had a tooth extracted. He was only her landlord, after all. Some people never knew their place.

'Oh, for goodness sake,' said Minna, suddenly impatient with the indelicacy of the charade, 'why don't you just ask me who I was with, and have done with it?'

'And how do you know I was even wondering? None of my business,' said Eddy, playing for time. Pride coming before a fall was not a lesson he had ever spent any time learning, and he was damned if he was going to admit to being eaten with curiosity ever since he had woken to find the pallet empty where Minna should have been.

'Come along, ducky,' said Minna, who was intolerant after no sleep, and daring after the bad behaviour she had pretended to for so long had finally become reality. 'A girl doesn't have to be Dick Tracy to work that one out. Have a little respect.'

'And what's that supposed to mean?' said Eddy, who knew perfectly well.

'Look it up in the funny papers, Sherlock,' said Minna, flipping her cowlick at him. A haircut that survived such a night intact had to be worth a king's ransom, in anybody's book.

'Oliver called,' said Eddy, which might have been changing the subject on any other day. That particular day they both knew better. So typical of greedy clever insatiable Oliver, who hadn't had such a cat to put among the pigeons for quite a month. Incorrigibly chattering Oliver, who had a codicil in his will requesting that he be buried with his telephone. One heard such terrible stories these days about people being rushed into their graves not half dead.

'Oh,' said Minna, just a crochet too offbeat for plausibility. 'And I suppose he simply happened to ring to discuss the Thelonious Monk revival?'

'No,' said Eddy, making strides in the art of the monosyllable that would have left Clint Eastwood breathless.

'Oh, all right already,' said Minna, stubbing out her cigarette and taking on the patient demeanour of a child who knows it has to swallow its medicine like a brave little soldier. 'So, do you want to tell me that I'm treading dangerous waters, out of my depth, skating on thin ice, betting out of my league, heading for a bad end? Would you like to warn me about the slippery slope, and there being no turning back, and the downward path being easy?'

'No,' said Eddy, who did.

'That's all right then,' said Minna, glad that the subject seemed to be closed. 'In that case, I expect I shall get changed.'

'By the way,' said Eddy as she left the room. 'Someone called Jay rang for you. Lunch, he said.'

'Lunch,' said Minna in rapture. 'How did he guess?'

'Lunch,' said Minna as she arrived, quite restored in a purple silk shift and electric blue dark glasses. 'How did you guess?'

'Oh, you know,' said Jay, self-deprecating just like mother taught him. 'Just an idea. Any old idea, nothing special.'

'An inspiration,' said Minna, settling the point. 'Any more ideas like that, Shakespeare, and David Hare had better look to his laurels, that's all.'

She sat down, turned a blinding smile on the waiter, and ordered a dry Martini, very cold, two olives.

Jay looked at her curiously, but held his council, which was after all what he was good at. Something was changed. Jay didn't hold much with the convention of the writer's eye, but it didn't take Einstein to notice that something was different. Eleanor of Aquitaine had met Mae West somewhere along the way and strayed into Lou Lou's territory. She never called him Shakespeare, and martinis before lunch? He wouldn't have been at all surprised if she had asked for it shaken, not stirred, just like James Bond. He smiled without quite meaning to, revelling in the unpredictable.

Minna saw the smile and let it ride. How she liked a man who didn't ask questions.

'So, blissfulness,' she said, toying with her olive in the unnecessary kind of way that had gone out in 1929, 'do you think I look just like Cedric in *Love in a Cold Climate*?'

Jay, whose education hadn't reached as far as the Mitford sisters, nodded emphatically, as if that had been exactly what he was thinking all along.

'Just like,' he said. 'Absolutely and completely like. Really.' He wondered if he could ever learn to wear dark glasses indoors and get away with it.

'Clever of you to notice,' said Minna judiciously.

'My job,' said Jay, more judicious still but with a hint of modesty becoming in a Young Artist.

'Talking of which,' said Minna, 'I thought you disapproved of lunch in places like this. What happened to Integrity in his Garret? Did he go out and win the pools?'

'Not quite,' said Jay, unconsciously puffing out his chest a little, like a pouter pigeon who has just made a conquest. 'I sold another collection of postcards.'

'Well now,' said Minna, smiling with pleasure.

'There's a cause for celebration. The utter cleverness of you.' She turned to the waiter, who was
making rather indiscreet eyes at the two feathers
she had chosen to hang from her ear that morning.
'Champagne for the gentleman, why not?'

'Why not?' said the waiter ardently, eager to
endorse her every whim. He hadn't seen two purple
feathers in one ear since Sid Vicious was a boy.

'So,' said Jay, who was learning fast to take this
sort of behaviour in his stride. Until he had met
Minna he had only had champagne once in his life.
At least, they said it was champagne, although the
label had indicated something called *vin mousseu*,
which didn't sound the same at all. 'Lunch is on
me, since I owe you.'

'The bourgeois is coming out again,' said Minna,
affecting melancholy. 'But I accept with good grace
and shan't rag you about it, since I see that some
habits die hard.'

'Rome wasn't built in a day,' said Jay, who knew
better.

'Can't wait,' said Minna, raising her glass to him
and flashing her eyes over the rim, just for the hell of
it. Jay rather wished she wouldn't do that. 'Here's to
you.'

'Here's to me,' he agreed solemnly. He really
wanted to raise his glass to her, but something
told him that she was not a girl to be crossed,
not today, not in this new mood. All the girls he
knew had two moods: quite cross and very cross,
but this creature gave mercurial a good name. How
clever he had been to think of lunch.

As they drank their champagne in the charity that
only lunchtime can induce, complicity tinged with

183

devil-may-care, the room filled about them. The circus carried on swinging, the performing seals begging genteelly for fish as they had since the day the media was invented. Most good Christian souls thought that God rested on the seventh day, but the *cognoscenti* knew that that was when He invented television. It was in this certain knowledge that the Italian-suited diners sauntered in for their lunch, shining American Express cards ready to take the weight of expense accounts that put Ivana Trump's clothes bill to shame.

English producers met with their American counterparts to mourn the decline of the British film industry and allowed themselves to be consoled by generous offers from across the herring pond. Agents met with agents to mourn the decline of the reading public and be reassured by five-figure deals for a mini-series. Scriptwriters met with directors to mourn the decline of the art movie and be mollified by contracts for a ten-part sitcom. Over Bordeaux and Beaujolais the spoken and printed word was shamelessly traded, each sell-out softened by a double Armagnac and a large cigar, which combination as everybody knows, always makes things better.

Oblivious to barter, unconsciously set above the commercial herd, Jay and Minna drank their champagne, armour-clad with dreams of pinnacles that aspiring playwrights might yet climb. The day when Jay would be tempted to sell his soul was still far off, and here in the long green lunch hour of fashionable London anything was possible. Purple feathers hung from ears and electric blue glasses and dry Martinis with two olives might seem like trifles to some, but not to Jay. To Minna, they were just what she felt like that morning, afterthoughts of a girl of whim, but to Jay, who had known the humdrum of the provincial north, they were revelations.

Just as they were starting their coffee and Minna was trying to order some chartreuse without Jay noticing, an award-winning playwright happened by their table and stopped to talk.

'Alabama,' said Minna pleased. 'Just exactly who I wanted to see. Sit down and have some chartreuse, I'm going to.' Safe now to go public, with Jay far too preoccupied with touchingly vain attempts to stop staring like a slightly retarded calf.

'Why not?' said Alabama, in the dry way which served so well to keep the unwelcome at bay. Minna, always welcome everywhere, took it as a yes please, and smiled kindly on the three waiters who were quietly battling to win the prize of bringing the famous Miss Skye a chair. 'I am on holiday, and Milo has had to rush off to some signing or other.'

'Men,' said Minna in disgust.

Finally they were settled, the chair arranged, the chartreuse brought, the waiters subsided.

'This is Jay,' said Minna, remembering her manners.

'How do you do?' said Jay, blinking ingenuously and trying to look as if he hadn't just left prep school.

'He writes plays too,' said Minna, delicious with joy, as if she had just come up with the answer to a thorny metaphysical problem that philosophers had been puzzling over for decades.

'Minna,' said Jay, embarrassed into some sort of coherence. 'Really.'

'Really nothing,' said Minna, blandly lighting a cigarette and watching the smoke float away to bother an executive producer who was trying to find his ulcer pills. 'Artists unite and all that.'

Alabama laughed and decided to rescue Jay from his embarrassment. She quite saw what Oliver meant about the Lodger, and she knew enough about the Vane family to recognize that the struggling young playwright was only just holding his head above water. It wasn't so long ago that she had been a struggling young playwright herself, and she hadn't grown so grand as to forget in a hurry. So she turned to Jay and asked him about his work and within five minutes Minna was gratified to find her gambit an unqualified success as the artists united before her very eyes in a corruscating discussion of plays and playwrights which seemed to consist, on Jay's part at least, of comparing them all unfavourably with Alabama. Oh, those strings, thought Minna fondly, see how they pull, and she sat back and drank her chartreuse and allowed herself a small moment of reflection on the surprisingly athletic nature of Irish torsos.

Alabama, who had been thoughtfully filled in by Oliver on his morning telephone round, saw Minna's eyes wander indecorously into the middle distance, and wondered for a moment quite what the formula was that had served Casey so well for the last fifteen years. She didn't dwell on it for long, since she was finding herself too charmed by Jay to let her mind wander. Alabama had a strict defence for would-be admirers and copyists, and she wasn't used to it being breached quite so easily. She was surprised to find it more pleasurable than disconcerting, made a mental note not to tell Oliver who would be too full of always having told her so, and settled down to enjoy herself. She was on holiday, after all, and who was she to dash aspirations that had been hers such a short time ago. So she smiled on Jay, and he smiled back, knowing too little of her reputation to realize his startling elevation to the chosen few, and told her about coming to London and his garret and his writer's block and how the third act, which had been giving him hell, was now flowing sure and sweet as a swallow flying south for winter.

And Minna sat and wondered at her utter wickedness, and the waiters hovered with more chartreuse and tried to work out quite who Jay was to be favoured with such luncheon companions, and across London Eddy sweated in an airless rehearsal room and hit E flat instead of F sharp and cursed all lodgers in general and his in particular.

At four o'clock the party broke up.

'Call me tomorrow,' said Alabama to Jay, giving him her number. 'And we'll see what we can do. Give Eddy my love,' she added to Minna before walking swiftly away, a tall uncompromising figure cutting through the hot Soho afternoon, motorbike helmet swinging from one arm. Jay stood in silent awe, watching her go, a heroine in black leather.

'What we can do about WHAT?' said Minna, rudely interrupting his worship. She had, after all, been quite silent for the last hour, letting him have a free rein, but now she wanted his attention again. Minna liked her place in the sun.

'Oh,' said Jay, shrugging his shoulders and trying to come down to earth. 'You know, my play. She wants to show it to her agent.'

'Don't,' said Minna. 'You don't say. You could knock me down with a feather boa. From the garret to the Garrick in one easy lunch. The great Alabama Skye helping a lesser mortal up the ladder of success, there must be a God after all. If I had a hat, I should eat it, but I look hell in hats.'

'You couldn't look hell in anything,' said Jay, with a touch of grandeur fitting to his new status.

'Sweet Shakespeare,' said Minna. 'I don't expect thanks, really I don't. You should get back to the muse and not spend any more time on a girl like me.'

'I must,' said Jay firmly. 'I must go and work. I have work to do, plays to write.' If he stayed up all night, he could just about finish the third act before tomorrow.

'Me too,' said Minna blithely. 'No rest for the wicked and all that. Danton waits for no girl.'

'Who doesn't?' said Lou Lou, drawing up in a squeal of ill-oiled taxi brakes and the aura of a ship in full sail. 'What ARE you two doing, hanging around on street corners? I thought they'd passed a law against that sort of thing. And you under age, Shakespeare. I'm shocked.'

'Look, princess,' said the cabbie, who knew a touch of class when he saw it. 'I'm holding up the traffic.'

'Don't be silly,' said Lou Lou imperiously, 'there's plenty of room. So,' she said, turning back to Minna, eyes shooting sparks of fascination, 'WHO was that delicious Irish you were with last night?'

'Was he Irish?' said Jay, whose mind was, after all, on other things. 'I didn't notice.'

'Darling heart,' said Lou Lou. 'You wouldn't have noticed unless he'd turned up carting a crate of Guinness and a shamrock between his teeth, singing When Irish Eyes are Smiling.'

'Not fair at all,' said Jay, unoffended.

'So,' Lou Lou said again, not to be deflected by any playwright, persistence incarnate in a black cab, 'where did you find him? Who is he?'

'Just a boy I know,' said Minna, which was true, after a fashion.

'Just a boy, my eye,' said Lou Lou, 'but I admire your discretion. What with that vision of loveliness and the to-die-for landlord you must have your hands full. The summer IS looking up.'

'Isn't it though?' said Jay, still thinking of Alabama.

'What's with Shakespeare?' said Lou Lou. 'Did he just bump into Harold Pinter?'

'Alabama Skye,' said Minna, with a speaking look.

'Oh, well,' said Lou Lou. 'I suppose that means we won't get any sense out of him for a week. What a life. I must fly,' she added, taking on a businesslike air. 'People to see, things to do. What it is, being me.'

She withdrew her head, which was a rather conservative shade of black today, back into the taxi which moved off into the traffic, obviously relieved to be gone.

'Well,' said Minna, wondering. 'And where's she off to in such a hurry?'

Jay shook his head. He didn't believe in trying to fathom the unfathomable, and as far as he was concerned, Lou Lou fitted right into the unfathomable category, and no mistake.

'I must go,' he said again.

'That's right,' said Minna approvingly. 'Kiss me and go. Let me know what happens.'

'Oh, I shall,' said Jay. 'I shall.'

11

'Hello,' said Casey, opening the door.

'Hello,' said Minna. 'Just passing,' she added, lying shamelessly.

'That's nice,' said Casey, taking her in and kissing her.

'So is that,' said Minna, when he had finished. She leant against the wall a little, wondering where he learnt to kiss like that. Years of experience, she supposed.

Upstairs, the great white room was full of early evening sun, muddling over the busts and bookshelves. A portable computer hummed on the table, and in the corner a delicate walnut cabinet stood open to reveal a fax, chattering quietly to itself.

'Three telephones,' said Minna. 'State of the art. Have you got any beer?'

'Of course,' said Casey, going into the back. 'Anything you want.'

'How cunning,' said Minna, following him. 'A kitchen tucked away. All mod cons and no stove. I expect you eat out a lot.'

'Oh, stop it,' said Casey, handing her a bottle. 'Give a boy a break.'

'Quite right. I can't really see you slaving over a hot stove anyway. You do have a reputation to protect.'

'Good of you to remember,' said Casey. They laughed at each other, full of nonsense, buoyed up on a tide of mutual attraction.

'It's part of my charm,' said Minna, settling herself on the sofa, just as if she had been invited. Casey watched her, wondering at a girl who played so few games. He would have called her, but he didn't have her number. He had been unsure how this particular dance would progress, thinking on it in a desultory kind of way while he worked, but he would never have guessed that she would simply present herself at the door like this, washed and clean and new in her purple shift, seeming so sure of her welcome. But then he supposed she had a right to feel sure of it, when he was finding himself so pleased to see her. He smiled to himself at the novelty of it all, and Minna saw his smile, and relaxed.

Into the middle of all this chemistry, one of the three telephones started to ring, oblivious to the atmosphere.

'It's Oliver,' said Casey, picking it up.

'Of course it is,' said Oliver, spry as you please and revelling in all these new developments. 'Is that Minna with you?'

'Yes,' said Casey. 'We're just having a drink.'

'Cocktails at six,' said Oliver in delight. 'How positively Noël Coward. I didn't know you were that kind of boy. Perhaps there is hope for you after all.'

'Well, thank you,' said Casey. 'I like to think so.'

'Now then,' said Oliver in his most business-like manner. 'I want you both to come to the theatre tonight. Say you're free.'

'I'll have to ask the lady,' said Casey ironically.

'He wants us to go to the theatre,' he said to Minna.

'Why not?' she said. 'I haven't a thing planned,' she added, as if it were unusual.

'That would be fine,' Casey said to Oliver.

'Oh, good. How lucky I am to get you at such short notice. I'll pick you up at seven. *Ciao.*' And he rang off.

'He's picking us up at seven,' said Casey, putting down the telephone, and switching it and its two brothers off. Minna watched him, trying to adopt a sophisticated expression that gave nothing away. 'That just gives us time.'

'Time for what?' said Minna, opening her eyes very wide, as if she couldn't possibly guess.

'You know,' said Casey, giving her one of those rogue Irish looks, the one that had roused her interest in the first place, the one that the kind of women who should know always said was quite irresistible.

'Here?' said Minna, dropping the pretence. 'On the sofa?'

'Why not?'

'Well,' said Minna, submitting with an artless sigh of pleasure. 'And what WILL the neighbours think?'

When Oliver arrived, they were ready for him, spruce and scented, wearing faces that suggested butter had never melted in their mouths.

'Just look at you two,' he said, seeing through it at once. 'Come along, I've got a cab waiting.'

Inside the taxi, Venice and Sebastian sat, wearing equally angelic faces, and just as improbable. After all, Minna thought to herself, it was the third summer of love. It said so in *The Face*, so it must be true.

Everyone said hello.

'Casey,' said Venice who was too interested for words in this novel ménage, but too well brought up to show it. 'What heaven to see you. It must be quite a month. How was New York? Did you see that ducky François? What's the news?'

'Oh,' said Casey, laughing reminiscently. 'I had dinner with him. He's distraught with love for the man who came to plant his roof terrace. He's trying to buy a house with a garden so he can gaze at him for weeks, sweating over bougainvillaeas.'

'Don't,' said Venice. 'Don't tell me.'

'That boy,' said Oliver sagely. 'I always thought he'd end up with a bit of rough. I could see it coming.'

'What about Carlos?' said Venice naughtily. 'Don't tell me you loved him for his conversation?'

'I thought he only spoke Spanish,' said Sebastian vaguely.

'That's the point, dolt,' said Venice fondly.

'That's very cruel of you, Venice,' said Oliver, taking on the slightly martyred face he adopted whenever Carlos' name was mentioned. 'Considering recent events.'

'Oh, well,' said Venice philosophically. 'I can think that he's having a madly gay time in Poland. He'll be back swearing undying love and begging forgiveness, you'll see.'

'I shouldn't have him back,' said Oliver with dignity. 'Not if he walked on hot coals and wore sackcloth for a month. Not if he got down on his knees and begged, but BEGGED.'

'Quite right,' said Venice approvingly. 'One has one's pride, after all.'

'I saw Ernst Poellenberg too,' said Casey.

'Surrounded by eight bottle blondes in Mortimers, but still pining for you, Venice, after all these years.'

'Well, poor lamb, he is only ninety-fourth in line to the throne,' said Venice, as if that excused everything.

'But frantically rich and at least three princedoms in the *Almanach de Gotha*,' said Oliver, who always knew these things. 'He gives eligible a new meaning. You should be jealous, Sebastian.'

'But,' said Sebastian with maddening logic, 'he's fat, forty, and he makes a noise when he drinks his soup.'

'There is that,' said Oliver, who liked to think of himself as fair. 'But still. That lovely castle with footmen behind every chair, and all those Monets, and wild boar hunting in sable coats, the romance of it. I'm almost tempted myself, despite the soup.'

'A little vulgarity does go a long way,' said Venice. 'Where are we going?' She peered out of the window in dismay, suddenly lost, finding only rows of terraced houses where the West End should be. 'I thought you said we were going to the theatre.'

'We are,' said Oliver cryptically. 'A little culture never did a girl any harm, even you, Venice.'

'But we're going the wrong way,' said Venice, who always felt rather disorientated if she strayed too far from SW1.

'We're going to Hampstead,' said Oliver, for all the world as if this were a regular occurrence.

'Hampstead,' said Sebastian vaguely. 'Is that on a hill?'

'Don't,' said Venice. 'You should have warned us. I'm sure I'm not at all suitably dressed.'

'Venice,' said Oliver firmly, looking with love at the confection of white slipper satin and chiffon in which Venice was artlessly draped, 'you would look suitable anywhere. A dream darling, that's all, so do stop fussing. I thought it might make a change for you, going north.'

'Stop trying to make it sound glamorous,' said Venice sternly. 'Going north, indeed. Will we ever get back? Do they have cabs in Hampstead? I mean to say.'

'You'll love it,' said Oliver soothingly. 'It's a new discovery of mine. I think you'll be interested.'

'All I can say,' said Venice, 'is that I hope it's worth it.'

The theatre was small, crowded, and smelt strongly of filter coffee. The clientele, earnest in earth tones, looked disapprovingly at Venice but pretended not to. After all, they were far too busy discussing ecological matters and when Anita Brookner was going to write her next novel.

'You would think they might approve,' said Venice carelessly. 'After all, white is very New Age. Don't they read *Vogue*?'

'Come along,' said Oliver, shepherding them into the auditorium with the slightly distracted air of a schoolmistress in charge of a geography field trip. 'They're about to start. Oh good, here's Roger.'

Roger Middlemarch, thought Minna, the darling of Cannes, in Hampstead for the theatre. There was more to this than met the eye. And why were she and Casey asked, all of a sudden? Curiouser and curiouser.

'Roger,' said Venice in reproach. 'What on earth are you doing here? Shouldn't you be having dinner with David Puttnam or somebody? Really, I can't think what has come over Oliver.'

Roger smiled and kissed Venice's offered cheek. He was urbane in dark blue Milanese suiting and he gave off a calm air of success that went well with his slicked-down hair and Cutler and Gross spectacles.

'It's his new discovery,' he said. 'He promised me it would be worth the trip.'

'Well,' said Venice, all at once conspiratorial, 'will you promise to take me out of here as soon as it's finished, back to civilization? I'm worried about my supper, and Sebastian must be fed.'

'Oh, don't be silly,' said Oliver. 'We've got a table at Orso for half-past eleven. Do you think I would let poor Nellie starve? Now do be quiet, they're starting. Watch the play.'

So they watched the play. It was a modern American work, in the Tennessee Williams mould, a combination of claustrophobia and histrionics, firmly in the physical school so favoured by Strasberg disciples, and quite powerful in its way. But the revelation was the female second lead, a study in thwarted desire, a girl who could have been born to play Blanche Dubois.

'Lou Lou,' said Minna in amazement. 'And I thought . . .'

'We all know what you thought,' said Oliver. 'It should teach you not to take people at their own valuation.'

'Silly old me,' said Minna, quite ready to be put in her place. 'No wonder she was in such a rush this afternoon.'

*   *   *

Afterwards, they went backstage to congratulate Lou Lou.

'Utterly angelic of you all to come,' she said, looking curiously naked as she wiped off her stage make-up with cold cream. 'Don't tell me what you thought. I can't bear post mortems.'

'Roger had to run,' said Oliver. 'That boy, he can't sit still for two minutes without remembering an appointment with George Lucas or I don't know who. Anyway he sent his love, and said to tell you how wonderful you were, and he'll call you tomorrow.'

'Oh,' said Lou Lou. 'Fancy.' Minna looked at her curiously, taken aback. She had never thought she would see Lou Lou at a disadvantage. Shy with success, her black bob damp with sweat, her face shiny with grease, she was quite a different reincarnation from the temptress whom Minna had found in that sleazy bar only a few short weeks ago.

'Come on,' said Oliver generally. 'We'll wait outside for you to change. If Venice has to wait much longer to get back to the bright lights I can't be responsible for her actions . . . '

The restaurant was nicely full of a post-theatre crowd when they arrived, everyone gossiping and preening and pretending not to notice that Jonathon Pryce was sitting on the next table. It was that kind of place. Oliver, looking round shamelessly, was pleased to see that his party rated highest in the room for consistent glamour. Venice, of course, could stop any kind of traffic on her own, but even more so with Sebastian on her arm, such a golden boy with his green eyes and his peacock blue suit cut two sizes too big. And the lodger was such a perfect slip of a thing with her sleek silver hair and her purple shift. Very modern, Oliver thought with pleasure, very modern and very young, shining with youth, and a perfect foil to Casey with his dark looks and his well-trained eyes. And then there was Lou Lou, cleverly understated tonight in unadorned black to match her hair, monochrome only relieved by the vivid slash of scarlet that was her mouth. Oh, how very clever he was, even if he did say it himself.

They sat down in a wave of chatter, congratulations showering over Lou Lou, who took them with a pretty self-deprecation, and Oliver ordered champagne, and Minna wondered how it was that he managed to turn everything into a party. But that was another of Oliver's secrets, another that he wasn't telling.

'Well,' said Minna, as the commotion died down and everyone fell to studying their menus, suddenly hungry. 'Why didn't you tell me that you were an actress?'

'What was to tell?' said Lou Lou, coming back into her old self as the champagne circulated. 'I was between jobs, and there's nothing more dreary to my mind than tales of failed auditions.'

'Lucky for us that you didn't fail this one,' said Casey, the gallant.

'Thank you, Irish,' said Lou Lou. 'I feel much the same myself. So there's no mystery,' she added to Minna. 'Just that a girl doesn't have to tell all of the truth all of the time.'

'Listen, learn and inwardly digest,' advised Oliver, who utterly approved of Lou Lou's brand of worldly wisdom. 'You're young yet, after all.'

'Not that young,' said Minna, who was suddenly rather tired of everyone telling her how young she was. She was having an affair with the wickedest man in London, after all, didn't that count for anything? She knew that sophistication didn't grow on trees, but she felt that she wasn't doing so badly, for a beginner, and she wasn't getting any credit for it.

'Don't knock it,' said Oliver. 'Wait until you've been round the block as many times as I have, darling, and then you'll see how much it takes out of you.'

'Depends which block you go round,' said Casey naughtily.

'Oh, you,' said Oliver. 'We all know you've sold your soul to the devil, so you don't count. I don't begin to know what it is with you Irish, you've all got the secret of eternal youth sewn into your suspenders. Must be something to do with the leprechauns.'

'The Littlehorns?' said Venice, who hadn't been paying attention. 'Haven't they become tax exiles?'

'Tax my foot,' said Oliver. 'They had to flee the country after he was discovered doing something quite unrepeatable to the chauffeur.'

'Don't tell me,' said Venice, impressed. 'How quite extraordinary.'

'Do you think they use cold pressed olive oil?' said Sebastian, who was still immersed in the menu, 'or the other kind?'

'Really,' said Oliver with a shudder, 'I wouldn't like to think what they used. I really wouldn't like to speculate.'

12

It was after Casey and Minna were a week into their affair that Minna thought to ask what Casey did. As far as she could make out, he spent a great deal of time on the telephone and the rest sending faxes to New York and Los Angeles. Since this was virtually what everyone who made money had done all the way through the Eighties, she simply presumed that he was in business of some sort. He seemed to have a great many lunch meetings.

It was a long hot week, the city sweltering in a heat haze. Every day Minna, who loved the sun, happily watched the thermometer climb into the nineties. Everyone complained. Drought warnings were issued, and the police were kept busy arresting people for using their hosepipes. Casey sat in his big white room with three fans going, talking on the telephone and arranging lunch meetings. Minna, who for some obscure reason of her own didn't altogether care for the idea of returning to Soho, lay among the pots of clematis and bougainvillaea that cluttered Casey's tiny garden, and turned brown. The disc jockeys on the wireless talked a great deal about summer in the city and soaring temperatures, and warned motorists about roads melting in Barnes. The city was emptying as August approached. Jay was working, and Lou Lou slept until tea-time, before leaving for the theatre, where her four-week run was playing to capacity audiences and approving reviews. Minna didn't even miss her books on the Revolution, which she had left in Soho. She liked being a mistress, and there was no question that that was what she was. Casey was not the kind of man who would have a girlfriend, he had a mistress. Minna knew it was a fine line, and she wasn't quite sure what the dividing point was. It was something to do with the kind of places he took her, or the way he didn't ask her any questions or expect her to ask any of him.

Or perhaps it was the separateness of their lives. Even though they were living under the same roof, they hardly saw each other during the day. Casey would get up early, make himself some coffee and read the papers before starting work, turning on all his machines which sat humming about him, while Minna would drowse in bed until the sun was hot enough for her. They would meet in the evening, and go out, heading up to Soho to the bars and the restaurants and all the life that was left in the city. As the residential areas became deserted, turning into miniature ghost towns as the moneyed classes flew off to any riviera they could find, the urban dwellers who remained huddled together in Soho, where the drunks still drank, and the bars still spilled over with players and the neon signs still promised thrills of the most unrealistic kind. So that was where Casey took Minna, and that was where they sat and drank until late in the clear warmth of the night, and talked about nothing at all. Perhaps that was the difference. It was as if they were happy not knowing very much about each other, still remaining strangers. Whatever it was, Minna liked it. She thought it all highly suitable and more than a touch grown-up and just what a girl needed. At least it gave her something to do, what with Lou Lou and Jay so unavailable, and the sun shining so hot.

At the end of the week Oliver, who judged that the honeymoon was now over and Minna was ready again for the outside world, called and suggested lunch. As far as he was concerned, if anyone had invented lunch it was him, and he didn't take such a responsibility lightly. Oliver went out to lunch religiously, seven days a week, come rain come shine. His mornings were spent telephoning most of his large acquaintance from his bed, just to see how the world was wagging. Then he would get up, dress with care, pluck his eyebrows, and go to lunch. As far as Oliver was concerned, the world was divided into two types of person: those who did lunch, and those who didn't. Minna, he felt, fitted comfortably into the former category.

'I am glad you called,' she said, when he rang.

'Not bored already?' said Oliver naughtily.

'Of course not. But Casey's gone off to a meeting, or something, and I've had enough sun for one week.'

'Lucky for me,' said Oliver. 'So you're free for lunch?'

'Oliver,' said Minna, in the worldly voice she was starting to affect as fitting to her new position as mistress of the wickedest man in London. 'I'm ALWAYS free for lunch. You should know that.'

'Silly of me,' said Oliver, chastened. 'How about La Famiglia at one?'

'I'll meet you there,' said Minna, and disconnected.

*   *   *

Thank heaven for Oliver, Minna thought, as she got ready to go out. He really was a godsend to a girl, in this heat. Her week in the sun had felt like a holiday, in this strange house, with this strange man. Their evenings together had a curiously Mediterranean feel, for all the world as if the dirty old streets of Soho were the pink sidewalks of St Tropez, and any moment the young Brigitte Bardot would come walking along, barefoot. It was the smell of heat rising off the pavements, and the irresponsibility of warmth and sex in the air. But now the week was over and she was brown and impatient for action. It was too hot to read, and there was nothing in the shops and no good films on at the cinema, and the theatres were stuffy enough to make a girl quite faint. Of course, Minna reflected, if she were a real mistress, the old-fashioned kind, the kind they don't make any more, she would have more than enough to do during the day, preparing herself for the nightly attentions of her beau. It would be hours in the salon and the hairdresser, and an endless round of shopping for négligés and silk underwear and tiny confections of peach satin. But Casey didn't seem to mind that she simply lay in the sun, and, for the moment, being brown and young enough not to care was enough. As a concession to her new status, she had gone out and bought quantities of Chanel No. 5 to put behind her ears and in the bath and on her body, which she thought almost the last word in sophistication. So overcome was she by her own chic that she ran out of ideas and had done with it. After all, as she said to herself, she didn't hear anyone complaining.

In honour of lunch, and as it was Oliver, she put on all her pearls and painted her lips in a rather fetching shade of fuchsia. As for the rest, she put on a plain white shift dress and a curiously dated pair of gilt sandals, the kind Twiggy and Jean Shrimpton and Penelope Tree used to wear in the Sixties, all those nights that they used to go out with David Bailey and Terence Stamp and all the other East End boys who used to be so much the rage. Then she admired herself for a brief moment, thinking how much Oliver would appreciate this vaguely androgenous look. She gave herself a faintly languorous look in the glass, just to prove she could, and then she went to lunch.

Oliver was waiting for her, charmingly punctual, sitting at the best table in the garden in a cream linen suit and a panama hat, and looking just like our man in Havana, which was the idea. He was reading Graham Greene this week, and it showed.

'Well,' said Minna, who wasn't. 'You look just like the Great Gatsby, or someone.'

Oliver was too polite to correct her. Anyway, he supposed it could just as easily be Fitzgerald, even Somerset Maugham at a stretch. He was a man of many parts.

'It's the heat,' he said, kissing her. 'It brings out the F. Scott in me. I'm in Mediterranean mood.'

'I'm surprised you didn't suggest we flew to the Hôtel du Cap for lunch,' said Minna, who knew the South of France well from her youth, when her summers had been spent in white lace dresses on the Cap d'Antibes, being cooed over by former kings and impecunious gamblers and fading screen stars and discontented ex-patriots. 'Why aren't you in the Mediterranean anyway,' she added, suddenly struck, her vague knowledge of the Season sharpening into curiosity. 'I wouldn't have thought that you would be seen dead in London in August.'

Oliver smiled appreciatively. She was learning fast.

'I thought it was time for a change,' he said, shrugging his shoulders in a delicate intimation of the utter controversy of his decision. 'I've had people begging me, but begging me to go on Aegean yachting parties, and to Salzburg for the music festival, and Effie Hampton spent half an hour on the telephone telling me that she would simply die if I didn't go to Long Island, but die, stone dead. But I am cruel and immovable, I am immutable, I am the Rock of Ages, I've turned them all down. I'm rather enchanted by it all so empty, to tell you the truth.'

'Keeping everyone guessing,' said Minna, laughing at the thought. 'How they must wonder what it is that's keeping you at home.'

'Or whom,' said Oliver naughtily. 'It never did people any harm, being kept on their toes. Shall we order a drink?' he added, smiling at the hovering waiter, who was the handsomest kind of Venetian, the kind that made one think of those dashing gondoliers in the Thirties who used to run off with English heiresses bored with guards officers and simpering débutantes and coming-out balls. Oliver wondered why no-one ran off with nameless Italians any more. He thought it a great shame.

'I expect I should have a bellini,' said Minna, who was thinking much the same thing. She knew that no-one drank anything else in Venice. Bellinis in Harry's bar and the ghost of Hemingway, who could ask for more?

'What a perfect idea,' said Oliver, as if she had just split the atom. 'Let's have two, why not? After all, it's not often one's in London in August.'

'An excuse for anything,' Minna agreed, slipping easily into the spirit of things, just as if she too had decided to stay in the city on an inexplicable whim, turning down endless invitations to Greek islands and South American ranches and Tuscan estates.

'Anyway,' said Oliver consolingly, 'it's not for long. I've got Venice in September, how I yearn for Harry's and lunch on Torcello, and before that a week with my decadent friends in the Wicklow hills.'

'Your decadent friends?' said Minna. She wondered what could be more decadent than Oliver himself. What kind of people could these be? Wife beaters, child molesters, white slavers?

'Yes,' said Oliver, smiling with pleasure. 'Good old-fashioned feckless Irish, you know the thing. Living in crumbling follies of houses but still keeping two butlers, drinking until dawn every night, breakfasting on eggs and Guinness, calmly watching the family fortune decline about their ears. Singers of songs and tellers of tales and to hell with tomorrow. I stay with them every year. A little loafing never did a boy any harm, a change being as good as a rest as Nanny always said, the old fraud. The nearest telephone is ten miles away, everything is done by telegram. It must be all that rain,' he added, on a meditative note. 'I rather think it turns them a little soft in the head. I always wear a hat when I go to Ireland, just in case.'

Minna tried to picture Oliver carousing amidst a gathering of charming good-for-nothings high in the Irish mountains, and failed. He was such an essentially urban creature that she couldn't begin to imagine him stranded in a remote hill village, far away from all the hallmarks of civilization. To her Oliver was Bond Street and Mayfair and the bar of the Ritz all rolled into one. She wondered quite how one achieved such a pitch of sophistication. Perhaps he had come out of the womb in white tie, ready for his first party. On balance, she thought not. It was the work of a lifetime, a triumph of artifice over nature. Some people devoted their lives to Art, some to Science, some to Good Works, but Oliver simply dedicated his to the pursuit of sophistication. He was an honourable last bastion against the growing hordes of barbarians, thought Minna, with a little pre-prandial flight of fancy. Oliver would always be the man with the perfectly chilled Martini, the finest cotton shirt, the cleverest florist, and the most avant-garde collection of paintings.

'Casey isn't that soft in the head,' she said, reverting to the Irish.

Oliver gave her his most avuncular look, the one to which he felt his age and experience entitled him.

'Casey is different,' he said. 'An exception to the rule. Besides, his family isn't starting to decline, it's been doing that since the sixteenth century. There hasn't been a natural death among them since 1714.'

'How romantic,' said Minna, delighted. 'Duelling at dawn?'

'Duels, suicides, fighting in any war they could find (even if it had nothing whatsoever to do with them) either out of natural pugnacity or to escape the bailiffs, bar brawls, poison, even the rack on one occasion. His grandfather was doing all right, looking ready to reverse the trend, but then his wife ran off with the second footman, he took to drink and cards, one thing led to another, and before you could say royal straight flush, he'd lost his house in a game of poker.'

'Don't,' said Minna. 'It's the most penny novel-ettish thing I've ever heard in my life. It can't be true.'

'True as I sit here,' said Oliver, who for the first time since 1973 was not exaggerating. 'You'll learn about the Irish. Most of them are still living in the last century. Milo's uncle still drives about Galway Bay in a coach and four and full Georgian coaching costume, and no-one finds it at all strange. So don't let Casey mislead you with that devil-may-care exterior. He might seem like the last of the buccaneers, but he's determined to reverse the trend of the last five hundred years. While his father sits drinking brandy in the Shelbourne, quoting Yeats and Brendan Behan through the bottom of a glass, Casey is doing battle with his genes. And he looks like he's winning too, now he's becoming such a big shot.'

'Is he?' said Minna with interest. She had never met any big shots, and wasn't altogether sure that she would recognize one if she did. 'What exactly does he do?'

Oliver let out a disbelieving laugh, and looked at her with admiration.

'Do you mean to tell me that you haven't asked?' he said. 'Darling heart, you are the utter end. I never met a girl with less curiosity, I rather think it's a most refreshing change.'

'Well,' said Minna, a little defensive, not sure that she liked the idea of being a refreshing change. 'It didn't seem to come up, and it's such a hack-neyed question, asking people what they do, as if it mattered. I hate it when people ask me, it used to make me so cross I'd make up the most terrible lies and tell them I was a nuclear physicist, or an undertaker, or something.'

'I couldn't agree more,' said Oliver. 'It's too bourgeois for words. But my sweet, if you will forgive me, there are ways and means of finding out these things without being quite so blunt. Still,' he added, endlessly indulgent as far as this ridiculously unworldly creature was concerned, 'I suppose I do see that it wasn't uppermost in your mind as far as that luscious Casey is concerned. To tell you the utter truth, my angel, if I had my hands on something that delicious, I don't expect I should be asking too many questions either.'

'Well, you do see,' said Minna, pleased that he understood. 'Besides, the days do just slide away, and suddenly it's a week, and you realize that you don't know very much about a person, but by that time it doesn't seem to matter any more. We're having a lovely time, so what is the point? He doesn't ask me anything anyway.'

'Ah well, he wouldn't,' said Oliver obscurely. 'It's just lucky that you've got me. I can tell you absolutely anything you need to know.'

Oliver was being slightly economical with the truth when he said this. He wouldn't be able to tell anyone how to change a plug, or fill in a tax return, or how to play the stock market, or why inflation was rising, or even if inflation was rising. What he meant by Absolutely Anything was the life histories of the three hundred or so people he considered worth knowing about. Regarding these, he could list accurately who was having whom, and where, who was committing adultery with whose wife, who had a bottle of gin stashed under the bed or a skeleton hidden in the cupboard. He could trace family trees back over five or six centuries, explain how too many cousins marrying cousins had led to eccentricity or madness, indicate whether a marriage had been made for convenience, money, social aggrandizement, or love, recall how a family had made or lost its money. He knew who liked boys and who liked girls and who liked both. He could tell stories of clandestine pregnancies, discreet bribery, secret backhanders, and hidden assets in the Cayman Islands. That to him was Absolutely Anything, and absolutely everything, a life's work of knowledge accumulated and stored away in his steel trap of a brain. People often said of Oliver that he would have been an absolute shark if he had ever considered going into business, and they were probably right, but as he pointed out if the subject was ever raised, it simply wasn't his bag at all.

'Well,' said Minna, who thought that he probably could tell her anything she needed to know, 'I shall remember that. It's always nice to know. So, you still haven't told me. What DOES Casey do?'

'My dear,' said Oliver, with a nicely judged little flourish of his cigarette. 'He's the Mister Fixit of the music world. Absolutely number one wheeler and dealer, that's all. He has a company called Catalyst, and that's exactly what he is, and everything besides. Agent, bagman, producer, talent scout, he does it all. He sets up deals, that's what he does, bringing people together, and he's getting to be the best at it, even I know that, and let's face it, darling, the music business is hardly *moi*. It's that sly Irish charm of his, people can't resist it, they find themselves saying yes when they mean to say no, and that's another rabbit in the hat, and no-one knows how he's done it.'

'Goodness,' said Minna, rather impressed. 'So that's what the three telephones are for. No wonder. And I just thought that he was showing off.'

Oliver laughed fondly at her. He really was too interested for words with this new liaison. He couldn't have guessed at anything more unlikely, not if he'd been given a padded cell and no calls for a week. Casey's taste in women usually ran to the kind of exotic creatures who looked as if they had been born in Studio 54, who went into forty-eight-hour shock if they broke a nail, who bought even their toothbrushes from Cartier. They were the kind of women who never read anything except for *Vogue* and the gossip columns, mostly to check what they had been doing lately, who thought nothing of flying to Rome for lunch, who could list the two hundred richest men in the world in their sleep. They were a breed apart, intimating by subtle dips of their eyelashes and kitten-like sighs that they were just tiny weak helpless things, when all the time they were perfectly capable of eating ten grown men for breakfast and still keeping their figures.

Oliver couldn't think of anything less like Minna, still a babe in arms by comparison, hardly aware of the little she knew. He rather thought that he approved of the change, although he wondered quite how it would develop. Even he, the Argus of the chattering classes, was a little at a loss to predict the outcome of this one. It really was too intriguing for words, and extremely well timed, with August being what it was. One never knew, Oliver thought, his febrile mind lurching from possibility to possibility, perhaps Casey would confound all the pundits and marry the girl. And if that happened, Oliver promised solemnly to himself, he was going to ask to be maid of honour.

Food seemed to be arriving now. That was the nice thing about this restaurant, the waiter always seemed to know what one wanted, hardly having to be asked.

'Lovely,' said Oliver appreciatively, tasting the Antinori. (He never drank any other Italian wine on the unimpeachable principle that the Marchese di Antinori was simply the most amusing man with a vineyard that he knew.)

'Well,' said Minna, raising her glass and giving him her best ironical look over it. 'Here's to London in August. A first.'

'You never know,' said Oliver extravagantly. 'Now that I have discovered you, it might become a habit.'

Minna laughed at him, old enough at least to know better than that.

'Flattering to think that I rate higher than a yacht in the Aegean,' she said. 'Really, I'm quite flushed with compliments.'

'To tell you the utter and absolute truth, darling,' said Oliver, confidential as a spy about to impart state secrets, 'if you had seen the assembled company, you wouldn't be all that tickled. The Gothenburgs and the Hampshires I love, but they're absolute maniacs for bridge, which I cannot take for a single second without going into a brown study, all that three no trumps and mine's a club and I don't know what else, it's almost as bad as golf. It's that English obsession with games, what Freud would say I DREAD to think.' Oliver looked round a little furtively as he said this, in case any of his game-playing acquaintances should be within earshot.

'And as for that old Darnley,' he continued, barely drawing breath, 'if he tells me ONE more time about the head shrinker he went to in New York who advised him to go and beat pliant youths in the seamier downtown bars, I think I shall scream. I mean to say, darling, downtown bars can be utter heaven, no-one knows that better than I, I love the Village with a passion, anyone will tell you, and I, of all people, have nothing what-soever against pliant youths, I absolutely dream of them, and I suppose all that tying up CAN be rather amusing, although I've never quite seen it myself, but then I expect I'm just an old-fashioned boy, but one doesn't really want to HEAR, does one? I mean, REALLY. I look at Darnley, with his frightful grizzled grey hair, and that ghastly mistake of a facelift that he thinks no-one has noticed, and I think of that poor pale wife with all those plain daughters, sitting at home on their own, not a man in sight, desperately selling Monets to make ends meet, and I want to weep, really I do. And instead of all that, I've got lovely you, you do see.'

'I quite see,' said Minna staunchly. She had never met any pederasts, although she had always thought that they sounded rather amusing, what with all that rushing off to Morocco every five minutes and pretending it was for the sun.

'So,' said Oliver, a living example of lateral think-ing, 'where is that enchanting playwright of yours?'

'Not really MINE,' said Minna, pleased that he should have noticed. 'But definitely enchanting.'

'Of course he's yours,' said Oliver patiently,

remembering her youth and more than happy to make allowances for it. 'Quite your discovery, you should be proud. Do tell where you found him, I absolutely long to know.' Oliver had a very taking vision of Minna stumbling over Jay, deep in study, in the reading room of the British Museum, or tucked into a secret corner of the London Library.

'In a café,' said Minna, shattering his illusions. 'In Soho. We shared a table, and he offered me a cigarette, you know how these things happen.'

Oliver, who had never shared a cigarette with anyone in his life, didn't know at all. But then that was what he loved about Minna, her Bohemian approach to life. Imagine letting oneself be picked up in a café, during daylight hours. He really didn't know that that kind of thing went on any more, he thought it had gone out in the Fifties, along with Tommy Steele and the skiffle craze.

'Well,' he said, 'clever, clever you, is all I can say. You must have a nose for talent. I hear he's terribly good.'

There was a slightly regretful note in Oliver's voice when he said this. It was one thing having a face as pretty as Jay's, but being good as well was an irresistible cocktail, and if there was one thing Oliver did know, it was when something was Out of Bounds. There were times when he really did wish he had been born a girl.

'Is he?' said Minna. 'I like to think so, but he won't let me see any of his work. I mean, of course I understand, but I do rather long to know.'

'But I DO know,' said Oliver joyfully. 'Alabama tells me that her agent is quite beside himself with excitement. Another Joe Orton, he says. A real find. Imagine, your Jay.'

'Oh,' said Minna, less pleased. She wasn't sure that she liked getting such news second hand, especially when it was she who had set the wheels in motion. Jay could have called her himself, she thought crossly, disregarding the fact that he couldn't possibly have known Casey's number. And Oliver knowing, of all people, when he had only met Jay once. It was too irritating. But then, she hadn't quite realized the extent to which Oliver had mastered the fine art of Knowing Things First. How could she know that he had been perfecting the age-old practice of keeping his ear to the ground since he left the perambulator, only to inform his mother that Nanny had been at the gin again. His sacred two hours of telephoning from his bed each morning were never wasted on trivia, but devoted to the indispensable pursuit of keeping himself in the know.

He had found Alabama in a rare state of excitement that particular morning, and had been surprised. Usually, she spent the first few weeks after one of her plays opened in a vile mood, taciturn and uncommunicative, uncomfortable that control of her work was finally out of her hands, her mind restless in search of a new idea, unsure even that one would come. Oliver, of course, suffered no such doubts, convinced as he was of the enduring genius of his cousin, so it was only he who dared approach her at these times, undaunted by the terse 'What?' with which she answered calls. Oliver was made of stuff far too stern to be put off by such treatment, and amused himself by lecturing her gently on the advantages of developing social graces at a late age.

'You may be nearly thirty, darling,' he would trill happily, 'and I won't say HOW nearly, to save your blushes, but it's never too late to learn to say "Hello, how do you do?" Why don't we start now, count to two, repeat after me . . . '

This morning, Oliver had been quite taken aback to find Alabama fresh as a breath of springtime and twice as spry, positively welcoming his call.

'I AM glad you rang,' she had said, even sounding as if she meant it. It was so uncharacteristic that Oliver had a moment of panic, and had to check his address book to make sure that he had dialled the right number and wasn't hallucinating. 'You'll never guess what has happened.'

'Milo has asked you to marry him?' said Oliver, stunned into foolishness.

'Don't be silly,' said Alabama, sounding more like herself, 'You know perfectly well that Milo's publicity agent says it would ruin his image, and then what would we live on?'

'Oh, well, darling,' said Oliver philosophically, 'you know, we'd all rally round. It would be worth every penny to see you in white, and as for Milo, I'd pay any money to see him tripping down the aisle all decked out in his morning coat, he's got just the right shoulders for it.'

'Oh, for God's sake, Oliver,' said Alabama impatiently. 'Enough is enough.'

Oliver had been badgering Alabama and Milo about getting married for the last year, ever since they had started living together. 'Living in sin is so Seventies,' he always insisted. 'Marriage is absolutely back In, I promise you, it's the new puritanism. Everyone's doing it, really the smartest people. I could always give you away, if you're worried about that.'

This morning however, his mind was running on other matters, and he could tell that Alabama was in no mood to be pressed. She would come round to the idea in time, it was just a question of planting the seed and letting it grow.

'So,' he said, 'why is it that you're so pleased I've rung? Not that I'm not flattered, but I can't help suspecting an ulterior motive.'

'Cynicism ill becomes you, Oliver,' said Alabama sternly, 'but of course you're right. I've made a discovery.'

'Another one?' said Oliver in alarm. The last time Alabama had made a discovery was when she had found an extremely nasty young actor in a play in Croydon, and had not only decided that he was London's answer to Marlon Brando, but that he was her answer to Prince Charming. The affair had been painful but thankfully short-lived, since as soon as Alabama had launched her protégé on his path to stardom he had trotted off into the accommodating arms of an older woman, which, as Oliver always said, had been a great stroke of luck, because it left the field clear for Milo to step in and comfort Alabama in her distress.

But still, however happily the whole business had turned out, Oliver did not want to go through all that again.

'Nothing like that,' said Alabama soothingly. 'Don't worry yourself. It's that nice young playwright friend of Minna's.'

'Really, Alabama,' said Oliver in reproof. ' "That nice young playwright friend", you sound like someone's maiden aunt. You may be approaching your prime, but you don't have to come on all Lady Bracknell with me. It doesn't suit you at all.'

'Stuff,' said Alabama, taking no notice as usual. 'Anyway, do sharpen your wits for two minutes and concentrate. Minna introduced me to him at lunch the other day, and he started telling me all about his work . . . '

'And we all know how much you hate that,' said Oliver, not to be denied.

'Well, yes,' Alabama admitted, 'Usually. But he was really rather appealing, this boy, and not a bore at all, so I was interested, and before I knew what I was doing I'd told him I'd show his stuff to Morty.' Morty was Alabama's agent, who managed to drink two bottles of hock a day and still be the best in the business.

'And you NEVER do that,' said Oliver, astounded.

'I never do that,' Alabama agreed.

'So, so,' said Oliver. He was really interested now. 'What did he say?'

'He loves it,' said Alabama. 'But loves it.'

'Don't TELL me,' said Oliver, riveted. 'Morty? The man who always says that if Shakespeare was still alive he wouldn't have him on his books? The man who insists that Ibsen was over-rated? The most fiercely critical man in London? It cannot be true.'

'We're meeting on Wednesday,' said Alabama. 'What do you think? Clever of that lodger to have such a nose for talent. I know you're thick as thieves with her these days, why don't you ask her if she knows any other struggling young artists?'

'Well,' said Oliver in awe. 'I just will.'

'So you see,' he said now to Minna, 'it's the big time for that one and no mistake. I mean to say, darling, once Morty has got hold of someone it's the West End and Broadway and Robert de Niro to supper and I don't know what else.'

'That's wonderful,' said Minna. 'I am pleased.'

219

Oliver, whose ear for nuance was as sharply honed as a prospector's nose for gold, gave her a sympathetic smile.

'Don't fret, my sweet,' he said, patting her hand in a comfortable manner. 'He won't go forgetting that it's all due to you. He's a good boy, that one, success won't go to his head. But there really is nothing more you can do for him now, much better to leave him in Alabama's hands, and then you can go to his first night and help him pick up the bouquets. You'll like that.'

'Yes,' said Minna, cheering up. 'I will. And he will be awfully good at being famous, don't you agree?'

'Darling,' said Oliver with feeling, 'the public are simply going to EAT him up, that's all. So grave and so shy, and still not looking a day over twelve and a half, they won't know what to do. He could have been invented for fame. And just think how impressed everyone will be when he has a play running to hysterical reviews and STILL remains that nice quiet boy who came out of the provinces. It couldn't be more perfect. I can hardly wait.'

'And just think,' said Minna, her equilibrium quite restored, 'people say nothing happens in August.'

Minna went back to Casey's house in a thoughtful mood. The summer, which had started off so quietly, suddenly seemed to be teeming with unexpected developments. Who could have imagined that the whim which had led her to knock on Eddy's door that day back in June would have led to all this? She was still in a state of shock from the revelation of Lou Lou's secret career (and vaguely ashamed of having assumed the worst), and now there was this interesting new development of Jay's discovery.

She wondered if young playwrights were found so easily. She rather thought not, on balance. It wasn't a thing she knew a great deal about, but she suspected that it usually took years of struggle, working in obscurity, putting on plays in church halls and primary schools and the outer reaches of the fringe, waiting endlessly for the great break that would propel them towards centre stage. After all, how many playwrights could one think of who were under forty? And now, here was Jay, hardly dry behind the ears, only just come to London, and he was being taken up by the most important man in the business.

He was the exception to the rule, the law that broke the average, how the press were going to love it. He would be dubbed Boy Wonder, and Young Prodigy, and everyone would ask him how he did it. And he was the boy who had offered Minna a cigarette in a café because all the other tables were full, she who had only been in Soho that morning because her house had been invaded by Americans. All coincidence and luck and fate from the start, and here was the world still wagging as if nothing strange had happened.

Walking back through the white Chelsea afternoon, Minna watched the scant flotsam of Londoners left behind by the departing tide of holiday-makers going about their business, and wondered if they too had plays or novels or collections of poems tucked away in their bottom drawer, waiting to be discovered. She wondered how many of them struggled away in secret hours of the night, cursing an ungrateful world which remained indifferent to their outpourings. She wondered how many of them had manuscripts sitting unread at the bottom of a pile on an editor's desk, how many of them desperately rifled through the post each morning searching for the letter that would begin with the magic words, 'Dear Mr Brown, We very much enjoyed your book . . . ' and how many of them instead had to make do with, 'Unfortunately, it is not quite what we are looking for at the moment . . . '

So now Jay was discovered, and judging by Roger Middlemarch's sudden interest in Lou Lou, she would be next, and that just left Eddy. But if Casey was such a big shot, as Oliver insisted, then he could do some of those famous deals of his, and then Eddy could start playing in some proper places instead of those murky little clubs where no-one saw him. Minna supposed she ought to take Casey to hear Eddy play one night. He must be doing something soon, he usually had more than one engagement a month. She should really find out.

She felt rather light-headed after the wine at lunch, and irresponsible from the glass of Strega that Oliver had insisted she had.

'My dear,' he had said, ordering up a glass of the most extraordinary looking yellow liqueur, 'it means witch in Italian, you must have some, you'll die.'

And he had been quite right, it was very delicious, so delicious that Minna had had a rush of blood to the head and asked for a second and now she was weaving about the streets with all her thoughts chasing each other in random directions, and far too restless to go back to Casey's and lie in the sun.

A taxi wandered past, looking for a fare, and slowed down to admire Minna in her Jean Shrimpton shift. Minna took this as a sign, although she wasn't quite sure of what, and hailed it. The driver drew up, smiling at his luck.

'Soho, please,' said Minna politely, giving Eddy's address.

She would go and see Eddy, and find out when his next date was, and then she could take Casey, and Eddy would be discovered too, and then August really would be full to capacity, and even Oliver wouldn't be able to bitch about how dull the summer in London was. It was all going to be perfectly splendid, and when they were all really famous and wrote their autobiographies they would dedicate them to her, because she was the one who had made it all happen. With a happy little sigh of omnipotence, Minna settled back in her seat to enjoy the ride. The cabby, admiring her in the driving mirror, gave an equally contented sigh, and forgot to curse the traffic.

'And there I was,' he said to himself, 'thinking the Sixties were over.'

13

'Hello,' said Eddy, opening the door. 'And there I was, not expecting callers.'

'It's tea time,' said Minna vaguely. She held up a brown paper bag by way of explanation. 'I've brought you a bun or something, I forget.'

'You'd better come in,' said Eddy, unimpressed. 'I haven't got any Earl Grey, or did you bring that with you too?'

'There's no need to be pompous,' said Minna, who on the strength of two glasses of Strega felt more than equipped to deal with Eddy in one of his moods. She had a very effective strategy for his kind of behaviour: she simply ignored it and carried on as if he was being charm itself. 'It really doesn't become you at all. Not the sort of thing that makes an aspiring musician look as if he has his finger on the pulse. You should brush up on your street talk, really you should.'

'Thank you for the hint,' said Eddy, who was starting to verge on frostiness. 'I shall remember.'

Upstairs, there were signs of disrepair. Beer bottles stood about at drunken angles, interspersed with empty pizza cartons and half-finished Chinese take-aways. A bottle of Tequila stood sentinel over Minna's revolutionary tracts, and in the kitchen the sink was piled with washing-up. Irene was obviously working to rule.

'Have you had the decorators in?' said Minna. 'Or is that enchanting daily woman of yours playing up?'

'She got a limited run in Weston-super-Mare,' said Eddy, his face as deadpan as if he were discussing a contract with the RSC.

'Clever, clever her,' said Minna. 'What is she playing? The back end of the pantomime horse? The widow Twankey? The beanstalk in Jack?' She had to admit, being a mistress did bring out the irreverent in her. She thought she rather liked it. No good being a ray of sunshine all your life.

'No,' said Eddy, with dignity. 'I believe it's the maid in a Ray Cooney farce.'

He tried terribly hard not to laugh. Minna really did think it was a heroic effort, but his sense of the ridiculous got the better of his bad temper, and suddenly they were both laughing fit to bust, and it was going to be all right. Thank God for Irene and her choice in plays, Minna thought to herself as she settled herself on the balcony and allowed Eddy to bring her some beer.

'That IS better,' she said, smiling at him in utter forgiveness against all the odds. 'You really are the most terrible bore when you're in a temper. Remind yourself to do it less often.'

'I wasn't in a temper at all,' said Eddy, lying through his teeth without a trace of shame. 'I was nursing a perfectly honourable anger. Perfectly honourable, utterly justified, quite called for.'

'Oh, really,' said Minna in exasperation. 'I'm not at all sure that I care for the New Pomposity. It's worse than the New Greenness, or whatever it's called when no-one is allowed to open their refrigerators for fear of killing off the rainforests. I mean it's all very well, but people have to eat.'

'Or drink,' said Eddy, looking rather pointedly at her.

'Oh, do give me a break,' said Minna. 'Isn't a girl allowed to go to hell her own way any more?'

'Some go quicker than others,' said Eddy, no longer talking about drinking at lunchtime.

'I see,' said Minna, who did think that she was being remarkably perceptive, considering the length of her lunch. 'So we're back to the slippery slope now, are we?'

'I never said anything about the slippery slope,' said Eddy, looking into the middle distance and trying to conjure up an aura of not caring less.

'No,' agreed Minna affably. 'I did. Which was very generous of me under the circumstances, considering that it saved you giving me a lecture. And with you being so Victorian, and all.'

'I was NOT being Victorian,' said Eddy crossly. He didn't like this new idea of hers at all, it conjured up terrible images of Gladstone cutting down trees in that Freudian way he had and asking ladies of the street home for tea with his wife. 'I was trying to do the crossword, that's all.'

'Crossword, my eye,' said Minna. 'I don't know why you took quite such exception to my behaviour. I never promised you a rose garden, and vows of chastity went out with the last century.'

'Chastity is making a comeback,' said Eddy blandly. 'Or hadn't you noticed? It's the New Morality.'

'Temptation is easy to resist if there's nothing to

tempt,' said Minna, equally bland, as if she were talking about the weather or the state of the pound. 'There's nothing wrong with a little respectable bad behaviour from time to time, among friends.'

'Oh, really,' said Eddy impatiently. 'And you wonder why I wasn't turning cartwheels, when you run straight into the clutches of the most notorious rake in London, hardly having been introduced.'

Oliver had really done his work well, Minna thought, laughing at Eddy's cross face. She supposed she could hardly blame him, what with it being the silly season and everyone away. He must have seized on her indiscretion as a godsend, a lone piece of intrigue in the desert of the summer recess. But even so, she did rather wonder why he had taken it upon himself to tell Eddy every last detail. He may be her landlord, but that didn't give him feudal rights. Am I my lodger's keeper, she thought to herself, defiantly epigrammatic in the face of all the odds.

'You're starting to nanny me again,' she said. 'And you did promise that you weren't going to do that any more, now I'm over the age of consent.'

'Age has no regard for the season,' said Eddy, drinking his beer and affecting a sudden overpowering interest in his shoe-laces.

'So you say,' said Minna inexorably. 'But I really am perfectly capable of looking after myself, although I expect it is very sweet of you to mind.'

'You're right,' said Eddy unexpectedly. 'It's one of those irritating cosmic jokes. The rest of us have to struggle, but you can trip into any old cesspool you like and still come up smelling of roses.'

'It's not that bad,' said Minna, who secretly agreed.

'It is,' said Eddy. 'Worse. You make a cat look hard done by, the amount of lives you've got.'

'Flattery,' said Minna darkly, 'is not you at all. Anyway, that's enough about me.'

She felt they were heading for treacherous waters, that any moment Casey's name just might come up, and then they would be stuck with it, and she would have to undergo ruthless questioning, and she really didn't feel up to it, not after lunch. Besides, she didn't feel that it was the kind of ménage of which Eddy would approve, not that that was any surprise. Eddy had never approved of anything she did, not since she was fifteen and running around town with eight boys at once, and half a dozen spare in reserve. Nothing had really changed, because here he was still not approving, looking askance at her fleeting dresses and her nocturnal habits and her choice of gentleman friend.

It really was rather unfair of him, when he prided himself in being utterly unjudgemental where everyone else was concerned, and always insisted that what people did was their own business. Except when it came to her, and then the judge and the jury were out in full force and never with a favourable verdict. She supposed that you couldn't please all of the people all of the time, but really. It wasn't as if she sniffed great amounts of cocaine, or allowed herself to be courted by gun runners or drug barons, or found herself in a different bed every night. Compared to most girls, she considered herself a perfect soul of propriety. She didn't make exhibitions of herself or fall down drunk in public or take men's ties off with her teeth, and she knew plenty of girls who did.

But none of that seemed to cut much ice with

Eddy, who inclined to take that same line of all those disapproving aunts and interfering cousins who had always said that she would come to a bad end. Perhaps they were all right, and she would come to a bad end, but it seemed an awful long way off still, and in the meantime she was determined to have a little fun. A girl needed some fun in her life, while she was young, because otherwise it was suddenly middle age and the change of life and all those terrible regrets for a lost youth that never was, and then where would she be?

'Tell me about you,' she said, with her best charm school smile, the kind they don't teach any more. 'How's the band?'

'Fine,' said Eddy. 'Working hard, you know. We're playing a gig night after next, at Le Cave.'

'Oh, yes,' said Minna. She knew Le Cave of old, not because she was a particularly devoted jazz aficionado, but because it was one of those dark discreet places down by the river where they let you get a drink at three in the morning, and when you're just out of school and taking the town by storm those were important places to know about. 'I haven't been there for years, is it still just the same? What time?'

Eddy looked at her suspiciously. He wasn't sure he liked this sudden show of interest in his work, so innocent and demure. He wasn't sure he liked this sudden tea-time visit for that matter, after more than a week, just to sit and talk about nothing in particular. She hadn't come to confide in him, or ask his advice, or weep on his shoulder. She had just come to sit on his balcony and drink his beer and tell him not to be so Victorian, and it was a long way from Chelsea just for that.

'Why?' he said, unwilling and not altogether gracious. 'Ten o'clock.'

'I might just come and see you, that's all,' said Minna, looking like all the cherubim and seraphim rolled into one. 'Don't look at me with that jaundiced air just because I'm showing some interest in your work. Give a girl an even break, why don't you?'

Eddy smiled reluctantly. That was another thing that annoyed him about Minna. However hard he tried, he could never stay cross with her for long. 'Oh all right,' he said, still a little grudging. 'Although I don't know how exciting it will be.'

'It will be fine,' said Minna. 'You're very good, you should be proud of yourself.'

'That's as may be,' said Eddy, self-deprecating to the last, 'but I still haven't made it to Ronnie Scott's, not after all these years.'

'It's not your fault,' said Minna, who privately thought that it was high time that Eddy faced facts and cut his losses and ditched the band and realized his full potential. He really did blow the sax well enough to break your heart, but the rest of them weren't in his league. She wouldn't employ them if she were Ronnie Scott, but then what did she know?

'Oh, well,' said Eddy, remembering to be philo-sophical, just like all struggling artists had to, 'it's a dirty job . . .'

'But someone has to do it.'

'Casey,' said Minna that evening, 'how would you like to go to a jazz club tomorrow night?' She batted her eyelashes at him a little, just to see how far she could bowl him over.

'Sure,' said Casey, who didn't mind being taken

for a soft touch. 'Why not? Anything you want.'

It was late, and they were in a bar drinking margaritas, and Minna was still carrying the torch for the Sixties in her white shift, and he would agree to anything she said. A girl who looked like that and drank margaritas without a second thought should never be contradicted. She should have anything she wanted, anything at all.

'It's a friend of mine playing,' said Minna casually. She wasn't going to give Casey any build-up, tell Casey that he was the best thing to blow a saxophone since Charlie Parker was a boy, and then have to worry about the performance living up to her description. She would just see what Casey thought. He could make up his own mind. And if he was such a big shot as Oliver said, then he must be capable of telling whether someone had what it took, in under five minutes. That was the whole point about spotting talent after all, knowing instantly, just like falling in love.

Minna drank back her margarita rather quickly and blinked her eyes at Casey so he would get her another one.

'Can't I buy you two?' he said. 'Let me get you two.'

'One is plenty,' said Minna, 'for the time being. One is enough for any girl, at this time of night. Don't let's get carried away, the barman might think that you're trying to get me drunk.' The barman was a flashing-eyed Cuban straight out of the underworld. Everyone always muttered about nefarious activities and mob connections and mysterious trips back to his native land, but all Minna knew was that he shook a mean margarita. He and Casey went way back.

'Don't worry about that,' said Casey. 'He knows me far too well for that. He *knows* I'm trying to get you drunk.'

'It's the simple Irish in you,' said Minna generously. 'Trying on such an obvious trick at your age, when you should know better.'

'I know,' said Casey happily. 'Some people never learn.'

Minna watched him wander off to the bar, and wondered if all big shots were like this. She rather thought not, but then she supposed that was what she liked about Casey. You couldn't put him down to a type. And he did know how to show a girl a good time. Perhaps she was treading dangerous waters, and perhaps he was the wickedest man in London, but she hadn't seen any sign of it yet, and she couldn't imagine anyone being less of a cad. But she wasn't quite so young as to think that you could really change people, and reputations don't come cheap, they have to be won, so perhaps the role of gallant was a very good disguise, and perhaps he might drop her just as suddenly as he had picked her up, but until then she was having fun, and whatever Eddy said, there was no harm in that.

'What are you looking so thoughtful about?' said Casey. 'Didn't anyone tell you that it makes me nervous when my women start thinking on me?'

'Hark at you, Casanova,' said Minna, giving him her most cynical look from under her cowlick. 'My women indeed, and you with a positive seraglio at your disposal, I'm surprised you have time to fit me in.'

'Ways and means,' said Casey, looking rakish. 'And of course, so worth the effort.'

'The charm of you,' said Minna, drinking her

margarita carefully through the salt. 'Don't let me put you out. And don't give me that look.' Casey had a soulful sort of little-boy-lost way with his eyes that he tried every so often. Usually it worked like a charm, making even the most worldly women want to take him home and mother him, but it seemed to leave Minna quite unmoved. 'It don't cut no dice with me.'

'It's ice, not dice,' said Casey, reverting to his normal look, which was quite fatal enough anyway, if only he had known it, being a cross between Errol Flynn on a bad day and Jack Nicholson on a good one.

'Ice, dice, where's the difference?' said Minna. 'Whatever it is, it's not being cut by that Little Lord Fauntleroy number. Besides, it dates you terribly, far too Seventies, we've seen it all before. You really should develop a new repertoire for the Nineties.'

'It won't be any good,' said Casey, gazing mournfully into his glass. 'I'm just an old-fashioned boy at heart.'

'Oh, really,' said Minna, laughing. How could this be the wickedest man in London? He was a perfect joke. 'I think you ought to switch to Jack Daniels. Tequila doesn't have a good effect on you at all.'

'Can't drink it,' said Casey, more mournful still. 'Too sour. It's always been the bane of my life. All I ever wanted to do was grow up and be Keith Richards and drink a bottle of Jack Daniels a day, but it just makes me sick to my stomach.'

'Well,' said Minna, quite without sympathy, 'I'm surprised you didn't just go and put your head in a paper bag and be done with it. Do you want to tell me next about all those school reports which said this boy will never amount to anything? Or shall we save that for pillow talk?'

'There really is no hope for me at all,' said Casey glumly. 'And I do think it's unfair on a boy to read his old reports behind his back. Stealing a march like that without so much as a word of warning.'

'And you at such a disadvantage?' said Minna sunnily. 'I bleed for you, really I do.'

'Oh, you,' said Casey. 'Just drink your drink and give a fellow a break.'

'I do love it,' said Minna, 'when you beg for mercy.'

Oliver rang Minna the next morning at eleven, having decided that she was simply crying out to be included in his daily round of calls. Besides, what with it being August and everyone going away, he was rather shorter than usual of people to call.

'How are you today?' he said, his cosmopolitan voice carrying strongly down the line. 'What are you doing? Tell me everything.'

'I'm having my coffee in bed,' said Minna weakly, 'and wondering if I shall ever feel strong enough to move ever again. Casey and I ran into a bottle of tequila last night, and I don't think that there are expected to be any survivors.'

'What heaven,' said Oliver in delight. One of the things he regretted most about the end of the decade was this frightful abstemiousness that everyone seemed to be embracing with such misplaced enthusiasm. Even some of the hardened spirits, the ones he had believed quite immune to any kind of propaganda, had started worrying about their cholesterol levels and their livers and their colons and all those other perfectly unspeakable parts of the anatomy that were supposedly under threat from all the things that made life worth living. It was all very well, this dashing off to aerobics classes and health spas and nutritionists and being told not to eat anything except for bean sprouts and the occasional slice of organic toast for a real treat, and it probably would keep one alive for an extra ten years, but as Oliver always said, who would want to live to ninety on such a soulless regime? He couldn't understand a word of it. He drank a bottle of Malvern water a day, had a facial once a month, and employed a perfectly charming Thai gentleman to come in every week and give him a massage, and as far as he was concerned that was quite enough to keep the body beautiful for as long as anyone needed it.

'Well,' said Minna doubtfully, 'it was rather heaven at the time, but I'm not so sure this morning. I'm rather wondering if it was worth it, I've got such a pain.'

'Where?' said Oliver with interest. 'Head?'

'All over,' said Minna. 'I really daren't move, for fear of setting off a terrifying chorus of disapproval in every muscle.'

'You poor darling,' said Oliver. He did rather love a woman who was so shamelessly and completely incapacitated by a hangover. Most would take an Alka-Seltzer and a quart of orange juice and carry on as if nothing had happened, but he was glad to see that Minna had absolutely no qualms about making a drama out of a crisis. 'You should try some *fernet branca*, it really does work.'

'Perhaps I should ask Casey to get me some,' said Minna.

'And how is the delicious Casey?' said Oliver, moving on to the main attraction.

'Oh, you know. Delicious. Very silly for a big shot.'

Oliver laughed in delight. Of all the things that amused him about this liaison, the fact that Minna remained so completely unimpressed by Casey was affording him the most entertainment. There was none of the desperate longing in her voice that Oliver was used to hearing from Casey's women. How well he remembered the endless telephone calls he used to get from the line of foreign beauties – Brazilians, Italians, French, Spanish, even a hauntingly lovely Czech, the kind of women used to keeping ambassadors and rock stars and movie moguls in thrall, all brought low by Casey.

They would ring Oliver at four in the morning and weep down the telephone and beg him to tell them the secret of keeping Casey's interest. Oliver could only give them cold comfort, because he knew there was no secret. Casey was a rover and he was easily bored, and for those kind of men one woman was never enough.

Casey himself remained outwardly baffled by the havoc he caused. 'I never promise them anything,' he said to Oliver. 'I don't make vows of eternal love or fidelity, I don't give them rings of engagement. I can't think what all the fuss is about.' Privately, Oliver thought that Casey knew a great deal more than he was telling, but he didn't press him. He provided such an interest in life that Oliver couldn't possibly wish him any different, and after all, these worldly beauties had broken enough hearts and bank accounts in their time to be able to take a little of their own medicine.

But they never gave in without a fight. There were always endless dramas, Oliver remembered fondly.

There was the Italian contessa who had sent her husband round to threaten Casey with a gun, and the Argentinian beef heiress who had arrived outside Casey's house in a floor-length sable which she shed to reveal nothing underneath, and refused to move until Casey came out and took her back, until finally the police arrested her for disturbing the peace. There was the Austrian princess who had thrown his bust of Voltaire clean through the window, and the young Spanish widow who had lost her husband in a bullfighting accident, who had cut the arms off all Casey's suits with her nail scissors. They had all gone down fighting, Oliver had to give them that.

And now there was Minna, who didn't seem to mind whether Casey was going to leave or going to stay, who sounded anything but desperate, and who was more interested in her hangover than the whereabouts of her admirer. It was all too strange and interesting and unexpected for words, and Oliver really couldn't have asked for anything more to amuse him during the normally dead month of August.

'Well, what did you expect?' he said. 'Robert Maxwell?'

'No,' said Minna, 'But I do think a little more *gravitas* might be rather more becoming for such a young Turk. Half the time he doesn't make any sense at all. Not that I mind.'

Oliver laughed with pleasure. Perhaps Casey could confound all the pundits by falling in love with the girl. Then he shook his head at his own folly. His brain must be going soft in the heat. Casey wouldn't know how.

'So,' he said, getting to the point at last. 'I want to know what you two have planned for this weekend.'

'Don't be silly, Oliver,' said Minna, in her most grown-up voice. 'We don't plan the next five minutes, let alone the weekend. It's all hand to mouth with us.'

'Well,' said Oliver, 'I did rather suspect that might be the case, but I thought I'd be polite and give you the benefit of the doubt.'

'Charmed I'm sure,' said Minna in cockney, which just showed what a change the summer was making in her. She never did accents. 'But you don't have to stand on ceremony with me.'

'So, if you are free,' said Oliver, continuing, 'I've had the most extraordinary idea. I thought we might go into the country.'

'Goodness,' said Minna. 'How alarming. I hadn't got you pegged for a huntin', shootin', fishin' kind of a boy. Have you had a rush of blood to the head with the Glorious Twelfth approaching?'

'It must be the heat,' said Oliver, pleased with the utter controversy of his decision. After all, he hadn't been to the country since he left prep school, not to speak of. 'But I have these friends that I'd quite forgotten about, and they have the most enchanting house in Norfolk, at least I hear it's enchanting, Caroline you know, the sort of place where George the Fourth stopped on a journey north, you can imagine the kind of thing. And there's a swimming pool and rose gardens and we can just lie about and pretend that we're in Italy, don't you think?'

'Sounds heaven,' said Minna, who liked the country. She could admire the roses and wander about the pool in an old-fashioned bathing suit and let Casey admire her legs, which wouldn't do him any harm.

238

'So shall I put you both down as definite?' said Oliver.

'Yes, please,' said Minna. 'Do you expect Casey likes country weekends?'

'Can't think,' said Oliver. 'I don't see him in plus-fours and croquet mallets, that's for certain.'

Minna laughed at the thought. 'Never mind,' she said. 'He's in a very pliant mood at the moment. I shall just tell him that it's all arranged. It's a wonderful idea, you are clever.'

'I know,' said Oliver modestly. 'I'm one of the unsung geniuses of the twentieth century, but what can you do? I'm dashing now, darling, I'll call you first thing tomorrow to confirm.'

'Fine,' said Minna, and disconnected. She lay back on her bed and wondered if her hangover might recede a little if she kept very still for an hour. On balance, she thought not. She supposed she would just have to adjust herself to living with pain. It wasn't always easy, being her.

14

'So where is this place?' said Casey that evening. 'This jazz club.'

'Le Cave,' said Minna. 'It means cellar in French. It's in a cellar, you see. Do you know it?'

'Of course,' said Casey, on his dignity. 'What do you take me for?'

'A ride, most of the time,' said Minna, with more accuracy than she knew. She lit a cigarette and blew out the smoke on a sigh of pleasure.

They were drinking in the bar of Blakes, because they had felt like a change from Soho all of a sudden, or rather Minna had, and in the mood Casey was in at the moment, her wish was his command. She liked this bar because it was underground, with no windows, and it was sleek and black and shiny, and it always felt like three in the morning there, whatever the hour. It was one of those dark sleek sexy bars, the kind they don't make any more, and the barman was the handsomest Scot you ever saw, and the clientele always looked promising somehow, as if they were famous, even when they weren't. Tonight it was quite empty apart from an itinerant brewing heir and his girl, drinking bourbon sours, straight up, and three rather drunk Americans who had just flown in from Los Angeles, and were clearly suffering from jet lag. They were talking happily at cross purposes.

'Did you ever see *The Cook, The Thief*?' said the first American.

'Did you know I used to live here?' said the second American.

'In London?' asked the third.

'No, here. In this bar.'

'You've got to say it. I mean Peter Greenaway gives obfuscation a bad name.'

'Great piece of real estate.'

'Grace Jones used to live here too.'

'I didn't get any of *The Draughtsman's Contract*, and that was supposed to be his easiest picture.'

'In London?'

'No, in this bar.'

'How long ago was this?'

'Oh, we lived here for years, me and Grace. She lived on the piano.'

'Visually stunning of course. But obscure, and how.'

'Eartha Kitt stayed a while too.'

'Then what happened?'

'I moved to Minneapolis.'

Minna and Casey decided that it was too hot for dinner, so they stayed in the bar drinking champagne instead, because Minna had declared that any more spirits might kill her off altogether at this stage, and because she had great faith in the healing powers of Dom Perignon. So they sat quite happily watching the Americans getting drunker and more confused, and pretending not to notice the brewing heir shamelessly making up to his girl, who sat very upright on her bar stool in an effort to maintain her composure.

'I know that girl's face,' said Minna idly. 'Didn't

241

she just have a book published. I think I've read about her.'

'Ask Oliver,' said Casey, 'He's bound to know.'

'Of course he is,' said Minna. 'He knows everything. I can't think how the Foreign Office missed him when they were signing people up. He would be a perfect godsend to the intelligence service.'

Later, they took a cab and went down to the river to Le Cave, which was hot and dark and stuffy and clouded with cigarette smoke and everything a jazz club should be. Minna rather imagined that it must have been like this on those hot summer nights in Kansas City in the Forties, when the great musicians were young, still playing unrecognized in steamy little bars just like this one. But for all that, for all its echoes of nostalgia and romance, it was just a seedy basement at heart, and half the people there only came because they could drink after hours. It wasn't the kind of place you would want to play your whole life, and it was an awful long way from the big time. Minna really thought that it was high time Eddy moved on. Ten years was a long time with nothing to show but engagements in dives like this. She was a great believer in celebrity, and she thought that Eddy was probably ready for a little fame, and he certainly wasn't going to get it in places like this.

Casey wandered off to the bar in that way he had, and came back with four bottles of Rolling Rock.

'No glasses, I do call that chic,' said Minna, noticing the waitresses noticing Casey, a momentary flash of interest lighting up their sullen faces. 'We are having a butch day.'

'Can't use a glass if you're as rough and tough as me,' said Casey. 'Think of my reputation.'

'I do,' said Minna truthfully. 'I was discussing it only today.'

'Oh?' Casey cocked one of his eyebrows at her, a trick he had perfected long ago, in his salad days when he first started chasing women. He rather thought it gave him a rakish air, a touch of irresponsibility. Whatever it was it had served him well over the years. Every one a coconut. 'And?'

'And nothing,' said Minna. 'I think it's all humbug, but then I may be wrong. I suppose I have to bow to Oliver's superior knowledge.'

'Oh dear,' said Casey, thinking how much Oliver knew and wondering quite how much he had told. It wasn't exactly that Casey didn't want Minna to know about his past, it was hardly any great secret, not after Oliver had finished with it, but there are some things a boy would prefer a girl not to know about him. 'Are my boats all burnt?'

'Not at all,' said Minna. 'Now I know that you are appalling to women and have left a trail of broken hearts from Mayfair to Montenegro or I don't know what, I am in a position of strength. Forewarned is forearmed and all that. I shall be calling in the troops at any moment.'

'Trench warfare,' said Casey, 'at its peak. I'm quaking in my boots. It is unfair of Oliver. He never tells me about all the hearts you've broken.'

'But all the best women work in mysterious ways,' said Minna, drinking her beer out of the bottle in the most distressingly unfeminine way. She thought with pleasure of the mortification of the maiden aunts and interfering uncles if they could see her now, drinking lager in a seedy basement with one of Europe's most notorious seducers. How they would be shocked to their steely backbones. How they would shake their heads and mutter under their breath and say how they had predicted it would happen. Oh, she was heading for the worst of ends, there was no question of that. Playing with fire and bound to get her fingers burnt, what could be done with such a girl? There was no hope for her, no hope at all. 'You should know that, with all your experience.'

'I do think,' said Casey with dignity, 'that you might be a little more impressed. Couldn't you look just a fraction more intrigued, or shocked, or something?' Casey knew all about his reputation, mostly because Oliver was at pains to tell him about it, lest he forget, and sometimes it puzzled him, because he had done so little to foster it. After all, plenty of men had strings of girls, many more than his baker's dozen, and treated them far more callously than he did. So why did they get away with it, while he was landed with this absurd epithet of a latter-day Byron? He had said this to Oliver once, who as usual had all the answers. 'Darling heart,' he had said, 'don't be so naïve. It's the women you choose. I mean, you're practically in the public domain now. You can hardly expect people to take no notice when jilted women break bottles over your head in nightclubs right in front of Dempster and all his cronies, or protest naked in the street. It's every gossip columnist's dream. If you had wanted a quiet life you should have stuck with those nice docile types from the Home Counties who practically BEG a man to walk all over them, you do see.' But of course it was too late for that now, and Casey was stuck with it, and here was Minna seizing on it with glee, and using it as yet another stick to beat him with. It wasn't at all what he was used to.

Those exotic worldly creatures whom he normally courted were only too delighted to perpetuate the myth, but Minna went straight for the feet of clay, and then laughed at him heartlessly, as if he had put it about himself, to impress people.

'Shocked?' she said now, hooting with laughter just to prove his point. 'Well, of course, I was a little surprised when you first asked me to swing from the chandeliers, and I wasn't altogether expecting requests to dress up as a French maid and spank you if you didn't eat up all your pudding, but you'll have to do worse than that if you want me to be shocked.'

'Oh, don't,' said Casey dolefully. 'How can I help it if I'm just a good Irish boy at heart? I longed to be the most depraved degenerate all my life, but I'm just not the type.'

'Well, don't worry, ducky,' said Minna, patting his head in reassurance. 'I shan't breathe a word. Just think how disappointed your public would be. I shall keep the terrible truth to myself, and all those mothers can go on warning their daughters against you. After all,' she added reasonably, 'I suppose they have to have someone to warn their daughters about, now that Mick Jagger is over the hill.'

'Well,' said Casey, 'I suppose there is some hope for me after all. I may be a disappointment as a Lothario, but at least I'm not over the hill.'

'That's right,' said Minna approvingly. 'Look on the bright side.'

At ten, the band came on, and Casey and Minna stopped the staccato *badinage* that passed with them as conversation, partly because it was too tiring to shout, and partly because the music was good. Minna had forgotten how good Eddy was. It had been such a long time since she had seen him play, not really since the old days, that first summer in London, when she had been almost in awe of him, the older man, with his cabin trunk and his saxophone. Minna had always had a thing about the saxophone, for her it had a strange kind of mystique, a forgotten glamour, a romantic aura of lost days and broken hearts and unrecognized genius. She wasn't at all sure where this idea had sprung from, perhaps it was a hangover from all those old black-and-white films she used to watch, but whatever it was, it had stuck stubbornly in her mind. She had only to hear the lone high note of the sax for her mind to be filled with a plethora of confused images: of girls in red lipstick waiting for men who never came, of desperate drinkers in smoky bars, of gamblers staking everything on black with reckless bravado.

'That saxophonist is good,' said Casey in her ear. 'Which one is your friend?'

'That saxophonist,' said Minna, with a hint of pride. He was good. He blew notes that could break your heart. He shouldn't be wasted all his life in dives like this. The audience seemed to like him too, falling quiet to listen, greeting each solo with bursts of politely restrained applause. Eddy remained unmoved by their enthusiasm. He was a workmanlike performer, no histrionics or flights of fancy marked his act. He simply stood on the tiny stage, his eyes half-closed as if to block out the crowd, playing with utter concentration, just as if he were alone in his room, blowing those notes for no-one but himself.

Minna looked covertly over to Casey, to see what he was making of it. He was concentrating on the music, his face still. She couldn't really tell from his expression whether he was liking it or not, but his eyes were on Eddy, which Minna took as a good sign. Perhaps that steel-trap big-shot brain was already turning over with ideas, thinking of deals that could be struck, introductions that could be made, percentages that could be earned. She hoped so. If nothing else, at least it would stop Eddy being so snooty about her choice in men friends.

When they had finished playing, gracefully refusing the audience's demand for an encore, Minna waved at Eddy to come over to their table.

'That was lovely,' she said. 'Sit down, have a drink, meet Casey. Casey, this is Eddy, my musician friend.'

The two men shook hands, a little wary, summing each other up, almost like rivals. Of course, Minna thought, the advantage was all on one side. All Casey saw was a tall dark boy who knew how to play the sax, but Eddy, informed so generously by Oliver, saw the wickedest man in London, the rogue Irish who was busy adding Minna to his list of conquests. She was going to need every ounce she had of attar of roses to come up sweet smelling from this one.

'Hello,' said Eddy, not altogether gracious. He sat down and accepted the beer Minna gave him, and looked about with a moody sort of air. He really was wasted, Minna thought. He would have done very well in the Fifties, when the angry young man had been so much in vogue. John Osborne could have written a play about him.

'Have you played long?' said Casey, whose grasp of etiquette was rather more comprehensive, and who knew the importance of making conversation.

'Long enough,' said Eddy, playing his cards close to his chest.

'Years,' said Minna, filling the breach. 'Eddy could play the saxophone before he could walk. Don't you think he's rather good?'

'Very good,' said Casey. 'It was a great set. Do you write your own stuff?' he added, as if he were really interested.

'Mostly,' said Eddy, lighting a cigarette in a curiously insolent gesture. He really wasn't going to get discovered if he carried on behaving like this, Minna thought crossly. It was all very well setting up a meeting with one of the most influential men in the business, but she couldn't do all the work herself, and Eddy wasn't exactly helping himself.

'Interesting,' said Casey, who was starting to wonder if it was something he had said.

'It's a living,' said Eddy, which was wide of the mark. It might have been a way of life for him, but no-one was ever going to make it into the Forbes top 100 playing in places like this.

Minna had had enough. Casey had seen Eddy perform, he could make his own judgement about that, but she wasn't going to sit here and watch Eddy dig his own grave out of some ridiculous pique about her throwing away her virtue on a libertine.

'We should really go,' she said, standing up abruptly and putting on the dizzy society manner which she used in tense situations. 'Come along, Casey.' She kissed Eddy rather breathlessly on the cheek. 'See you soon, my sweet,' she cooed, enjoying his look of utter fury. 'We simply MUST do lunch. Look after that ducky sax of yours.'

And then she swept out of the club, up the steps

and into the street without a pause, dragging a bemused Casey in her wake.

'What was all that about?' he said, rather at a loss. He had never seen her imperious before. What an unexpected girl she was.

'Oh, you know,' said Minna carelessly. 'Musicians. They're all very well, but not much good for small talk. Besides, I was getting claustrophobic in there. Let's go somewhere else and get a drink, why don't we?'

'Anything you say, darling,' said Casey obediently. He never called her darling.

Minna punched him on the arm.

'Don't you start,' she said threateningly. 'A girl is allowed to have a whim from time to time. It's all part of our charm, ask anyone.'

'Absolutely,' said Casey, opening his dangerous blue eyes as wide as they would go. 'It is charming. I'm charmed to hell and back. Now, where would you like to go?'

'Let's go to the Ritz,' said Minna.

So they went to the Ritz, and Casey proved his worth by buying Minna another bottle of champagne, and when they had finished it they somehow didn't feel like going home, so they took a room, one of the big balconied ones that overlook the park, which had happily fallen vacant because the Parisian art dealer due in it that night was stranded at Charles de Gaulle, and they kissed all the way up in the lift, and Minna thought to herself that she really could get used to being the mistress of a big shot, and quite forgot about Eddy and his sulks and people being discovered, and concentrated like all good heroines on the matter in hand.

15

Minna wasn't quite sure what her next step should be in propelling Eddy into the big time, although she wasn't altogether certain that he deserved such attention after his recent behaviour. But still, she was a girl who prided herself on her fairness and her open mind, and she liked to think that she understood about talent and genius and the artistic spirit, and how those who had it could not be expected to behave like ordinary mortals, so she made allowances and decided to forgive him. (Minna was very good at making allowances, she sometimes wondered if she should take it up professionally.) She wasn't sure whether she should encourage Casey to do something, make a call or set up a meeting. She knew how important meetings were, everyone had them, breakfast meetings, lunch meetings, brunch meetings, it was how everything happened.

As it was, Casey saved her the worry of having to decide by bringing up the subject himself. They were lunching together for once, since he had had a cancellation, and halfway through the coffee, just as Minna was wondering if it would be very irresponsible of her to ask for a glass of Strega, he looked at her rather directly and said, 'Did you take me to hear your friend play on purpose, or was it just another of your enchanting feminine whims?'

'Oh,' said Minna, who tended to forget that he

wasn't quite such a fraud as she liked to think. 'Well, on purpose of course. I mean, you being such a big wheel and all, I thought it a pity not to put it to good use.'

'You are a disgrace,' said Casey. 'And I was thinking that you loved me for my mind.'

'Poor you,' said Minna. 'Yet another illusion shattered. Can I have a glass of Strega?' she added, sneaking it in while his mind was on something else.

'Of course,' he said, absently summoning a waiter and ordering their drinks. 'So what do you think I should do about him?'

'What do I think?' said Minna, surprised. 'I don't think, silly. I'm purely decorative. You're the one that does the thinking.'

'But what do you expect me to do?' persisted Casey.

'Oh, I don't know,' said Minna. 'What do you do with saxophone players? I just think that it's the most terrible waste that he's still playing with that second-rate band in those second-rate clubs when he's quite obviously better than that. There must be more to life.'

'Perhaps he doesn't want any more,' said Casey, who knew people who didn't. 'Not everyone does. It's safe, playing that circuit, not everybody wants to stick their neck out. It's much more frightening, aiming for the top.'

'He does want more,' said Minna, who had no doubt in her mind about that, at least. Eddy might be difficult as hell, but he had ambition running strong in him. She knew that. She knew that was why he had forsaken his assured place in society. If he didn't want it all, he would still be running around with the chattering crowd, drinking in chi-chi nightclubs every night, one of those aristocratic blondes on his arm, and the envy of his peers. If he was ever going to settle for second-best he would never have strayed from the lotus-eating he enjoyed in his youth. 'He's just too proud or too cynical or too something to do it for himself. He won't get rid of the band, he must know that they're holding him back, and he won't prostitute himself by flirting with the right people, and he's not getting any younger.'

'So you thought you'd do it for him,' said Casey, smiling at her. He could hardly remember what it was like, seeing things so simply. But then, he didn't think he ever had. To Minna, life was as black and white as those films she liked so much, and he supposed it always would be. It wasn't to do with being young, it was just that she was a different breed.

'Well, yes,' said Minna patiently. 'It seemed the obvious thing to do.'

'He must be a very good friend of yours,' said Casey, wondering if he were jealous or not.

'Don't be silly,' said Minna, hearing the doubt. 'We've known each other for ever. He was at school with my brother. Nothing sinister in that. So,' she added, reverting firmly to the matter in hand, 'what do you think?'

'Well,' said Casey thoughtfully, 'it just happens that he is exactly what I am looking for at the moment, which is typical of your luck.'

'Not luck at all,' said Minna, in reproof. 'It's judgement all the way.'

'But he will have to give up the band, for the moment.'

'Oh,' said Minna airily, making other people's

decisions without a qualm. 'He won't mind that so much, not if you tell him he must. He's not really a performer anyway. He doesn't crave the roar of the greasepaint and the smell of the crowd. He just wants to play his music, and he can only do that at the moment by playing gigs. What do you want him for anyway?'

'I'm looking for someone to do a film score,' said Casey casually, just as if it were the kind of thing one went shopping for in Harrods, just as if he didn't have hysterical producers screaming at him down the telephone every day, just as if he hadn't sent out over twenty demo tapes which weren't quite what they were looking for. 'And I think that he'll do.'

'Well,' said Minna, who had known all the time that it was going to be all right. 'Don't look at me. I can't play any instrument, not to save my life. Get on the blower, and set up a deal.'

'So, what's happening about it?' said Oliver the next morning, perfectly breathless with interest.

'Well, of course he's jumped at the chance,' said Minna, 'And they're both frantically rushing off to meetings with producers and directors and I don't know who else, and sending sample tapes off in twenty different directions and I suppose that he's going to be fearfully famous.'

'You ARE clever,' said Oliver, in awe. 'I never knew someone for making things happen like this.'

'Well, I rather agree,' said Minna, who was feeling pleased as punch and really rather impressed with herself. 'But of course Eddy isn't being at all gracious about it. He nearly spoilt the whole thing to start off with by being so rude to Casey, and then he had the cheek to blame me.'

'Scandalous,' said Oliver in horror. 'How could he do such a thing? Some people never learn.'

'Oh, he said it was all my fault because I didn't tell him what Casey did, and of course he was rude because he had heard all about Casey's reputation from you, and he doesn't approve of those sort of womanizers, and I don't know what else. It all sounded too much like the lesson for today. I mean it's all very well, him bleating on about my virtue, but now they're absolutely thick as thieves and I can just go hang for all Eddy cares.'

'Sauce for the goose,' agreed Oliver, not having the grace to blush.

'So now of course, Casey is the most splendid cove imaginable, and it wouldn't matter a hoot if he left me at home and went off and seduced half of London, as long as he gets Eddy his deal. Double standards is what I call it, in plain English, and I can think of some rather pithy Anglo-Saxon too, but I won't go into that now, since it's still breakfast time.'

'It's jealousy, I suppose,' said Oliver. 'It never becomes a man.'

'Don't be silly,' said Minna. 'He's got nothing to be jealous about. I was only his lodger, and that was on sufferance.'

'If you say so, darling,' said Oliver, in a rather irritating I-know-better sort of way. 'But I think that there's rather more to it than that.'

'Oh, don't,' said Minna. Oliver always read too much into a situation. It was all sex with him, just like Lou Lou. 'You've been reading too much Jane Austen. Eddy just thinks he's my mother, that's all. If it was down to him, I'd be married to one of those respectable men who do something clever in the City, sitting in the borders in twin set and tweeds, and well out of harm's way.'

'Don't speak, angel,' said Oliver, in genuine alarm. 'The very thought makes me feel quite faint.'

'Anyway,' said Minna, moving on to more agreeable matters. 'What about this weekend then? Casey's simply longing for it, couldn't you die? I really hadn't imagined him to be the house-party type, had you? He says that he trusts your judgement, and that it's bound not to be too pastoral. He doesn't sound very keen on the country, he says that it rots the soul.'

'He's quite right,' said Oliver. 'But he doesn't have to worry his pretty head. There isn't going to be anything too pastoral about this weekend, I can promise you.'

'Pity,' said Minna. 'No wall building, or wild oat picking, or rounding up young bullocks? No, no,' she said, hearing Oliver's gasp of horror at the mention of bullocks. 'Only teasing. Anyway, I'm delighted to be getting away. I can't be bothered to deal with Eddy in this mood, and I'm bored of looking at Casey's pots. I never thought that I'd say Thank God it's Friday.'

'Don't worry, my sweet,' said Oliver. 'I shan't tell a soul.'

So, on Friday afternoon, they set off for Norfolk. Casey had rather surprised Minna by pulling a 1954 soft-top Mercedes out of his garage and piling her and her suitcase into it.

'Goodness,' she said, as they headed down the road to Oliver's house, 'if I didn't know you better, I'd say you minded about your image.'

'You know how hard I work at impressing the

ladies,' said Casey in the post-Oxford drawl that worked on everyone except for Minna. 'A little drive out to a country hotel in this baby normally works wonders.'

'Good thing I'm not available,' said Minna blithely. 'Otherwise we'd end up in Bray or I don't know where and then what?'

'What indeed?' said Casey, letting his mind wander.

'Don't be disgraceful,' said Minna. 'And keep your hands on the wheel, IF you don't mind.'

'How I love it when you lecture me,' said Casey, leaving his hand where it was.

They stopped to pick up Oliver, dressed from head to foot in vintage Ralph Lauren and looking more like the Great Gatsby than ever, and took the Cambridge road.

'Isn't this heaven?' shouted Oliver from the back seat. 'Am I not utterly brilliant to have thought of it?'

Oliver was right about the house. It was enchanting, tall and symmetrical, built from gracefully weathered red brick and half obscured with climbing roses. Long sloping lawns ran away at either side, and beyond a ha-ha bright chestnut horses grazed in the sun. A broad sweep of gravel stopped in front of the house, crowded with cars.

'Oliver,' said Minna, looking at them accusingly, 'is this all you?'

'Well,' said Oliver in self-deprecation, 'I did take the liberty of asking a few other people. A mere handful, a bagatelle, that's all. Not a HOUSE party.' A house party, in Oliver's book, was still the kind of thing that Sybil Colefax would not have sniffed at, and involved at least twenty guests, quantities of servants, and gentlemen not travelling with their luggage. Anything less was just off the cuff, not worthy of a name.

'All I can say,' said Minna, who harboured no illusions about Oliver's notion of entertaining, 'is that they must be very hospitable, these friends of yours.'

'Oh, darling,' said Oliver, 'you'll die for them, that's all.'

At that moment, the front door opened, and a tall and statuesque woman came down the steps, Juno without her peacocks. She wore the kind of wide trousers and matelot vest that used to feature so strongly in the fashion plates of the Thirties, those outdoor shots that Norman Parkinson liked to take in the South of France, and her beautiful, faded face was half-obscured behind the biggest pair of dark glasses that Minna had ever seen. She looked for all the world as if she had just stepped off the yacht of some peripatetic playboy, and was simply waiting for someone to take her down to the casino for a game of *chemin de fer*.

'Darlings,' she said, in a deep, faintly throaty voice. 'You've arrived just in time for tea, you are clever.'

She kissed Oliver fondly.

'Minna, Casey,' he said. 'This is Marie-France, your hostess. Say hello nicely.'

They all said hello nicely.

'Now come down to the swimming pool,' said Marie-France, 'and have some tea. You must be quite exhausted,' she added, as if they had just travelled five hundred miles over inhospitable terrain to get there.

She led them away from the house, through orchards and walled gardens, past ornamental ponds and follies and box hedges, down to the swimming pool, which was a perfect blue octagon flanked by a pavilion in the Palladian manner and a rose garden filled with statuary. Tea was laid out on a round stone table, and gathered round it, like a *tableau vivant* arranged by a masterful hand, were the Skye sisters, Sebastian, Milo, Lou Lou and Jay. Venice, dressed in her country wardrobe of a floral printed dress, faintly reminiscent of the Fifties and the end of rationing, set off by a wide straw hat dressed with peonies and a drape of chiffon, was concentrating on pouring Lapsang Souchon into paper-thin china cups.

'Well, hello,' said Minna, waving prettily. 'Isn't this a surprise?'

'Knowing Oliver,' said Alabama, in a dry aside.

'At last,' said Lou Lou, raising her cigarette holder in greeting. 'We'd quite given you up for dead.'

'It's all Casey's fault,' said Minna. 'Don't look at me.' Casey gave a resigned look and kissed Lou Lou.

'Can I sit down next to you?' he said. 'Out of the line of fire.'

Marie-France watched them with an indulgent eye. 'I see that you all know each other,' she said. 'Now where's my old husband? Ring that bell, would you ever, Venice?'

Venice rang a tiny bell that sat on the table, and right on cue, a rather dishevelled figure, slightly stooped, emerged from the rose garden and ambled towards them.

'Sweet Granville,' said Marie-France. 'He's been reading his Pliny to the roses again. August is such a relief to him, with everyone on holiday. The rest of the year I can never get him out of his study, he's so busy with writing his books and his thesis and the Prime Minister ringing up every two minutes asking him how to run the country or I don't know what else.'

'Dearest,' said Oliver sympathetically. 'It's the price you pay for being married to the cleverest man in England. I mean to say, no-one told you it was going to be easy.'

'Especially not my mother,' said Marie-France, laughing. 'You remember my mother?'

Oliver nodded with feeling. 'I remember,' he said faintly.

'All that fuss,' said Marie-France. 'Still, I don't complain, really I don't.' She looked wistful for a moment. 'It's just it would be nice, just once, to have a meal on time. Here you are, darling, we were just talking about you. Sit down and have some tea.'

The professor smiled on them all rather vaguely, as if wondering quite what this group of strangers was doing, taking tea in his garden, made an oddly gallant little gesture of lifting his hat to the ladies, and sat down next to Alabama. Within moments they were deep in conversation about Aristophanes.

'There,' said his wife with relief, 'he's happy. He's utter heaven,' she added confidentially to Minna, as they sat down, 'but don't expect too much small talk. He's becoming something of a recluse as he gets older, so his social graces are not quite what they should be, but you won't mind that, darling, will you?'

'Not at all,' said Minna, impressed. She wished she had paid more attention to her Carlyle. How typical of Oliver not to mention that some sweet friends of mine in the country just happened to be the most famous intellectual in England.

'So,' she said, taking a cup of tea and turning to Jay, 'you beast, why didn't you tell me about your play? I'm most put out, I can tell you.'

'I wanted to,' said Jay, fixing her with his grave regard. 'But every time I rang up your landlord told me that you were out.' Across the other side of the table, Casey smiled to himself. 'He's not very accommodating, is he, your landlord? I had to give up in the end, it was becoming embarrassing.'

'Oh dear,' said Minna, all contrition. 'You poor thing, of course I forgive you, you must have been quite terrorized. So, anyway, tell me everything, I long to know. Oliver teases me hideously about being first with the news. Is it true that Alabama's agent loves it?'

Jay's eyes went involuntarily over to where Alabama sat, deep in conversation with the professor. Minna saw the look, and thought privately to herself that it was high time Jay got himself a girl, or the webs being woven would be in danger of tangling. Hero-worship was all very well, but Minna didn't trust the subconscious, and Milo didn't look like a man to be crossed in love, for all that reasonable exterior. It was always those with the most patient demeanours who turned out to be the most dangerous, as any reader of the crime pages knew.

'Yes,' said Jay dreamily, 'it is true.' He could still hardly believe it himself. 'Wasn't it good of her to send it to him? I thought she was joking, I mean, how could she be serious, he's the best in the business, and I'm just nothing, a nobody, unproven.'

'Not a nobody,' said Minna. 'Full of promise,

anyone can see that. I always said so,' she added staunchly, 'and look how right I was.'

'Well, yes,' said Jay, who still found it hard to get used to his work being admired. 'I suppose you were. And it is all thanks to you, after all. If you hadn't introduced me to Alabama and started all the wheels in motion, I'd still be struggling in my garret, wishing on the new moon, just like everyone else.'

'Well,' said Minna, full of self-deprecation now she had her due. 'You know. Garrets may be amusing for a little while, but we couldn't leave you there for ever. Anyway, I had to get you noticed somehow, I'd already started planning my wardrobe for your first night, and I couldn't let that go to waste, could I?'

'No,' said Jay seriously. 'Certainly not.'

'So what happens now?' said Minna, who wasn't altogether familiar with the procedure by which aspiring playwrights were catapulted into the spotlight.

'He wants to take me to America,' said Jay, who was rather bemused by the whole thing. 'He's setting up a deal for two of his plays to go to Broadway, Alabama and someone else, and he's going to put me in as part of the package, while no-one is looking.'

'So you're going to be on Broadway?' said Minna in disbelief.

'Not quite,' said Jay, laughing at her astonished face. 'It will be off-Broadway, if it works, the fringe, you know, the outer reaches. The Bronx, probably,' he added, making a little joke to cover up his excitement.

'I'll bring sandwiches and an armed guard,' said Minna.

'I don't really understand it,' said Jay, 'but

261

Alabama says Morty did always have very unorthodox methods, it's all that hock, and Morty says that it's all perfectly simple, and the Americans will do anything to get Alabama, so they'll take me without too much fuss, and it will be much more of a start for me than Croydon or somewhere, and no skin off anyone's nose.'

'And actually, people say the Bronx is becoming very chic, these days,' said Minna.

'Well,' said Jay, looking doubtful. He wasn't sure that this wasn't going a little too far, even for Minna. 'If you say so.'

'I do,' said Minna happily. 'So you're really off to New York. Just think.'

'I do,' said Jay, who did. 'Isn't it the oddest thing?'

'Not odd at all,' said Oliver, who didn't like to be left out of any conversation for long. 'Considering the brilliance of you. And just think what a perfect couple you and Alabama will make in America. My dear, all those poor sweet Yanks are simply going to EAT you up, that's all.'

'Oh, do stop, Oliver,' said Milo, who had rather taken to Jay. He was such a relief after the unmitigated horror of Alabama's last discovery. 'They've got enough to think about without having to worry about being eaten alive by hordes of ravening Americans.'

'Darling,' said Oliver with dignity. 'It shouldn't be a worry. Personally, I couldn't think of anything nicer than being devoured by all those heavenly uptown boys with their Harvard haircuts and their Brooks Brothers suits and their button-down shirts. My idea of bliss, that's all.'

'I knew a Harvard boy once,' said Venice nostalgically. 'He was rather a duck, except that he would keep talking about committed relationships and taking a flyer on the bond market, neither of which I knew anything about.'

'Well, darling,' said Oliver, dwelling for a moment on the blond perfection of Harvard boys, 'I suppose you can't have everything.'

'I certainly can,' said Venice, looking dotingly on Sebastian, who was concentrating on adding pepper to his cucumber sandwiches and smiling happily at finding himself in a house where they still cut the crusts off.

'Well,' said Oliver, relenting in the face of such perfection. Any girl who wore hats like that in this day and age deserved to have her cake and eat it. 'I expect that YOU can, angel, but then you are a law unto yourself.'

Venice looked pleased, and discreetly admired her reflection in her teaspoon. She knew better than to deny it. False modesty never did a girl any good, in her opinion.

Gradually, the tea party broke up. Alabama and the professor went off to sit in the rose garden and discuss Ovid, and Milo and Sebastian changed into whites and went off to play a set of rather gentlemanly tennis. 'They're so sweet,' said Venice. 'They spend so much time conceding points to each other that it takes hours for one of them to win.'

Marie-France took Oliver on a tour of the garden. 'I want your advice about borders, darling,' she said, taking him by the arm.

'You couldn't have come to a better man,' said Oliver spryly. 'I am a veritable Vita Sackville-West, let me tell you. If Violet Keppel had met me, she

263

would never have had to marry that dreary Captain Trefusis.'

'The tragedy of it,' said Venice. 'You being born twenty years too late. Just think what a twist history might have taken.'

'In more ways than one,' said Milo as he strode past on his way to the tennis court.

'That Milo,' said Oliver, shaking his head. 'No respect. Come along, Marie-France, on, on. To the borders.'

Casey lay down in the sun and went to sleep.

'He's awfully tired, poor lamb,' said Minna, with unaccustomed indulgence. 'He's been up until all hours making international telephone calls to Eric Clapton and David Bowie and I don't know who else.'

'Goodness,' said Lou Lou, who was looking more like Louise Brooks than ever in drop-waisted white muslin and ropes of pearls. 'What does he do, this Irish of yours?'

'He's in the music business,' said Minna. 'He makes deals,' she added with portent. 'Oliver says he's a big shot. I don't understand a word of it.'

'Well, I never,' said Lou Lou, impressed. 'So you haven't been sitting and twiddling your thumbs while the city burns.'

'Not as such,' said Minna cagily, looking across to see if Jay was listening. She felt that this really was girls' talk. But he was not paying any attention, too busy dreaming of Broadway and his new agent and all the plays he was going to write. 'Not at all, in fact. And he's going to get Eddy a job, as well.'

'A job,' said Lou Lou, laughing. 'Any more like you, and they'll have to shut down the labour exchange.'

'No, but really,' said Minna seriously. 'He's taking Eddy to Los Angeles to write a film score. Apparently Eddy is just exactly what Casey has been searching for. Isn't it too much? You must admit it's better than playing in those seedy little clubs.'

'I suppose,' said Lou Lou, who rather liked those seedy little clubs, but quite saw Minna's point, what with one thing and another. There were limits, after all. 'And all thanks to you.'

'Not really all thanks,' said Minna, with becoming modesty. 'I just took Casey to hear him play, that's all.'

'That's all, that's all,' said Lou Lou, laughing her wicked Tallulah Bankhead laugh and throwing her pearls over one shoulder to emphasize her point. 'Look at you, launching us all into the limelight like this and then pretending that it's nothing.'

'Not you, though,' Minna objected.

'Of course me. You introduced me to Oliver, and if it wasn't for him I should never have met Roger, and if I hadn't met Roger he wouldn't have been able to cast me in his next film.'

'No!' said Minna, sitting up very straight in astonishment. 'You mean to say that I've been here all this time and you didn't tell me.'

'No-one knows yet particularly,' said Lou Lou, a little shy. 'It's not the kind of thing that a girl comes out with at tea. There's a time and a place, after all.'

'Well, just imagine it,' said Minna. 'I AM impressed. But when did all this happen? When do you start? Does this mean you are going to meet Robert de Niro? Will you introduce me?'

'If Eddy is off to the City of Angels, it will probably be him doing all the introducing,' said

Lou Lou. 'Power lunching with Michelle Pfeiffer before you can say Darryl Zanuck.'

'But I want to hear more about you,' said Minna, who didn't want to think about Eddy having lunch with Michelle Pfeiffer. 'When did you hear?'

'A couple of days ago,' said Lou Lou, smiling broadly at her luck. 'Roger called me. We start shooting in Paris next week,' she added, trying heroically not to look smug. 'Gay Paree and the Tour Eiffel and La Coupole and I don't know what else.'

'What heaven,' said Minna. 'Just think. The Tuileries and the Place des Vosges and the bar of the Ritz and Gérard Dépardieu and *café au lait* and Yves St Laurent and the Left Bank and all the things that make life worth living. And lovely clever Roger who wins all those prizes at Cannes.'

'Yes,' said Lou Lou. 'Lovely clever Roger.' She had that kind of look in her eyes when she said it that made Minna think that perhaps the *Face* really was right, and that it was the third summer of love after all. 'So what about you and this Irish?' said Lou Lou, changing the subject in a way guaranteed to confirm all Minna's suspicions. 'Is it love? Oliver says he's never seen Casey so docile with a girl. I must say, he looks an utter pet to me, but my mama didn't tell me that appearances are deceptive for nothing. You know what they say, it's always the quiet ones. Look at Doctor Crippen.'

'Just do,' said Minna, laughing. 'Casey has got the most shocking reputation, it is true, Oliver has told me everything.'

'Bless him,' said Lou Lou.

'But I haven't seen a sign of it yet,' said Minna.

'He's the most perfect gentleman, I never saw a man buy so many bottles of champagne.'

'Stranger and stranger,' said Lou Lou, interested. 'There must be an ulterior motive. He must be after something,' she added, with a meaningful look.

'No, no,' said Minna, with one of her sudden flashes of clarity. 'It's really very easy. He's perfectly charming to me because I'm not in love with him.'

'Ah, well,' said Lou Lou, shaking her head with the wisdom of ages. 'That makes all the difference.'

'You do see?'

'I do,' said Lou Lou, woman to woman. 'Nothing ever changes, does it?'

'No,' said Minna, 'but then I don't expect that's such a bad thing. And anyway, in this particular case it happens to suit me perfectly. There I am, having a scandalous affair with the wickedest man in London, think how my credibility soars, and in fact I'm just having a lovely time and a lot of fun and letting him feed me foie gras and inanities.'

'And he does look so pretty,' said Lou Lou, who thought there was a lot more to this than met the eye, but would have died rather than say so.

'There is that,' said Minna, who had never been the kind of girl to pretend that her mind was on higher things. She knew all about the importance of character, and how that lasted even when the looks had gone, but she did like something pleasing to look at in the morning, she couldn't help it. 'And he does have such a way with those Irish eyes.'

'Don't,' said Lou Lou. 'If I didn't know about the Irish, I'd be jealous.'

They dined late that evening, gathered round a long mahogany table overlooked by the disapproving

267

ranks of Marie-France's ancestors, cardinals to a man. Granville dusted off some fine 1964 claret which he had been sent by some senior statesman or other and quite forgotten about, along with an equally good Pouilly-Fumé for the fish, so everyone was in exceedingly good spirits. The talk sparkled round the table, growing more scandalous with each glass. Reputations were discussed and discredited, gossip traded, rumours brought up and enlarged upon.

'Of course,' Oliver said of one poor unfortunate, 'none of us could ever understand what she saw in him. I mean to say, there she was going steady, if you can call it that, with that ridiculous film star with the teeth, and even if I can't happen to see it myself, people tell me he's devilishly attractive, and ten million in the bank covers a multitude of sins, and so she's quite set up, and then off she goes with that dreary Andrew Charcoal. I mean to say, what CAN she have been thinking of?'

'She got the wrong side of the family,' said Milo, who wasn't above a bit of gossip in spite of being the newest of the Young Literary Sensations. 'She thought he was part of the electronic Charcoals, you know all those terrible fat ones who made all their money in pocket video games or something just as bad, I can't remember.'

'No,' said Oliver in delight. 'Don't tell me. And he's only a second cousin twice removed, and I can't think that estate agency pays frantically well.'

It was that kind of dinner. Whenever anyone's name came up, Oliver knew something salacious about them.

'Oh, darling,' he would say, 'that old rock star. *Quelle blague.* The last I heard of him, he was chasing an under-age chambermaid round the corridors of a hotel in Mexico City.'

Or,

'So there she was, convinced he would marry her, already practising her English accent and how to ask the butler to bring in the fish, and before you can say off the bone, he's upped sticks and run off with a twenty-three-year-old shopgirl from Surrey. And now he thinks of himself as an absolute Tom Jones, and insists on telling all his friends that love means never having to say you're Surrey.'

And,

'Oh, don't talk to me about that one, she's the most frightful old mantrap, an utter Jezebel, really, she'll go to bed with anyone with a title. She's the only girl who's seduced Tony Ramhurst since he left Oxford, I can't think how she did it when everyone knows that he only likes Italian boys. In the shrubbery, apparently. I've never been able to look at those box hedges since.'

That was the kind of dinner it was.

Afterwards, the men had port and cigars and discussed the state of the government and the ways of the world, while Oliver and the girls drank great balloon glasses of Armagnac as if it were sweet sherry and picked apart the new autumn collections which were terribly old hat this year, not a thing one hadn't seen before.

'If only the poor dears had called and ASKED me,' said Oliver, casting aside copies of *Vogue*, the picture of despair. 'I could have TOLD them. I mean, really, it's so last year I could die. It's like pulling one's fingernails out. Who's going to wear it all?'

'Wear what?' said Granville, wandering in with an empty decanter. 'We seem to have finished the port, Marie-France, do you think that's rather shocking?'

'Good for the blood, darling,' said Marie-France soothingly.

'Ah,' said Oliver, 'well, that's what poor old Freddie Waterloo used to say, before the accident. And look what happened to him.'

'Not STILL gossiping, Oliver?' said Sebastian naughtily, sitting down next to Venice and putting his hand on her knee.

'Oh, you,' said Oliver in reproach. 'Well, stop spooning and make polite conversation then, if you must. I promise to sit up straight and listen, really I do. I'll even take notes if it will make you happy.'

In the end, they stayed up very late, and drank a great deal of a 1914 brandy that Granville found, rather to his surprise, in the back of the drinks cabinet while looking for some angostura bitters. It was after three when they finally went to bed, and everyone got rather hysterical creeping round the corridors with the lights out, which wasn't made any better by Sebastian getting the wrong bedroom and trying to get into bed with Oliver by mistake. As Oliver was to say later, when the story had become part of his repertoire, it was the most exciting thing that had happened to him since he left school.

Everyone rose late on Sunday and ate bacon and eggs and croissants and halves of melon in the kitchen which was tiled and pale and faintly Roman. Venice watched Sebastian do the crossword in under twenty minutes, which she always said was the reason that she had fallen in love with him in the first place, while Milo and Alabama bickered over the arts pages and bitched genially about the critics. Casey read the business section and let Minna tease him about it, and Oliver talked Lou Lou through the fashion shots in the colour supplement in preparation for all the clothes he said she must buy while she was in Paris, instructing her in the mysteries of couture and the Faubourg St Honoré. Jay didn't read the paper, but ate seven pieces of bacon in abstracted silence, still dreaming of all the plays he had to write and all the audiences he had to win over. Marie-France, who today was looking as if she were about to go to a nightclub in Monte Carlo in red palazzo pants and a pink shirt knotted at the waist, wafted in and out with great baskets of flowers slung rather incongruously over her arm. There was no sign of Granville.

After breakfast, everyone wandered up to the swimming pool. It was too hot to do anything but sit about in the shade and gossip, and Oliver went about with his self-appointed task of keeping everyone up to date on any scandal they might have missed, and even Alabama and Milo stopped discussing Lorca to listen, although they pretended not to.

Finally, even Oliver was exhausted. 'So the three of them settled down together, happy as grigs, and as far as I know, they're there still,' he finished. 'Could you imagine.' His voice tailed off wearily into the heat. Across the lawn, the roses danced and bobbed in the haze, shimmering in patterns of pink and white. Basking in the heat, drowning in it, Minna could hardly bring herself to walk over to the pool.

'It never was this hot,' she said. 'Never in the world.' She felt like Daisy in *The Great Gatsby*, longing for air-conditioned hotel rooms and mint juleps and cold baths. Except that this was not a claustrophobic heat, but benign, bathing them in its incandescence, washing away memories of the bitter English winter.

It really was rather like being abroad, Minna thought to herself later as she changed for lunch, with the sun so hot and the garden so beautiful and the day so still and quiet. She couldn't imagine what cold felt like, or that it would ever be cold again. She felt rather odd, a little disorientated, as if this were the last weekend of the holidays, with all of them gathered together for the last time before they went their separate ways. Everything had changed, shifted a fraction, moved on. The long hot lazy days of summer would soon be over and everyone was going back to work. She wondered what she should do when they had all gone, and she was left on her own again. She wondered who she would gossip with, who would take her to lunch, who would sit up with her until the dawn.

But she didn't dwell long on it. Minna was not contemplative by nature; something would happen, as it always did, so she pushed the problem from her mind and concentrated on her reflection which was reassuringly familiar and touched now with colour from the sun, and she painted her lips and put on the pretty Italian dress that Casey had bought her, a clever boat-necked creation in burnt umber, and very sophisticated Minna felt. Then she ran her hands through her hair so it fell a little dishevelled into place and smiled ravishingly at herself and went downstairs where she found Granville making bullshots in the drawing room.

'Hello,' he said, smiling at her vaguely but with great charm, as if he had noticed her for the first time, which was probably the case, knowing academics. 'I'm afraid I haven't been much of a host this weekend, you must forgive me. But the only thing I'm really good at is making these noisome cocktails, do you drink them?'

'Love them,' said Minna, smiling right back, and wondering whether he had forgotten that he was still wearing his hat, or whether he always wore it indoors.

'Bullshots,' cried Oliver, arriving in a cloud of Monsieur Givenchy. 'Granville dear, you are a genius and I don't care who knows it. And you've got the proper bouillon, how did you manage it? The beastly EEC, or whatever they call themselves, have banned it because it's got too many additives or they kill the cows the wrong way or I don't know what, so you have to get it smuggled in, rather like brandy in the old days.' Oliver was reading *Jamaica Inn* this weekend, and was terribly taken with the idea of all those butch Cornish smugglers lurking about hidden coves in the dead of night waiting to receive contraband Remy Martin from France.

'Really?' said Granville in astonishment. 'I rather thought that Marie-France got it in Partridges.'

'Not any more,' said Oliver darkly.

'Cocktails, what heaven,' said Venice, wandering in in a charming lace confection and her hair still piled up on her head from swimming. 'Sebastian loves bullshots, they're his absolute Achilles' heel.'

'Really, Sebastian,' said Oliver naughtily, 'I thought Venice was your little weakness.'

'Could I have sherry with mine?' said Sebastian, ignoring this remark. 'It's a terrible habit with me.'

273

'Oh, Granville, really,' said Marie-France, coming in from the garden with a basket full of roses. 'You've still got your hat on. What will people think?'

'We shan't think a thing,' said Oliver. 'We're the perfect houseguests. Eat what we're given, speak when we're spoken to, I'm surprised you're going to let us go back to London, ever. Shall we just stay after lunch, and let the air out of our tyres. Granville would love that, wouldn't you?' He looked over at Granville, who took no notice whatsoever, far too busy measuring out Sebastian's dash of dry sherry.

'Now don't tease, Oliver,' said Marie-France severely. 'You know that we love having you. Now do let's go into lunch before the soufflé falls.'

'Oh, don't,' said Oliver, leading the way, his hand on his heart, 'my nerves. I shall have the vapours. The soufflé falling indeed! You KNOW I hate it when that happens.'

Later, driving back, Casey said, 'We had a nice time, didn't we?' and Minna, half-asleep and drowsy with wine, thought he said the last time, and felt a little pang of sadness. But then, she always felt like that on a Sunday night, a hangover from childhood, and the dread of going back to school, so perhaps that was it.

16

Back in London, August rolled on, inexorably moving towards autumn. As if to herald the change of the season, the exodus started.

Lou Lou went off to Paris to start shooting, as she now so grandly called it. She left in a private aeroplane from the city airport, with Roger on one arm and an Hermès bag on the other, perfectly balanced, and Minna and Oliver went to wave her off, fluttering their handkerchiefs in *adieu*. Jay had left the day before, got his package, just as Morty had promised, and set sail for New York with just one small bag and the complete Shakespeare to accompany him. 'Don't worry,' he said as Minna fussed over him, 'Alabama will be there, and I'm booked into a hotel in the Village. Just think, me in Greenwich Village.'

'Give my love to Allan Ginsberg,' said Minna, who hated to see him go. 'Don't grow your hair and turn in to a beatnik. Remember to eat plenty of greens and say your prayers before bedtime. I knew I shouldn't have come to see you off, I'm hell at goodbyes. I should have made do with that lunch.' The week before they left, Minna had taken Jay and Lou Lou to a last lunch at their favourite haunt where they had all got terribly drunk on Chablis, behaved extremely badly and quoted extensively from Yeats. Weaving out into the late afternoon, they had promised each other eternal friendship, undying loyalty, and that they would write. They had sworn categorically that they would not say goodbye at the airport. 'I just couldn't resist.'

'Of course,' said Jay, soothingly, standing up very tall and looking protective. 'It's all right, your mascara has hardly run at all.'

'It's supposed to be waterproof, dammit,' said Minna, blowing her nose. 'And don't forget to go down to the Tribeca Grill and make eyes at Robert de Niro for me. Don't fall off the Empire State Building. Don't drink the water, and DON'T make friends with the roaches.'

'Yes, ma'am,' said Jay, saluting smartly. 'You'll have to let go of my lapel now,' he added kindly. 'They're calling my flight.'

'Don't mug any pigeons,' said Minna, to his departing back.

Later in the week, Eddy left for Los Angeles to write his score. He took with him his cabin trunk and his saxophone, leaving his flat barer and more empty than ever. Minna, going round for tea, sat on a packing case and watched him rolling up his life. It didn't take long. Suddenly awkward, they talked in a desultory way about nothing at all, the unspoken questions still hovering just over their heads, neither of them knowing how to crack the ice.

'I should go,' Eddy said at last.

'You should,' said Minna affably, glad they agreed on something. 'Did you remember to pack your thermals? They wear nothing but Damart on Sunset Boulevard, it says so in the guide books.'

'Of course,' said Eddy. 'I wasn't born yesterday. Thermals and thick socks, just like Mother taught me. I shan't catch any chills.'

'That's good,' said Minna. She stood a little on one leg, unsure what to say next. 'Good to keep warm.' She stood on the other leg, admiring her perfect balance.

'Goodbye then,' said Eddy. 'I expect I'll see you when I come back.'

'I expect you shall,' said Minna, looking up. 'If you ask very nicely. I might even turn out to strew your triumphant path with laurel wreaths, if I'm in that kind of mood.'

'Don't start counting your chickens,' said Eddy, who didn't walk under ladders.

'Oh, you,' said Minna, joshing. 'You've got fame written all over you. It'll be fine, you'll see.'

'Perhaps,' said Eddy, crossing his fingers.

'Of course,' said Minna, reaching up to give him a peck on the cheek. 'Goodbye then,' she said.

Casey was the last, two days later, flying off to Los Angeles to look after his prodigy. 'There are some things you can't do on the telephone,' he said. He said he had deals to do and contracts to sign and that he wasn't sure how long he'd be away, and perhaps he would have to go to New York after, or even Chicago, he couldn't really tell. Minna, understanding perfectly, told him not to worry so, and in an uncharacteristically domestic gesture, even packed his bags for him before kissing him goodbye.

She didn't go to the airport with him, and he didn't ask, and she was glad. It wasn't the same as with Jay and Lou Lou, she couldn't flutter her handkerchief *adieu* or cry over his lapels, it wouldn't have been seemly. So, as usual, nothing was said, but as she told Oliver over lunch later that day, they seemed to understand each other perfectly well without explanations.

'I think it's rather better that way,' she said. 'Less turgid, you know. Otherwise the whole thing turns into *The Three Sisters*, and no-one ever gets to Moscow. Although,' she added, smiling at the waiter as he poured her Chardonnay, 'I still don't really see why he had to run off quite so quickly. He could have waited until the end of the summer at least.'

'Of course he couldn't,' said Oliver, who had seen it all coming. 'He was in danger of falling in love with you, and you do see how Casey of all people couldn't afford to let that happen. I mean, darling, think of it. He'd be quite unmanned. That's why he went off in such a rush, and Eddy and his deal were the perfect excuse. It's plain as the nose on your face. Except,' he added quickly, 'that you have a very pretty nose.'

Minna moved back into her brother's house, because the Americans had moved on to a lightning tour of the rest of England, lured by the charms of Shakespeare's birthplace and Pepys's bed and the very spot where the martyrs had been burnt, before heading back to Fifth Avenue. The house was tidier and cleaner than it had been, and Minna didn't have the heart to muddle it up again, so she lived in one room and ate out.

Oliver, who hated to see waste, took her up, and even managed to rustle up a hardy band of people who had bucked convention and stayed in London, so they had someone to see in the evenings, and there were even a few parties for them to dress up for, and a few trusty swains for Minna to flirt with, which she did with an instinctive grace, as if remembering her schoolgirl French. Oliver could see that her spirit wasn't in it, but even so, he had to admit that she did it beautifully, turning heads everywhere she went.

But then it was September, and the summer really was over at last, and even Oliver was gone. Starved of the cosmopolitan company he most enjoyed, he decided to go straight to Venice. He begged Minna to come with him.

'I can't tell you what it'll be like, darling,' he said, over their final lunch. 'Quite the most stunning apartment, right on the Grand Canal, bang next to the Gritti, it couldn't be more convenient. And then, Harry's every night, the best food in Italy that's all, and there's always someone's yacht to go dancing on. Even Effie Hampton is coming this year, and her boat is the envy of everyone, you can't miss it. And you would look so perfect in Venice, I can just see you now, please say yes.'

'It's no good, Oliver,' said Minna, who didn't know much, but knew what she liked. 'The high life just isn't me, really it isn't. I haven't enough clothes for a start, and I can't bear shopping, all those terrifying women forcing one into olive green and magenta, and I've had enough parties in the last two weeks to last me for a year, I can't talk fast enough to keep up, and those were mere cobbled-together affairs by your standards, think how far I would sink at the real thing.'

'All right,' said Oliver, knowing when he was beaten. He shook his head sorrowfully. 'I shan't press you. Although I do think that you might grow to love it if you tried a little harder and put your mind to it. And you would be so good at it, I can just imagine it, a triumph, that's all.'

'No,' said Minna, who didn't think it worth the effort. It was a life's work, and she would rather stick with the Revolution and count her blessings. 'Not a triumph at all. I just like a quiet life.'

'Oh, don't,' said Oliver. 'It's not THAT bad. You'll be telling me next that you want to settle down in a cottage in the country, and grow roses over the door, and cultivate a vegetable patch, and keep bantams for the eggs.' And he had laughed blithely at the very idea, and they had finished up their lunch in great charity, and talked of other things, and he had taken himself off to Venice, where he amused himself, among other things, by ringing up Minna every morning and telling her who he had seen the night before and exactly what they were wearing, down to the last corset.

With even Oliver gone, Minna sat in her house and returned to her books on the Revolution. She bought some cashmere to drape over her little dresses, for there was the beginning of a chill in the air, and went a great deal to obscure foreign language films at the cinema and wrote long rambling letters to Lou Lou and Jay. They wrote back, copious literary letters from Jay, written from various historic points of the city, and short pithy ones from Lou Lou, full of Parisian jokes and sentences that started 'Roger says'. Oliver sent pictures of the Cipriani with a black arrow pointing at the terrace and the words, 'I am drinking my bellini HERE' scrawled on the back in purple ink. Casey didn't write (he insisted he had never learnt how), but called from time to time, mostly to tell her, down a succession of bad lines, that he was going out to dinner with Bianca Jagger, which Oliver said was too typical for words.

'What a way to get over a broken heart,' he said in delight. 'I mean, darling, REALLY.'

All her writer and artist and musician friends started to return from Bali and Nepal and Christmas Island, and suddenly the telephone was busy again as they all called up and told her to come round straight away and see their photographs, which they showed her with great explanation and embellishment before dashing off to compose another symphony inspired by the mountains or write another novel suggested by the native tribes, or just to see their agents, who had missed them terribly during their travels.

But most of the time she sat and thought rather confused thoughts about Eddy on his balcony and Casey in his big white room and the differences between them. She thought about the summer and everything that had happened, and how it seemed to have left her with even less to do than she had before, and how she minded now where she hadn't before. She thought about Lou Lou with her film, and Jay with his play, and Casey with his deals, and Oliver with his lunches, and Eddy with his score. She thought about cottages in the country and roses growing over the door. She thought about life in the city and how things never quite turn out the way one planned. She thought about human beings and how strange and difficult they are and how little she really knew. She thought about missing the obvious and making things more complicated than they need be and ignoring the most blatant signs.

When she had finished all this thinking, she rang up Oliver.

'Lucky to catch me,' he said, spry as you please. Minna could hear the clink of ice against cocktail shaker as room service shook him his first dry martini of the evening. 'Effie Hampton has just docked her yacht. Darling, let me tell you, a Mondrian in the BATHROOM, that's all.'

'Oliver,' said Minna seriously, getting to the point before she lost her nerve. 'Do you think that I might be in love with Eddy?'

'My sweet,' said Oliver, pleased, 'of course you are. You're the last to know.'

'Do you think it's almost too much of a cliché?' said Minna, clinging to the last vestiges of her reputation. 'I mean to say, I rather suppose I've always been in love with him, since I was twelve.'

'Darling,' said Oliver seriously, 'it's heaven. It's too much. It's to die for. I'm dying, I'm dead. It's Enid Blyton.'

'And,' said Minna, pleased, 'do you suppose that he might feel the same about me? Or not?'

'Of COURSE he does,' said Oliver, quite forgetting about Effie Hampton and her yacht in his delight. 'Why do you think he's been in such a temper all summer? All those dark moods and long silences, too John Osborne for anything. I'm surprised that he survived after you went off with Casey. That WAS clever of you, angel, just think, until all that terrible green eye that he came down with, Eddy could convince himself that he didn't care.'

'Goodness,' said Minna, who wasn't above taking a little credit where it wasn't due. 'That was rather brilliant of me, wasn't it?'

'Inspired, darling,' said Oliver sincerely. 'If I were a poet, I should write an ode to you.'

'So what should I do now?' said Minna, accepting without question Oliver's position as expert on matters of the heart.

'Get on the telephone,' he said, without pause. 'Never forget about men and their silly old pride, tripping them up every time, I sometimes despair of my sex, really I do. So you will have to call him. Imagine,' he said, giving a little moue of rapture, 'all those long distance calls. The romance of it, I'm overcome with jealousy. Will you promise faithfully to let me know every development as it happens. I mean BULLETINS.'

'Of course,' said Minna. 'And thank you.'

'Don't thank me, darling. It was utter pleasure.'

After this conversation, Minna did a little more thinking, and came to the conclusion that life is earnest, life is real, and far too short for hesitation, and then she drank off three fingers of brandy to give herself courage and rang up Eddy in his hotel room in Los Angeles and said a great many revealing and intimate things to him down the telephone line, and he said a great many back, and when they had finished, she put down the receiver, and sat back and waited.

Late in October, Eddy flew back to England. The score had been a great success, and everyone was pleased with him, and now he had a bewildering range of offers to think about and a nice fat cheque in the bank to keep him going while he thought. He was written about in the trade papers and discussed at Hollywood lunches and asked to all the parties, and then talked about some more because he never went.

He was pleased to be back, he thought, as he walked out of the airport into the reassuringly grey and windy London afternoon, and he was even more pleased that Minna was waiting for him.

'Here,' she said, leaning out of the window of a vast limousine and waving at him. 'Don't you think it's the most vulgar thing in the whole world? I couldn't get a cab to save my life,' she added, making a little joke to cover up the fact that she was suddenly shy, now that he was here at last, and not just a voice on the end of a telephone line thousands of miles away.

'It's perfect,' said Eddy, not talking about the car. 'Can we go to Soho please?' he asked the driver.

'I am glad you haven't picked up one of those terrible transatlantic accents,' said Minna, who was still determined to make conversation.

'No,' said Eddy, who wasn't. And then he looked at her for a while, and she gave up her attempts at small talk, and then he kissed her, because he had wanted to for five years and he was fed up with waiting.

When he had finished, he looked out of the window at the dirty London streets and the tramps and the traffic and the loaded buses and the rubbish-strewn pavements, and then he turned back to Minna.

'What would you think,' he said slowly, 'about living in the country?'

THE END

OUT TO LUNCH
by Tania Kindersley

'CRISP AND VERY FUNNY'
Sunday Telegraph

The Skye sisters were just about the most devastating duo on the London scene. Venice was seriously and dangerously beautiful, Alabama was brilliantly bright. Venice wouldn't be seen wearing anything without a couture label. Alabama – the most gifted playwright of her generation – never wore anything but torn jeans and a biker's jacket.

When Venice was fired from her third job in a month, she decided she would just *have* to find a sugar daddy – it was the only way of surviving in a cruel champagne world. And Alabama's life wasn't totally without problems either. But the *jeunesse dorée* of London were shattered when Venice started reading the *Spectator* and quoting James Joyce, and Alabama began wearing Yves St Laurent and holding court in unaccustomed splendour. What were the outrageously inviting Skye girls up to?

'A WICKEDLY WITTY TALE OF LOVE, MODERN MANNERS AND, NOT SURPRISINGLY, MONEY'
Me

'JUST TOO IRRESISTIBLE FOR WORDS'
Tatler

0 552 13708 1

CASTING
by Jane Barry

'Heartbreakingly funny . . . tremendously entertaining'
She

Dee Devlin is sick of rotating her underwear to the dictates of her diary, sick of watching men search for their socks at one in the morning – sick to the back molars of always being the mistress, never the wife.

Yet how does she locate Mr Single in a world full of married men? At forty, she's missed the boat on 18–30 holidays. A Lonely Hearts ad generates only one congenial companion from a stack of no-hope replies – a six-foot transsexual called Ann. And, despite her friend Gilda's advice, Dee fails to detect an Adonis amongst the would-be waiters and Father Christmases who daily audition for commercials at the Soho casting studio she runs. Is Gilda right – should Dee set up a casting session to find Mr Single? Or should she console herself with her five-carrier-bags-a-day shopping habit and the companionship of her designer cat, Mabel?

'Frothy, soapy and bags of fun. And, in between the laughs, she puts her perfectly manicured finger squarely on the agonies of being single in a world full of couples and married men'
Cosmopolitan

'Fast, furious, wise, full of hurt and funny – I loved it'
Fay Weldon

0 552 13648 4

A GLIMPSE OF STOCKING
by Elizabeth Gage

Unforgettable women, capable of unforgivable acts.

ANNIE – the beautiful actress who will stop at nothing to get to the top.

CHRISTINE – the cool temptress who practises her art in the boardrooms and bedrooms of America's most important and influential men – and women.

ALETHEA – the evil and twisted widow who will change their lives for a second time – in a way they'll never forget or forgive.

'Easily as shocking as the last scenes of *Fatal Attraction*, and a lot more plausible . . . A gem'
Chicago Tribune

0 552 13266 7

A SELECTED LIST OF FINE NOVELS
AVAILABLE FROM CORGI BOOKS

☐ 13648 4	CASTING	Jane Barry	£3.99
☐ 14044 9	STARLIGHT	Louise Brindley	£4.99
☐ 13558 5	AMBITION	Julie Burchill	£4.99
☐ 13952 1	A DURABLE FIRE	Brenda Clarke	£4.99
☐ 12486 9	RIDERS	Jilly Cooper	£5.99
☐ 13264 0	RIVALS	Jilly Cooper	£5.99
☐ 13552 6	POLO	Jilly Cooper	£5.99
☐ 13877 0	A DARKER SHADE OF LOVE	Anne Dunhill	£4.99
☐ 13830 4	THE MASTER STROKE	Elizabeth Gage	£4.99
☐ 13266 7	A GLIMPSE OF STOCKING	Elizabeth Gage	£5.99
☐ 13644 1	PANDORA'S BOX	Elizabeth Gage	£5.99
☐ 13255 1	GARDEN OF LIES	Eileen Goudge	£4.99
☐ 13872 X	LEGACY OF LOVE	Caroline Harvey	£4.99
☐ 13917 3	A SECOND LEGACY	Caroline Harvey	£4.99
☐ 14104 6	LOVE OVER GOLD	Susannah James	£3.99
☐ 13708 1	OUT TO LUNCH	Tania Kindersley	£3.99
☐ 13880 0	THE VENETIAN MASK	Rosalind Laker	£4.99
☐ 13333 7	THE PRESIDENT'S WOMEN	June Flaum Singer	£3.99
☐ 13504 6	BRILLIANT DIVORCES	June Flaum Singer	£4.99
☐ 13523 2	NO GREATER LOVE	Danielle Steele	£4.99
☐ 13525 9	HEARTBEAT	Danielle Steele	£4.99
☐ 13522 4	DADDY	Danielle Steele	£4.99
☐ 13524 0	MESSAGE FROM NAM	Danielle Steele	£4.99
☐ 14163 1	THE SNOWS OF SPRINGTIME	Sally Stewart	£3.99